"Your brother—the baby's father— washed his hands of the entire problem."

Nora's voice rose slightly. "Are you aware that he even suggested abortion?"

Jake nodded. "I am. Isabel's phone call threw him for quite a loop. That doesn't excuse him, but I know he came to regret that suggestion almost immediately after he made it."

"And yet you're the one who's come to her, when it should be him—"

"My brother's dead, Miss Holloway. He died a few days after he received the phone call."

"I'm sorry. I didn't know."

"I sat by my brother's hospital bed for almost two days. He wanted to find Isabel and tell her he'd made a huge mistake. There's no doubt in my mind he would have married her and given his son a name...." Jake expelled a long sigh. "Toward the end, when he knew...he asked me to make sure she and the baby were okay. Of course, everything's changed now."

Nora's heart cramped suddenly. "What do you mean?"

Jake gave her a hard, level look. "I'm sorry, but I can't let you adopt my brother's baby."

Dear Reader,

It's hard to believe that the millennium is nearly here. When I was a kid, it seemed so far away. I was sure that by the year 2000 we'd be zipping around town in spaceships, our meals would be prepared by robots and we'd all be living in geodesic domes. As a fan of history rather than science, I thought it all sounded pretty scary and undesirable.

But here we are on the eve of a new century, and I'm delighted to see that one aspect of life hasn't changed much over the years. Falling in love is still unpredictable. It can't be bottled or scheduled or forced, and it can still sneak up on two unlikely people who think they know exactly what the millennium will bring them.

As I wrote this book, I liked the idea that I was creating two such characters in Nora and Jake—a heroine who sees only loneliness in her future, and a hero struggling to put the past behind him to make a new life. Their expectations don't include a baby, but what better way for two deserving lovers to kick off a brand-new year!

I hope the millennium brings you happiness and lots of wonderful books that warm and touch your heart. Somehow, the future just looks a little less scary when it's filled with love.

Happy New Year!

Ann Evans

Books by Ann Evans

HARLEQUIN SUPERROMANCE

701—HOT & BOTHERED
752—THE MAN FOR HER
805—HOME TO STAY

DREAM BABY
Ann
Evans

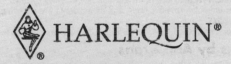

HARLEQUIN®

TORONTO • NEW YORK • LONDON
AMSTERDAM • PARIS • SYDNEY • HAMBURG
STOCKHOLM • ATHENS • TOKYO • MILAN • MADRID
PRAGUE • WARSAW • BUDAPEST • AUCKLAND

ISBN 0-373-70870-X

DREAM BABY

Visit us at www.romance.net

Printed in U.S.A.

For Evan and Holly Marsh, who gave me the opportunity to experience the love, excitement and delight of children firsthand, and who continue to enrich my life today.

CHAPTER ONE

New Year's Eve, 1998

NORA HOLLOWAY WENT to bed early.

Without waiting for the ball to drop in Times Square, without a thimbleful of alcohol in her system, without making a single resolution

She went to bed before the first skyrocket had a chance to arc over Blue Devil Springs's postage stamp of a town square. Praying for deep, dreamless sleep—and knowing that it was probably a futile wish.

An hour before 1998 escaped into the record books, she awoke sweaty and breathless in her bed, her head full of familiar images—long dark corridors, the sound of a baby crying, and herself, confused and frightened and unable to change any of it.

She sat upright, disoriented, but only for a moment or two. She knew why the baby dream had visited her tonight.

That afternoon she'd sorted through a box of junk she intended to donate to the Memorial Day garage sale. She had expected to find nothing of value, certainly nothing that would cause her heart to miss a beat. But instead it had yielded a treasure trove of mementos. The dried, crumpled remains of the orchid she'd worn to the prom. A clutch of blue ribbons her brother, Trip, had won in crew. Letters she had written to Mom and Dad from college.

Nothing startling. Nothing dramatic, although it was a little bit of a surprise to find pictures of Peter in the box as well. Peter, looking strong and handsome, with that absurdly charming smile that she'd fallen victim to right from the first. He seemed so achingly young in the photographs.

The sight of those objects brought no pain. Only regret for what might have been. She'd been smiling when she reached into the box to retrieve those faded images.

But as she picked them up, her fingers brushed something soft, and when she saw what it was, the smile froze on her lips.

How stupid to have forgotten what she'd done with the half-finished, cross-stitched birth announcement. The one she'd taken with her to the doctor's office that rainy day five years ago—five years ago to the day. It was such a small thing— too small to be framed on the nursery wall, Peter had said. But Nora had kept stitching anyway, because the cheery colors and its pattern of childishly simple icons for a little boy made her feel good, made her feel like the mother she couldn't wait to become in just four short months.

Seeing the announcement again this afternoon had brought it all back. Soiled, fading, the fabric

sat in her lap as though it were a snake that might
strike her. The name she and Peter had chosen for
their son still stood out plainly. JEREMY
WILLIAM. Jeremy for Peter's father. William for
hers.

Only the boy hadn't lived to carry the weighty,
paternal pride of such an important name. He'd died
the day of the accident. Along with Peter. Along
with so many half-formed dreams she'd had for the
future.

Now in the darkness of her bedroom, Nora's
hand fumbled for the bedside lamp. She squinted
against the bright glare, shoving handfuls of tangled
dark hair out of her eyes so that she could read the
clock radio: 10:58 p.m. Almost 1999.

A few homemade bottle rockets zinged in the
distance. It was probably her neighbor down the
road, Walt Clevenger, eager to start the celebration.
She'd dated him two years ago and knew how impatient he could get. Rifle shots cracked from the
direction of the national forest. The rangers would
be on the revelers in the blink of an eye. Alan Harcourt, the first man she'd gone out with after Peter's
death, didn't let campers get too rowdy.

Her heart was no longer pounding, but it would
be impossible to get any sleep for a little while, not
with all the noise.

She flipped on the television as she made her way
into the kitchen. The sound woke Larry, snoring
noisily at his favorite spot on the rug by the big
stone fireplace. The mongrel, the last of three moth-
eaten pups she and Trip had saved a few years ago,

snuffled a complaint and then followed in her foot-steps. Sensing his motive, Nora plucked a sliver of ham off the leftovers plate in the fridge and tossed it to him. Larry's front paws barely left the floor as he caught the morsel in midair.

Hunched over the open refrigerator door, Nora was about to pull a soda off the shelf when her hand brushed against the small bottle of champagne she'd set out earlier in Cabin Five. The honey-mooners she'd expected to check in today had called to cancel their weekend stay at Holloway's Hideaway, the resort cabins Nora and her brother had inherited from their parents. The trip to Paris the lucky couple had received as a wedding gift from their families far outweighed anything the Hideaway and tiny Blue Devil Springs could offer.

"C'est la vie," she said and snagged the cham-pagne bottle. She kicked the door closed with one bare foot, pulled a clean glass off the kitchen counter and headed for the living room.

Her attention strayed to the television, where two giddy cohosts were superimposed over the crowd of revelers in New York's Times Square.

"...and you can really feel the excitement in the crowd, even from up here, can't you, Mary Beth?" the male announcer nearly shouted. "I don't think I've ever seen a new year greeted this enthusiasti-cally, and we've still got almost an hour to go be-fore 1999 gets here."

Mary Beth smiled her plastic talk-show host's smile and nodded. "I think you're right, Bill. Each year, as we've gotten closer to the start of the millennium, people seem more and more excited. I can't wait to see what next year brings, when we actually hit 2000. Can you?''

"Yes," Nora muttered as she twisted the wire champagne seal. "I can."

Larry jumped when she popped the cork. Hunkering down into the huge, plush cushions on the couch, Nora poured herself a glass of champagne, then tweaked open the small card she'd attached to the bottle just yesterday. She frowned at the silly sentiment she'd painstakingly written inside:

Karen and David—Congratulations on the start of a wonderful new life together.
Nora and Trip Holloway, your friends at the Hideaway

With her glass full of champagne, Nora tipped an imaginary toast outward. ''You missed your chance, Karen and Dave. All the best, anyway.''

It had been a long time since she'd had any reason to drink champagne. The liquid tickled her throat as it went down, but didn't seem to have much flavor. She poured another glass, inspecting the label and wondering if she ought to offer wine to newlywed guests instead. She'd heard the new bed-and-breakfast on the other side of Blue Devil Springs greeted every arrival with fresh-baked cookies and a chilled bottle of Chablis. If Holloway's Hideaway was going to make it into the millennium, they might want to shake things up a bit.

Curling her bare toes along the edge of the coffee

table, Nora sank back with a sigh. The millennium. God, she was so tired of hearing that word. As though just because a year started with a two instead of a one it was more important, or carried some kind of magic...

She had a headache by the time the festivities in Times Square peaked. Larry was curled against her hip, and Nora ran a hand through the dog's soft fur. "You know what my New Year's resolution is, Larry? To stop watching Bill and Mary Beth."

Outside, celebratory gunshots went off again. From the direction of town there came the *zing!* of ascending fireworks. The one-minute countdown was on the television screen now. Bill and Mary Beth disappeared, giving way to wide views of the boisterous crowd, but their voices continued to offer nonsense and excitement. Thirty seconds. Twenty-nine, twenty-eight, twenty-seven—1999 was only moments away.

She supposed it was an overactive imagination that made her stomach feel queasy when the countdown was over, and the crowd in Times Square went wild. There were lots of shots of people kissing and yelling and waving frantically toward the television cameras. Bill and Mary Beth hugged each other as if they actually meant it. Nora closed her eyes against the sight of it all and laid her head back against the couch cushion.

She hated the fact that 1999 was here at last. Only twelve months until the year 2000.

She had thought she'd be enjoying motherhood by that time, caught up in Tupperware parties and

PTA meetings. She and Peter and her brother, Trip, would have made Holloway's Hideaway at Blue Devil Springs a premier resort destination, and she would have managed all that around Little League and school plays. It wasn't a particularly grand or exciting life plan, but it had always seemed perfect to Nora. The most wonderful future any woman could imagine.

But that dream had shattered five years ago, and whatever internal deadline she'd planned for herself by the millennium was far out of reach.

Financially, the Hideaway was barely hanging on. Trip, frustrated by trying to make ends meet, had fought with her frequently over selling the place. Even the arrangement they'd come to, that she would buy out his share of the Hideaway over a period of years, had not satisfied him, and two months ago he had taken off to pursue his own dreams. Peter and little Jeremy William were lost to her. And given the limited male companionship she'd enjoyed in the last couple of years, not to mention that old, ticking biological clock...

In the middle of the night, when she was really honest with herself, that was the thing that hurt the most—the thought of never having a baby of her own to love. She had loved Peter, but theirs had been a whirlwind courtship, and the marriage vows had barely been spoken before the accident occurred. She had mourned him, but the truth was, she had hardly known him at all.

But the baby—Jeremy William would have been the most desired, most treasured child in the world, and the knowledge that Nora would never hold him in her arms, and perhaps no other as well...

How could she face the start of a new century without the hope of a baby in her life? The thought was unendurable.

Another bottle rocket went off in the distance, and Larry growled low in his throat. Nora drew a deep breath, refusing to dwell on such dour thoughts.

She glanced toward the television one last time, where the cohosts were laughing over the antics of people on the street. "Happy New Year, Bill and Mary Beth," Nora whispered. A moment later she sent them to oblivion and tossed the remote on the huge cypress knee coffee table.

Larry growled again. On her way back to the kitchen, Nora stopped to listen. Although it was nearly too faint to hear over the crackling pop of distant fireworks, Nora was sure someone was knocking on the front door.

Because of the hour and her present state of mind, she was tempted to ignore the summons. It seemed unlikely that one of her neighbors had come by to wish her Happy New Year, and she wasn't expecting any late arrivals. The newlyweds had been her last hope for the weekend. Still, she pulled her housecoat over the long T-shirt she used for a nightgown. If someone wanted a bed for the night—had taken a wrong turn or broken down on the road—she couldn't afford to refuse them.

Larry led the way to the bolted double doors, his toenails clicking on the plank flooring as he *woofed* threateningly. Nora tightened the grip on the collar of her robe.

"Sorry. We're not open," she called out as she flipped on the outside lights.

"Not even for me?" a feminine voice full of tentative humor asked.

Surprised, Nora slipped back the bolts and pulled one of the doors wide. Isabel Petrivych had spent her college breaks for the past three years working at the Hideaway, and although she wasn't expected back on the payroll until spring break, she would always be a welcome visitor.

"Happy New Year, Nora," the girl greeted brightly.

"Happy New Year to you, too. What are you doing here?" Nora asked.

The girl's long black hair was unbound, falling in an ebony waterfall over one shoulder. She tossed it back in a reckless gesture and grinned hopefully. "I guess I didn't know where else to go."

They both jumped as the sudden *pop-pop pop* of fireworks exploded in the night sky.

"Why aren't you out partying?" Nora asked as they watched the last streamers of red and blue twinkle out of existence over the pines.

Isabel turned back to face her, and suddenly Nora caught the glimmer of tears welling in the young woman's eyes. "Partying is the last thing I should be doing right now. That's what got me into this mess. I've been so stupid…"

Isabel's voice broke with emotion as she swiped

the tear away with the back of one hand. She laughed, but the sound was choked, desolate.

Nora's heart sank to the pit of her stomach as she gazed at that sweet, troubled face, and when she spoke, she rushed into speech herself, "Izzie, what is it? What's happened?"

The girl shook her head, more wildly this time. "Oh, Nora, you're not going to believe this…" She grimaced shakily. "I'm pregnant."

CHAPTER TWO

May 1999

THE KID HADN'T SAID a word in over two hundred miles.

Jake Burdette slid another glance away from the road, just to make certain his son hadn't fallen asleep or turned to stone or gone into some sort of cosmic trance.

Nope, Charlie was still with him all right, still seated in the front seat of the car, still so uncommunicative Jake might as well have been keeping company with an upscale kids'-store mannequin. One twelve-year-old boy dressed in clothes that were too tailored, a haircut that was too precise, a suitcase that was too expensive and an adolescent chip on his shoulder as big as a house.

Since the moment Jake had picked him up at Thea's in New York—his private school term barely over—then flown down to Norfolk, and on to Orlando, conversations between the two of them had been increasingly one-sided. Nothing more than shrugs and grunts and a few uh-huhs ever since they'd hit the interstate. Not even the eye-popping excess of billboards advertising Florida's theme parks got a reaction, and Jake's suggestion that someday they might return for a trip to Walt Disney World was met with a complete lack of interest.

Jake stifled a huge sigh and glanced out the window.

There was no doubt that this little side trip to Florida had come at an inconvenient time in Jake's life, a time when he really needed to focus all his attention on Charlie.

But right now, he had to keep his promise to his brother.

And Florida wasn't that bad. After inching through the traffic congestion of Orlando, they'd headed north, past Thoroughbred country in Ocala, through the long corridor of rolling land that made up Florida's panhandle. The area made you realize not all of the state had given way to the big developers. It was woodsy and wild, and it reminded Jake of some of the wonderful places his grandfather had taken him and his brother, Bobby, camping in Virginia.

To a spoiled snob of a city boy like Charlie, it must look like the backside of the moon.

Maybe Jake should tell him about a few of those childhood trips. They needed to start someplace. He opened his mouth to speak, but in that moment there was the familiar sound of electronic music. Charlie had pulled the video game out of his backpack. The kid could go hours on that thing.

So much for a folksy tale to bond them together.

An hour later Jake pulled off the interstate to gas

up. Charlie was still smashing invaders from some high-tech planet—evidently meeting with success, if all the beeps and metallic crashes emitting from the video game were any indication. Still not a word of conversation. The only change in the boy's stony countenance was the occasional frown of displeasure he gave the game in his hands.

Jake watched him covertly as he ran gas into the sports car's tank. His son had a sweet forehead, wide and unblemished and intelligent. Without trying very hard, Jake could remember when the boy was four and had suffered through chicken pox— chicken pops, he'd called them—and Jake had sat by the side of his bed and stroked and stroked Charlie's forehead until the boy had dropped into a restless sleep. Where had all that trusting innocence gone?

He screwed the gas cap back into place and then leaned against the passenger door. "You want a soda from the machine?"

Still fighting his video war, Charlie shook his head. There was the descending sound of a sudden defeat, and with a sigh of complete disgust, Charlie switched off the game and tossed it into the back seat. He stared out the front windshield.

"Sorry," Jake said, guessing that he'd broken the boy's concentration, and therefore caused him to lose the war. Jake turned and headed toward the convenience store. He seemed destined to remain on his son's enemy list.

But for how long? How long would it take to reestablish a relationship that had once been taken for granted? He couldn't give up. Charlie was his now. Thankfully, Thea had seen the wisdom in avoiding an ugly court battle.

From the interstate they bumped onto the cracked, paved road that led to Blue Devil Springs. "Almost there," Jake remarked, trying for a cheerful tone.

No response. No surprise there.

"Look, Charlie…Charles," he corrected himself when the kid turned an annoyed glance his way. "I know you'd rather be back in New York with your mom. I know you're angry because you're with me now. I don't expect you to understand all the reasons behind that decision, but someday when you're old enough…"

He stopped. God, he sounded so much like his father. And the kid would resent a lecture. A different approach was definitely in order.

"You know, after I take care of business in Florida, and we get home to Norfolk, you might find you like it. It has beaches. And we can go to the mountains, up to Washington…"

Again he stopped. He sounded pathetic, trying to find favorable comparisons between the two places.

He searched his son's profile, looking for some chink in Charlie's armor and not finding any. The kid's jaw was tight with tension, and his gaze out the front window seemed impenetrable. And then suddenly the boy's mouth gaped open a little, and he muttered something unintelligible under his breath.

Jake discovered why when he jerked his glance back to the road.

They'd reached the town of Blue Devil Springs.

Town was probably too big a word for the place. It wasn't much. A few cross streets made up all of the downtown area, a collection of businesses that bore simple, unvarnished pronouncements like Ed's Hardware, Painted Lady Antiques, the Cut 'n Curl, and a small establishment called simply the Pork Store. If Andy and Barney and the whole Mayberry crowd had been looking for a place to retire, this could have been it.

He drove slowly past the main intersection Looking closer, he saw that Blue Devil Springs wasn't a complete loss. There was a certain charm and Southern grace about it. There were lots of big oak trees dripping moss and a pretty Victorian band shell in the center of a small park. The grass there was green and lush. It wasn't a ghost town bypassed by progress. The people on the streets looked energetic and involved in life, and overall, the place had an open, friendly feel.

Beside him, Charlie was still in a trance of stunned surprise.

"I know what you're thinking," Jake said. "Don't panic." The boy rolled his eyes, but remained silent. "I'm getting hungry. Let's see if we can find a place to get some food and information."

They discovered some activity around what seemed to be the only red brick building in town — the Whispering River Café and Outfitter's Post. Colorful rows of kayaks and canoes leaned against the building, and several huge tubs of dainty flowers led the way to the entrance.

The interior of the store wasn't the dark, backwoods outpost Jack expected. It was bright, upscale, full of environmentally correct merchandise. As Jake led his son toward the back of the store where the café seemed to be, they wove past listening posts of New Age music, stacks of camping gear and a bulletin board fluttering with offers for guided float trips down the river.

The café was also a surprise. The room was small, but bathed prettily in mild sunlight coming through large arched windows. Unframed artwork decorated the walls. There were leafy alcoves for privacy. According to the menu posted at the entrance, vegetarian dishes seemed to be the heavy favorites.

They found a table for two against one wall. Almost before they sat down, a tall, good-looking fellow in jeans and a Save-The-Planet T-shirt placed menus in front of them and promised to return in moments.

For the first time, Charlie seemed to be interested in his surroundings, and Jake realized it was the artwork that drew the kid's attention. Charlie's gaze traveled over the numerous canvases that lined the walls, then settled on the one right beside their table. And suddenly Jake could see what had caught the boy's interest.

Trendy as the Whispering River might be, whoever had decorated the place had made one huge mistake. The artwork was awful. Amateurish. They were all oils, the majority of them landscapes, but there wasn't a stroke of talent in any of them that Jake could see.

Like Charlie, he peered closer at the one nearest them. It was a Florida beach at sunset—lifeless and boring, with wheeling seagulls in the sky that looked unpleasantly like flying worms. Jake's eyes slid down to the artist's signature. NLH, it said, and Jake noted that several of the surrounding works bore those small slashing marks in the right corner. He hoped to heaven that NLH hadn't quit his day job.

He shook his head. "I guess now we know who actually buys all those Starving Artist paintings," he muttered.

He hadn't expected a reaction from Charlie, so it surprised him when the kid gave a little snort of amusement. Not an all-out laugh, really, but it was a more encouraging response than Jake had elicited from the boy so far.

He said softly, "You know, when you were five, you drew this great picture of a fish. Your mom put it on the refrigerator." He motioned in the direction of NLH's landscape. "In a head-to-head comparison, I think yours is better. At least I could tell it was a fish."

Charlie turned his head to look at his father. "Mom still has that picture," he said coldly. "It's in a box with a bunch of my old stuff. Guess that's all she's gonna have of me now."

Jake felt his heart rate slow to a crawl. So much

for connecting. One step forward. One step back. "You'll still be visiting your mother."

Charlie's gaze was openly dubious. "You won't let that happen."

"That's not true. I want you to keep in contact. But there have to be some guidelines to your visits. She can't just…there has to be someone looking after you." Jake unfolded his napkin carefully and placed it across his lap. Criticizing Thea wouldn't accomplish a thing except send Charlie further away. Quietly he added, "Right now your mother's career is very important to her, and she doesn't always think about her responsibilities."

"Like you thought about yours five years ago?"

Jake lifted his head and met his son's eyes. He wasn't in the mood for apologies and justifications, but neither would he allow Charlie to believe everything Thea had probably told him about his father.

"When your mother and I broke up, I had a job that kept me out of the country for months on end," he declared firmly. "Bridge construction often takes place in locations that barely have indoor plumbing. I couldn't drag a little boy off to an environment like that. It seemed best to let your mother have full custody. She gave up modeling when she married me, and I had no idea she was so involved again. I thought—"

"She's famous," Charlie flared. "She doesn't need you for anything. She's a supermodel, and everyone loves her." He turned his attention back to the painting on the wall, and Jake watched while muscles jumped and twitched along the tight ridge of Charlie's jawline.

The boy was right. Everyone did love Thea. If you could believe half of what you read in the tabloids.

While heavily involved in rebuilding the family construction company, Jake had heard all about his ex-wife's life. The New York parties that ran until all hours of the night. Rubbing elbows with the Hollywood elite. He was glad he wasn't part of that lifestyle, but he'd never begrudged Thea any of it. She'd always been a good mother. There was never any mention of Charlie in those tabloid stories and Jake had been confident his son was safe. That Thea had never drawn him into her social life.

Until he walked away from a Nigerian newsstand six months ago with an American paper in his hands and saw the media coverage of Thea's latest New York party. A glittering montage of celebrities and social arbiters all laughing, drinking, pressed close to one another. And in the middle of it all, his son Charlie. He knew in that moment that for four years he'd been fooling himself, and that as fathers went, he'd been pretty damn negligent.

It was an interesting bit of irony to discover that he'd failed miserably as a father on the same day that he was to make a catastrophic mistake with his own brother as well. That afternoon Jake had been furious with Thea, and three telephone calls to his lawyer in the States that wouldn't go through hadn't helped. The hill crew had yet to check in, and after the road foreman had asked a second time what they should do about it, Jake had snapped at Bobby to take care of it. Bobby, who'd never questioned a directive his older brother gave him. Bobby, who had always looked up to him and counted on Jake...

The waiter brought tall glasses of water to the table. He didn't carry a pad to write down orders, and the small badge over his left breast said his name was Ben. Beneath it was a button that proclaimed, "Yes, I'll remember what you want."

"The special today is sliced turkey on mixed rye and pumpernickel," he said with a genuinely friendly smile. "The soup is tomato bisque. Can I get you something to drink?"

Charlie swung his attention from the painting on the wall and scowled up at Ben. "A blind man could paint better pictures than these!"

"Charlie!" Jake snapped. "Apologize."

He and Ben exchanged glances, and Jake had the oddest notion that the man knew the boy's anger was not really directed at him. "No, that's all right," Ben countered. "Everyone's an art critic. To tell you the truth, I'm not that crazy about them myself." Then, with a wink, he added, "But you ought to see the artist."

Charlie had subsided into sulky silence. Jake tried to fill the void. "Good-looking, huh?"

"Nora Holloway's one of the prettiest girls the Springs ever produced. So what if she ought to be painting barns instead of beaches?"

"So the owner thinks he'll win her over if he buys a few of her paintings?"

"I'm the owner," the waiter said with a light

laugh. "No, we tried a few years back, but it was plain as pudding we didn't click. So what can I get you two?"

Jake ordered a rare burger, and Charlie asked for the special with instructions on just how much mayonnaise he wanted on his sandwich and a fussy inquiry as to the freshness of the lettuce. Was it possible to get alfalfa spouts instead?

Jake sat back in his chair and wondered when the little boy who had eaten mud pies in the dirt had become so picky.

Silence descended while they waited for their lunch. Charlie took out a pen and started doodling on the place mat—nesting circles with spikes along the edges. Jake hid his annoyance by studying NLH's painting again. He hoped Ben was right about her looks, because she sure as hell had no gift with depth perception.

The meal came, and it looked delicious. Without a word, Ben went off to snag ketchup and mustard for Jake's burger.

A layer of glistening hamburger juice covered the top of his bun, and Charlie's lip curled in repulsion when his father made no attempt to pat it dry. "Gross." Then he sighed heavily. "How long are we gonna stay in this place?"

"Just until we find the lady I told you about. I promised Uncle Bobby I'd find her, make sure she's all right. I'm sorry the sitter fell through and I had to drag you down here with me, but as soon as I take care of this, we'll be on the next plane out.

Unless you'd like to have a little vacation. School's over. We could kick back and do some fishing.''

Charlie looked horrified. ''That's your idea of a vacation? Fishing?''

''We'd do what you want to as well, of course. What did you do on your last vacation?''

''Mom took me skiing in Switzerland. We stayed with an Italian count.'' Charlie's mouth quirked. ''In a castle.''

Jake didn't care to admit that even though he could speak fluent Italian and had been around the world more times then he could remember, he'd never learned to ski.

Thankfully, Ben returned to the table, placed the condiments in front of Jake and then rocked back on his heels. ''Everything look okay?''

Jake nodded around a mouthful of burger. With one hand, he motioned Ben to stay. Taking a swallow of iced tea, he asked, ''I wonder if you'd know a woman in town named Isabel Petrivych? Not a full-time resident. Her friends at college say she comes up here quite a bit to work for some hotel during school breaks.''

''Hotel?'' Ben echoed with a shake of his head. ''There aren't any once you get away from the interstate.''

''I only met her once, but she's attractive—dark hair, dark eyes, a slight Slavic accent. By now she must be noticeably pregnant and—''

''You mean Izzie?'' Ben interrupted with a sudden grin. ''Yeah, I know her. And she's more than 'noticeably' pregnant. She's about six months gone."

"Do you know where I can find her?"

"Anyone in Blue Devil Springs can tell you where to find her. She and Nora have got this town buzzing, what with their plans for the baby."

"Nora?" Jake prompted. The inquiries he'd made to find Isabel hadn't mentioned the involvement of another woman.

Ben pointed toward the painting on the wall. "NLH. Nora Lyn Holloway. She and her brother own Holloway's Hideaway about three miles down the road. Their cabins are built around the headwaters of Blue Devil Springs. Once it boils out of the ground, it feeds into three rivers. Cleanest in the state, and you've never seen prettier."

Jake put down his burger to give all his attention to Ben. "And this woman is helping Isabel with her pregnancy?"

"More than that, from what I hear. The two of them have met with Nora's lawyer and are ironing out the final plans."

"Final plans for what?"

"Adoption." Ben tossed a look over his shoulder, conscious of other diners waiting. "Can I get you two anything else?"

Charlie shook his head. "No, thanks," Jake replied absently. Uneasiness clogged his throat, and he suddenly felt his appetite vanish.

Absently he watched his iced-tea glass sweat a water ring on his place mat. Adoption for Bobby's child? Jake had never considered that possibility.

As little as he knew of Isabel, he'd assumed she planned to keep the baby. That meant the child could be told about his father. Adoption, on the other hand, would effectively sever the link to Bobby. Jake didn't like the sound of it at all.

The remainder of the meal passed without incident and in silence. Jake left a generous tip on the table and took the bill up to the register, where Ben was doing double duty as the cashier.

Ben handed Jake his change. "Thanks for coming in."

"There is one more thing I need, if you don't mind," Jake said. "Directions."

"Sure. Where you want to go?"

Jake inclined his head toward one of the paintings directly behind the cashier station. "NLH. Where do I find her?"

HALFWAY TO a sitting position, Isabel groaned and shook her head. She fell back on her elbows.

Nora smiled encouragingly, though she had just finished a punishing series of sit-ups herself. This would never do. Isabel had managed only ten easy crunches today, and if they were going to keep to Dr. Brewster's recommended regimen of exercise for expectant mothers, they had to do better than this.

Drawing her legs up so that she could rest her chin on her knees, Nora eyed the girl speculatively. Isabel was a brilliant medical student. Someday she'd make a wonderful doctor. But she was one stubborn pregnant woman.

"Come on, Iz," Nora pressed. "You can do it. One more time."

They were seated on the huge Indian rug that lay in front of the resort's registration desk. Throwing Nora one last sullen look, Isabel maneuvered backward until her spine was against the wall of the desk. "I don't want to," she replied, crossing her arms across her breasts.

"Of course you don't. But you need to. Remember what Dr. Brewster said? Strengthening your abdominal muscles will—"

"—make the delivery easier," Isabel finished for her. "Yes, I know, and I don't care. No more crunches today."

"It'll also make it easier to get your figure back after the baby's born. You want that, don't you?"

Isabel cast a disgusted glance downward. "Too late. It will never come back."

"I'll do them with you."

"That doesn't make me feel any better. You sit there looking like a model on a workout video, while I look like I've swallowed a basketball."

"No, you don't. You look beautiful," Nora said and meant it. "Glowing."

"It's the sweat—" The girl's face suddenly transformed to surprise, and her hands flew upward to clutch her stomach. "Oh!"

Nora moved to Isabel's side quickly. "What's the matter?"

"The baby kicked really hard." She massaged the swell of her abdomen, grinned sheepishly after a long moment, then captured Nora's fingers in hers. "Give me your hand."

At first Nora felt nothing. Then suddenly, beneath the thin material of Isabel's blouse, she felt the slight roll of the baby as it shifted in the womb. It was such a small thing, no more than a sliding pressure against her fingertips, but it stalled Nora's breath in her throat.

She lifted her eyes to Isabel and smiled. "So strong," she said. Her fingers tingled, eager to feel that movement yet again, but the baby had settled down, and the jump of life had disappeared. "Is it wonderful to feel him move inside you?"

"No. It's unnerving. Scary. Like an alien creature is trying to take over my body." Catching sight of Nora's budding frown, she added, "Don't look so upset. Not every woman instinctively longs to have a baby, you know."

"You might learn to love him as you reach your due date."

"I won't," Isabel said in such a precise, cool way that Nora's frown deepened. The girl scooped a handful of dark hair away from her face and flung it back over one shoulder. "I don't see motherhood the same way you do, Nora. I've never wanted children, and God knows, I had even less reason to want this child after I spoke to Bobby in December."

Five months ago, when Nora had found Isabel at her front door, the girl had tearfully confessed that a two-day love affair with a young engineer on his way to a job overseas had produced a child. But when she'd called him in Nigeria to give him the news, the jerk had encouraged her to have an abortion, even volunteering to send the necessary funds by Western Union. Horrified by the suggestion, Isabel had told him just what she thought of that idea and then fled to the only person she knew she could turn to and trust with her secret—Nora.

"I made such a horrible mistake," Isabel continued with a rueful shake of her head.

"Don't say that."

"It's true. My parents had such high hopes for me. I am the oldest child. They saved for years to give me a good education in America." Isabel dropped her head, her gaze fastened on her swollen stomach. "If they knew—If I wrote and confessed how I have disappointed them..."

"You could never disappoint them," Nora said. She reached for Isabel's hand, drawing the girl's eyes upward again. "They love you. Perhaps you should give them the chance to show you how much."

"No," Isabel replied firmly. "This is what's best for everyone. Bobby and I got carried away by a night filled with too many stars and two many glasses of wine. I've seen what happens to children whose only mistake in life is to be born in the wrong place at the wrong time. I can't do that to a child."

They had argued this point more than a few times. Isabel was determined to give the baby up for adoption. She had very clearly defined career goals to become a doctor and the tenacity to make them a reality. Her parents had sent her to the United States for an education in the hopes that she would return to her war-torn homeland to help rebuild it. It was a noble, lofty ambition, and it would not be an easy life. Especially for a young woman with a small child.

"It doesn't have to be that way. You don't have to go back to Bosnia."

"Yes, I do. I owe it to my family. And my country."

"Izzie, what if—"

"No," Isabel cut in. "I've made up my mind, and I'm not going to change it. I deliver a healthy baby and begin my internship at Blakely-Forbes, and you become the wonderful mother you were always meant to be."

The mother you were meant to be. The words settled around Nora's heart, full of unbelievable good fortune and frightening possibilities. Could it really be so easy for her to become a mother at last?

Two months ago, after the prenatal visit that had confirmed the baby's sex as a boy, Isabel had suddenly posed the idea, one she'd evidently been considering for some time. They had been having lunch at the Whispering River. Nora had just slipped a bite of chicken salad onto her fork, and Isabel's words stilled her hand in midair.

"I would like you to adopt my baby."

The café was noisy, full of diners, and Nora shook her head, not sure she'd heard correctly. "What?"

"I'd like you to adopt my baby."

"You aren't serious."

"Don't say no right away," Isabel added quickly. "Just think about it."

"There's nothing to think about. It's impossible."

"Why?"

"It just is."

"Why? Because you're not married? Single women have been adopting children for some time now. Many come from my own country—out of orphanages where they would surely have died. At least in this case you'd know who the mother was, and I can promise you, in spite of the fact that Bobby doesn't want the baby, he comes from a good family. Virginians. Aren't those founding fathers or something?"

Nora shook her head, knowing that her gaze on Isabel must be incredulous. "Izzie, I can't adopt your baby."

Isabel set her water glass down and looked back at her with clear, determined eyes. "Nora, for as long as I have known you it has been your dream to have a child. Why not my baby? Give me reasons."

It was crazy. Too fast. She couldn't just adopt her friend's child. Could she?

The answer was yes, according to Nora's family attorney, John Forrester. Nora, who had greeted the new year certain that she was destined to remain childless for life, could be celebrating next Christmas as a mother. The idea—so frightening, so wonderful—had taken hold and now had such a tight grip on her senses that most nights Nora could hardly sleep for thinking of all the ways she would love this child.

Isabel drew her attention back to the present with a touch of her hand. "Nora," she said softly. "Have you changed your mind? Do you not want this child?"

Nora's stomach was full of sudden butterflies, but she responded in a low, unshakable voice. "I want this child with all my heart."

Isabel smiled. "Then together we will make it happen." With a toss of her head she climbed carefully back to her feet, dragging Nora with her. "Now, please, no more torture today. Ten crunches are enough."

"All right," Nora conceded as she slipped back into her sneakers. "But twice as many tomorrow."

Brushing wisps of hair out of her eyes, Nora tightened the ponytail at the back of her neck. Isabel toed the rug back into order where it had bunched up, while Nora maneuvered two enormous leather chairs back into place. Placing them at just the right angle, she glanced out the wide front window, past the front driveway and the narrow grassy slope where railroad-tie steps led down to the spring pool. Through the trees, the water was no more than a cool, inviting glimpse of crystalline blue. It was still a little too chilly for swimming. Memorial Day really kicked off the beginning of summer, and right now there was no movement down there. Not even a canoe sliced through the water of the river.

Nora cut her eyes to the left, down the line of Cabins One through Three, where the Hideaway's only guests, a couple from New Orleans, had checked into Cabin Two a couple of days ago. "The Pullmans' car is gone. Wonder where they're off to."

"Oh," Isabel said from behind the registration desk. "I knew I forgot to tell you something." When Nora swung around, she grimaced and said, "They checked out."

Nora frowned. "When?"

"While you were fixing the air conditioner in Cabin Six."

"That's a day early. Did they say why?"

"Mr. Pullman said his office called unexpectedly." Isabel wrinkled her nose, clearly indicating she doubted that story. "Mrs. Pullman said the quiet made it impossible for them to sleep at night."

"Damn," Nora muttered. She walked to the front of the registration desk, leaned over the counter and pulled the reservation book in front of her. What she saw there didn't make her feel any better. "We don't have anyone else booked until Friday."

Determinedly optimistic, Isabel rushed into speech. "Unless we get a walk-in, that gives us three days to relax. You can paint, and I can soak in the tub. Try to get my belly to stop itching." She must have seen something in Nora's face, because her tone became anxious. "What's the matter?"

Nora's breath escaped in one long sigh. "Izzie, I can't provide a good home for the baby if the

Hideaway continues to lose money this way. Cabin Six is going to need a new compressor. Four has a water leak in the bathroom, and I'll be darned if I can find it.'' With a flick of her wrist, Nora turned the reservation book around so that Isabel could see as she flipped through the pages, stopping on the weeks of June, July and August. Too many blank spaces where names ought to be. "The summer should be completely booked by now.''

She shut the book with a snap, leaning dejectedly against the counter. "Maybe Trip is right," she said almost to herself, remembering the last argument she'd had with her brother. "Maybe it's time to sell the place.''

Isabel gasped. "You don't want to do that. You love the Hideaway.''

"I do. And *I'd* eat bread and water before I'd let it go. But a baby needs things, expensive things…''

"The baby needs someone to love him. And that he will have. You mustn't give in to Trip's demands. He has his own selfish reasons for wanting you to sell.''

Nora smiled at her. Isabel made no secret of her opinion of Trip. "I know he's not without his faults, but he's still my brother and the only family I have left.''

"Better to be completely on your own, perhaps,'' Isabel grumbled.

Nora decided to ignore that remark. How could Isabel hope to understand the relationship Nora shared with her brother? The girl had grown up in a large family, with so many siblings jockeying for position, vying for their parents' attention.

But childhood had been completely different for Nora and Trip. The Hideaway had gone through years of financial difficulties, and although loving, Nora's parents had been too busy trying to keep the family business afloat to spend much time catering to the whims of their children. Trip had been a demanding baby, and Nora, a lonely little girl of eight had gladly taken on the task of looking after him. Through sickness and poor grades and driving lessons, he had relied on her, and though Trip was spoiled and self-centered at times, Nora still thought of him as the scared little boy who needed her.

It was probably too late to change the way Trip was, but was it too late to change her life? Was she only hanging on to the Hideaway out of stubbornness? Since her father had died, six years ago, and her mother shortly after that the profits had grown smaller and smaller each year. Bracing her head on her arms, she grimaced. "I don't know, Iz. Maybe it's just time to ''

"Oh, no!"

Nora straightened. Isabel's face had gone white. "What's the matter? Is it the baby again?"

"Oh, it can't be. What is he doing here?"

"Who?"

The girl gripped Nora's forearms tightly. "I can't see him. I won't." Her frightened eyes flew to the window. "Don't let him see me. Don't even tell him I'm here."

"Who?" Nora asked, a bud of panic beginning

to bubble to the surface of her own senses. While she stood in stunned silence, Isabel practically leaped from behind the registration desk and disappeared through the doorway that led to the private quarters of the lodge. "Where are you going?" Nora called after her. "Izzie, for Pete's sake, don't tell who—"

A car door slammed, and Nora whirled to look out the front window. A car had pulled into the semicircular driveway, and a man was just coming around the front of the vehicle. In the passenger seat, Nora caught a glimpse of a young boy, but her gaze quickly swung back to the man.

She lost him for a moment when he reached the front doors. That damned beveled glass! It turned his body into nothing but cuts and angles. Then he was inside, walking toward her in a purposeful stride.

He didn't look dangerous. Determined, maybe. Nora could see the hard set of his chin, the way his eyes scanned one side of the room and then the other before fixing steadily on her. For no reason she could name, Nora suddenly wished that she was dressed in her three-piece suit, the one she'd worn to the IRS audit last year.

Only this guy didn't look like an auditor, or any kind of government employee for that matter. His clothes were too casual, his tan was too dark and his golden-brown hair a little too long to meet any policy manual's expectations. He had strong features—the kind of genetic marvel that great ancestry could bestow upon a person. Any woman would want to know more about this man. So why was Isabel so—

Realization dawned about the same time that the man came to a halt directly in front of Nora.

Even in her advanced stage of pregnancy Isabel was gregarious, outgoing. She'd never have run away from a great-looking guy like this. Unless…

This man had to be the father of her child. The irresponsible, insensitive Bobby. He was older than Nora expected, but it had to be him.

Nora's heart bumped a little—the man was wonderful to look at—but she ignored it. Whatever reason Bobby had decided to show up on their doorstep now, Nora's allegiance lay with Isabel. And the baby.

Her baby.

CHAPTER THREE

JAKE COULD TELL right away that the woman was going to be difficult.

He didn't know what he had done to put her off him so fast, but he didn't much care. He gave her a once-over look meant for intimidation.

"Can I help you?" she asked.

Her words were pieces of crystal. He kept his own tone firm, but pleasant. "I hope so. I'm looking for a young woman named Isabel Petrivych."

"Isabel Petrivych," the woman repeated slowly, as though trying the name on for size. Then she shook her head. "I'm sorry—"

"Ben at the Whispering River Café told me I could find her here."

That threw her, he could tell. She wasn't a very good liar. The base of her neck went pink, and she swallowed, trying to regroup like an actress who realized she'd just muffed a line. "Oh. Well, Isabel was here. But she's not now."

"That's odd. I thought I saw her as I was coming up the walkway." Jake jerked his head toward the wide picture window. "It's a pretty good view from the front driveway."

"You must have been mistaken. It's just me here today."

The cool flatness of her tone irritated him. His eyes narrowed, taking in her sleek, toned length. The electric-blue leotard did marvelous things for her body—and a few unexpectedly pleasant things to his. He looked away, annoyed that he was noticing how attractive she was when he was trying so hard to be imposing. "So you're working out alone."

"Yes."

"But Isabel will be back." He made it a statement, not a question.

"Who knows?"

"I'm betting she will be," Jake replied with a tight smile. He bent to retrieve a pair of sneakers that lay on the floor nearby. They were small, and even though he'd met Isabel only once, he distinctly remembered her as petite. "She might need these," he said, taking a chance. When the woman looked momentarily stunned, and then opened her mouth to speak, he shook his head and tossed the sneakers on the desk. "Don't bother. You're at least a size eight."

"Seven, actually."

He started to smile at the response, then caught himself. "Look, I don't know you, or why you and Isabel have decided to play this little game—"

"I'm Nora Holloway. I own this place."

"Ah, yes. NLH. The artist."

"I beg your pardon?"

"I saw your paintings at the café. Ben was right."

"About what?"

"You are pretty."

It was her turn to look annoyed, which was a shame because the compliment had been a sincere one. The generous mouth, large, brown eyes—the bones in her face were the kind you wanted to linger on. He liked the thick auburn ponytail that swayed back and forth over her shoulder, and that cute little trio of freckles across her collarbone. Too bad she was turning out to be such a royal pain in the butt.

"Mr...."

"Burdette."

"Mr. Burdette," Nora Holloway said succinctly. "I've told you that Isabel isn't here. I don't know when she'll be back, so there's really no point in waiting."

"All right. Then I'll need to rent a cabin for the night."

"There isn't one available."

Jake turned to gaze out the front window again. "Looks pretty quiet out there," he observed. He pointed toward the wooden Vacancy sign that sat only a few feet away from his rental car, then smiled back at Nora. "And that's not what your sign says."

"We don't rent by the night. There's a three-night minimum."

"Three nights will be fine, then."

The pinkening at her throat had gone to red, but

she managed to harpoon him with an arctic glare. "Actually, we're closed. The season hasn't officially started yet."

He fished out his wallet and placed two one-hundred-dollar bills on the desk. "Then maybe I can give you a reason to open up early. *Un*officially."

Those dark eyes were smoldering now, and he knew that the offer of money had insulted her. The thin sheet of glass that had sprung up between them when they'd met had turned into solid steel.

"You're wasting your time," she said coldly. "And mine."

He was raw and improvising and suddenly out of patience. "We're in agreement there, lady, so listen up. I've come a long way to see Isabel, and I'm not going home until I do."

"Well, you can't stay here."

"Well, I think I'll wait, all the same."

He turned away from her, feigning interest in a wall covered with scattered pictures. The photographs looked as if they dated from the Eisenhower administration. Grainy, black-and-white, but all of them obviously taken nearby.

"How's the fishing around these parts?" he asked as he peered at a young boy holding up a good-size catfish for the camera.

"It's good. If you know what you're doing."

"Who's this?" He tapped the picture glass.

"My grandfather." She gave him a put-upon look. "As an innkeeper, I have the right to refuse anyone—"

He swung back to face her. "Look, I'm tired. I've just spent five hours cramming my six-foot, two-inch body in a roller skate of a sports car because my son liked the looks of it better than a roomy sedan. He's out in the car, by the way, and if you think *I'm* unbearable, you ought to take *him* on. The point is, I'm not getting in that toy and heading back to the interstate. Not when there are perfectly good accommodations right here."

"I don't want to call the sheriff, but—"

The door beside the registration desk, previously half-closed, suddenly flew back, and Isabel Petrivych appeared in the doorway. "Oh, stop... Enough!" she gasped out.

There was a long moment of silence, then Nora Holloway took a step in her direction. "Izzie..."

The girl's eyes were fixed on Jake. Her bottom lip disappeared between her teeth for a moment, then she said softly, "You wanted to see me. Here I am."

She hadn't changed much since he'd met her last year. Except for the pregnancy, of course. She still had deep blue eyes and long, dark hair that curled attractively down her back. Bobby had always been a sucker for women with hair like that, and Jake had guessed the moment his brother had introduced them that there might be more between them than just two people who'd met at the same political rally.

However, he'd never expected it to amount to anything. Bobby was leaving with Jake for Africa in a matter of days. They were going to build a bridge between two warring townships in the hill country, in a place so hot that the wind smelled like fire. The government had promised protection; the bridge was seen as a symbol of progress in the peace talks, and Jake had kidded Bobby unmercifully about being eager to see how his brother fared living in a place where the nearest comforts of home were miles and miles away.

The bridge was up and in use now. Shining hotly in the naked sun, forged together with a fair amount of tears and sweat...and blood. He'd brought Bobby's body home, and now he needed to do this one thing for his brother.

"You have seen me," Isabel said. "Now you can leave."

"No," Jake replied. "I can't."

"Why have you come here? I want nothing from you."

"I want to make sure that you're all right. That you aren't alone and—"

"I'm not alone. I have Nora to help me."

He was aware of the Holloway woman moving forward, as though responding to some unspoken cue. He resented it, that little movement to protect Isabel. As though he could ever be a danger to the girl who carried in her womb all that was left of his brother. He ignored her, keeping his attention focused on Isabel.

"We need to talk," he said firmly. "Just the two of us."

"There is nothing left to say."

"The hell there isn't." He crossed the room in

long, easy strides, but before he reached Isabel, Nora Holloway moved between them. "There are decisions that need to be made."

"And I have made them," Isabel snapped. "Go away!"

Nora's hand was suddenly on his chest. It was such a small, graceful hand, but it felt like a barrier of steel against his shirt. He frowned down at her, and something crossed her face that Jake hadn't seen in her eyes before. Genuine anger, iron determination...something.

"Don't get in the middle of this," he said finally.

It was clear she intended to ignore that advice. "Isabel's past the stage where the baby can be aborted, if that's what you had in mind."

That statement surprised him a little. So she knew about Bobby's foolish response to Isabel's news. What else did she know? "That was a mistake—"

"It certainly was. And you're not going to come into my home and upset Isabel with any other solutions you think might ease your conscience." She shook her head, and her eyes were filled with disgust. "You ought to be ashamed—coming here now. Where were you when she needed you the most?"

Jake jerked back. "Wait a minute. You think—"

"No, you wait a minute," she said, advancing on him a little. "Isabel doesn't deserve this. Only the worst kind of bastard would turn his back on a woman carrying his child—"

"Nora—" Isabel began.

"Miss Holloway—"

"—and if you think you can make things right now, you're in for a big surprise."

Jake took a step back. "So are you. Miss Holloway, I'm not the father of Isabel's child."

The woman's mouth tightened. "So now you want to deny that you're the father? I suppose we should have expected that."

He looked over at Isabel again, searching for help. The girl moved forward to touch Nora's elbow. "Nora," she said softly "This isn't Bobby. This is his older brother. Jake."

The Holloway woman's fierce expression melted a little; her eyes lost their fervor. Her hand came off Jake's chest as though it had been singed.

"Oh." A tenuous smile tried to form, but it failed miserably and then disappeared. "I'm sorry. I thought—"

"Yes, I know what you thought. That's part of the reason I'm here. To clear up a few things." To Isabel he said, "I'd just like to talk to you. That's all."

Isabel's mouth was still a slash of displeasure, but after a long silence she nodded. Nora picked up on this small signal and moved away from Jake. "I think I should leave you two alone," she said, then added quickly, "Isabel, I'll be in the rehab shed if you need me."

"Thank you," Jake began.

But Nora Holloway was already out the front door, a bright blue blur.

WITH THE LAST LEVEL of Space Scow conquered, Charlie sat in the car and stared down at the video game in his hands. *"I hate him,"* he muttered to himself.

Well, maybe *hate* was too strong a word. He really didn't know the guy well enough to hate him. Dislike, maybe. Yeah, that was it. Intense dislike. You couldn't burn in hell if you only disliked your father, could you?

He'd have to ask Marisela, his mother's housekeeper. The old woman was Catholic and knew everything there was to know about God and what he'd let you get away with. She'd know whether Charlie was in big trouble or not.

If he ever saw her again. Which might be never, now that his father had taken him away from his mother.

No. Stolen! That was the word. What was that phrase he'd heard somewhere…? Like a thief in the night. Yeah, that was the way it had been.

Only his father had come to his mother's Manhattan apartment in broad daylight, and his mother hadn't been weeping and wailing and carrying on about the loss of her son. Thea was much too dignified for that, and crying only made you look foolish, she'd once told him, so he really hadn't expected her to try to stop his father. She had other ways to deal with him. Charlie was sure she had an armload of lawyers looking over their new custody agreement right now, finding a way to get him back to New York and…and civilization.

Away from here. This place was creepy. Too

quiet. Lots of dark wood and hanging moss. All the little cabins made it look like a ranch, but there wasn't a single horse or cowboy in sight.

Maybe he'd get out of the car and poke around. Or maybe not. Who knew what was out there? He was comfortable in the city, where the doorman always looked out for him, and security cameras were in every corridor of the apartment building. Here, there could be grizzly bears in the woods that surrounded the main house.

The idea made him shiver, so he forced himself to think about his mother. He pictured her missing him in New York—with no one but her personal assistant, Anthony, and Marisela to talk to in the apartment. No one to ask her how the latest photo shoot went and actually care about her answer.

He looked out the car window, growing more impatient by the minute. He sure hoped they weren't going to stay in this dump for the night.

NORA SLOWED her pace as she went down the front steps of the lodge, giving herself time to regather her composure. Her breath was captured inside her like a square, solid box pressing against her rib cage. Her cheeks felt fiery, and she turned her face into the exquisite relief of a passing breeze.

She'd never been much of a fighter. Never confrontational. Even as a child she'd been the peacemaker in the family.

So what had she been doing just now? Lying through her teeth to a total stranger. Hearing her voice get higher and higher as she became more

and more defensive. Ready to lay a flying tackle on
this interloper if he so much as lifted a threatening
finger in Isabel's direction. Even now, the adrenaline was still pumping, pumping in her veins, until
she felt almost light-headed with the force of it.
And why—for God's sake?

She felt silly, embarrassed by the assumptions
she'd made about Jake Burdette in there. Not the
father, but the baby's uncle. He must think she was
an idiot. Oh, it was comical, really...

Only she didn't feel like laughing. Not at all.

Beneath all the feelings of humiliation and stu-
pidity lay a tiny trickle of fear, slipping through her
insides, leaving her cold and frightened.

Why was he here? What did he want? Why now,
when she'd just begun to really believe that her life
could be different, that her life could be made up
of all the wonderful things she'd ever dared to
dream about. John Forrester was drawing up the
necessary paperwork. A safe delivery. A petition to
the court. A few signatures. Then the dream of
motherhood would become a reality.

Deliberately she settled on the bottom step and
drew in a deep lungful of air. Okay, she told herself,
okay. Burdette's coming here today didn't have to
be a bad sign. It didn't mean he was here to effect
some sort of reconciliation between Isabel and his
brother. He was probably just trying to do the right
thing by her even if his younger brother wouldn't.
Maybe he planned to give her some money. Pay
her doctor bills. Offer her a place to stay until the
baby came.

Yes, that was why he was here. He looked like a man who took his responsibilities seriously. And in spite of that aggressive attitude, he had kind eyes—the soft hazel of autumn leaves. A man with eyes like that wouldn't hurt you, not deliberately. She had to remain positive, upbeat.

Closing her eyes, she willed herself to focus on the images nearest her heart—the baby. What he would feel like in her arms. His sweet smell, the softness of his hair, the whisper of his breath as she held him against her neck. Was there anything more heavenly than that—?

"Is my father ever coming out?"

Nora opened her eyes. A boy squinted down at her, his hands fisted on his hips, a look of pure annoyance etched across his childish features. He wasn't a bad-looking kid, but he was clearly in the pit-bull jaws of adolescence—no patience with adults and little desire to develop any.

Nora stood, brushing off the seat of her leotard. In spite of his preppy, clean-cut appearance, the boy looked tired, and Jake Burdette lost a point in her parenting manual. "Your dad might be a little while. Would you like to come for a walk with me?"

"Why should I? I don't even know you."

She stuck out a hand. "Nora Holloway. I own this place."

He took her fingers in a reluctant handshake. "Why?" he asked in a voice richly steeped in sarcasm.

It looked as though the kid had inherited some

of his father's manner. Nora didn't rise to the bait. She'd spent too many years winning over unenthusiastic boys and girls who had been dragged to the Hideaway by parents who were determined that they experience "the Great Outdoors." She smiled at him. "Not your kind of place, huh?"

"Not in a million years."

"Oh, well. Do you like animals?"

He shrugged. "I guess."

"I have a shed behind the main lodge where I take care of wild animals that have been injured. Want to see it?"

"Not really." With overt disinterest, he plucked a handheld video game out of his back pocket and began a slow march back to the car.

She wondered if Jake Burdette knew what a poor job he'd done in raising his son. "Well, you're on your own, then," she called after him. "So long."

She didn't look back as she walked behind the main lodge, but she could feel the boy surreptitiously watching her. He might not want to acknowledge it, but she suspected he had a kid's natural curiosity about where she was headed and what she was doing.

Her spirits lifted a little as she trooped down the short, grassy pathway that led to the building at the edge of the woods. The rehabilitation work she did with the animals in the shed usually took all her concentration. Maybe it would help keep her mind off Jake Burdette and what he might be saying to Isabel right this moment.

As kids, Nora and Trip had cobbled together a

playhouse from scrap lumber, setting it far enough away from the main lodge to escape their parents' watchful eyes. Five years ago, enlisting almost no outside help, Nora had expanded the playhouse, turning the modest structure into a rehab station that could house a small number of wounded animals. As a wildlife rehabilitator licensed by the state of Florida, she usually had half a dozen patients, but right now there were only four, with an eagle scheduled to come in from a nearby vet's office sometime soon.

The door to the shed creaked a little as she opened it, announcing her arrival to her charges. There were screeches and the flutter of wings from the cages holding an orphaned crow named Jeckle and a mockingbird named Begger, a chattering trill from Bandit, a raccoon who'd suffered numerous cuts when he'd been mauled by a dog, and a sniff of interest from the direction of Marjorie's pen.

"Hello, you guys," Nora said softly as she moved down the line of cages. "How are you doing today?"

The windows in the shed were small, but the sunlight sifting through them was strong enough for Nora to see that each of the animals was faring well. Within the next two weeks, they would all be able to be returned to the nearby national forest. Even Marjorie.

It was with some reluctance that Nora moved closer to the pen where the deer was penned. She knew she'd made a mistake with the fawn, an unforgivable error for a rehabber to make.

Marjorie's mother had been killed on the road, and the animal had been brought to her when she'd been hardly old enough to stand, malnourished and soaking wet. Nora had bottle-fed her, had wrapped her in blankets and stroked her for hours until the poor thing had stopped shivering. The fawn's sweet brown eyes had looked up at her defenselessly, trustingly, as though she knew Nora was trying to save her life but didn't know what to do to help.

And in that moment, Nora had done something every rehabber was supposed to avoid at all costs—she had fallen in love with one of her charges.

The fawn needed her as no other animal had. Nora brought the creature back from the brink of death at least half a dozen times during those first few days. In the first critical week, she had spent more time out here on a cot in the shed than in her own bed. But gradually the fawn had begun to rally and thrive.

Now, after six months, she was ready to be reintroduced to the wild. Nora knew in her heart it was past time, really. If she kept Marjorie much longer, the deer would lose all her instincts for survival.

Nora moved to the pen's entrance, but went no farther. Too often the deer had lifted her head over the edge of the door for a scratch, or had taken food from Nora's hand. Exhibiting such tame and trusting behavior was sweet and desirable in a deer park, but unacceptable for a wild animal. Knowing she was responsible for this kind of human imprinting, Nora was doing her best to reestablish some boundaries between the two of them.

The deer ran her body against the wire pen, obviously hoping for a friendly rub. Nora backed away. "I'm sorry, little girl," she said. "No more human contact. You've got to stay wild."

As though disappointed, the fawn snorted noisily, then wandered to the back of the pen to paw through the hay. She looked so healthy now, muscled, sleek, with none of the nicks and scars so many deer in the woods suffered. Nora watched the animal for a long time, wondering where she'd find the strength to send her off to join others of his kind.

While Nora stood there silently asking how she could have allowed herself to make such a mistake with Marjorie, she became aware of another presence. Actually, she heard the boy long before he appeared in the open doorway of the shed. He walked like a city kid—noisily, with total disregard for the beauty of the silence and his surroundings. From the corner of her eye she saw him move tentatively forward, inspecting the place.

Without glancing his way, Nora pulled a bale of hay off the small stack the feed store had delivered last week.

The boy moved into her line of vision, observing her silently for a long time. Then he asked, "Are you...like...one of those weird old ladies that keep eighty-two cats in their house?"

Nora straightened. "Gosh, I hope not. Come back in fifty years, and we'll see." She motioned behind him where a rusty box of tools sat on a wooden feed bin. "Hand me those wire cutters, will you?"

It took him longer than it should have to figure out which tool she meant. Finally, he lifted the wire cutters cautiously and held them out to her with a questioning look.

"Those are the ones," she told him. She slid the cutters under the wire binding the hay together. One snip, and the bale began to fall apart into flakes. "Feel like helping out?"

"I don't want to get dirty."

"I can see why," Nora replied, eyeing the expensive cut of his slacks and shirt. Who dressed a kid—especially a boy—like that? "Maybe you'd better not. I need someone who can really dig in and help me out."

The boy seemed to consider this statement for a moment or two, then he shrugged. "I'll be careful, and I guess there's nothing better to do."

"Can you tear this hay into pieces?" With one hand she indicated a second small pen she'd recently finished constructing. "Then spread it around the floor there?"

He nodded and began pulling apart the hay, methodically placing it in layers across the dirt floor of the pen while she retrieved medicines from the small refrigerator under one of the counters. She noticed that he was very careful not to allow the straw to touch his clothes.

"Don't you have anyone to do this for you?" he asked.

"I do now. What's your name?"

"Charles."

He said his name precisely, as though he thought it held special meaning. She inclined her head toward him. "Welcome to the rehab shed, Charles. Don't talk too loud and don't move too suddenly. It frightens the animals. And if you want to hang on to all your fingers, don't put them in the cages. All right?"

He nodded again. "So what's a rehab shed?" he asked when he was about halfway through the chore.

"A place where sick wild animals get better. Every year a few run into trouble—cars, hunters with no sense, predators that beat them up pretty badly. If the problem is fixable, they're brought here so I can nurse them back to health."

"So they're your pets."

She thought of Marjorie and shook her head firmly. "No. A rehabber isn't allowed to turn them into pets. They have to remain wild. Otherwise they won't know how to survive once you've released them." From the sink in one corner, she added a few drops of water to the medicinal base she planned to use on Bandit's cuts. "Want to meet them?"

He nodded, and she led him to the cages while she gently stirred the yellow concoction into a paste. "This is Jeckle," she said, inclining her head toward the crow, then the mockingbird. "And that's Begger. They were both brought to me as orphans."

Charles wrinkled his nose as he peered into

Jeckle's cage. "Why are you bothering to save him? He's just a crow. They're everywhere."

"You see little boys everywhere, but wouldn't you want someone to save you if you were in trouble?"

"I'm not a little boy," Charles said in an aggrieved tone. "I'm nearly a teenager."

"Well, Jeckle is important to me. All creatures are."

The kid looked up at her with sudden speculation. "Do they pay you lots of money to do this?"

"They don't pay me at all. I do it because I want to." She moved on to the raccoon's cage. The animal looked at them with sharp, beady eyes. "This is Bandit."

"Are you gonna cut his head off?"

"Good grief, no!" Nora stared at the boy, wondering what kind of horrid imagination this kid liked to indulge. "Why would you ask that?"

"You know," Charles said in a seemingly earnest tone. "Rabies. Isn't that how they find out if they have them?"

Nora frowned. "Bandit doesn't have rabies. He had a run-in with a dog. I'm mixing up this paste right now so that I can put it on those cuts you see."

"Oh. What if he bites you? Is there a chance you'll get rabies?"

"Are all kids your age so gruesome?"

The boy opened his mouth to reply, then seemed to change his mind. After a few seconds he spoke.

"I've just never seen many wild animals up close before. I live in the city. At least, I used to."

"That explains a few things," Nora muttered.

Charles asked a few more questions about the raccoon and its chances for survival. Unexpectedly, they were thoughtful, intelligent inquiries, and he listened closely to her answers. Nora began to suspect that he was enjoying himself.

"This is Marjorie," Nora said as they moved on to the deer's pen. "Her mother was killed on the road."

"She doesn't look like a Marjorie."

"Well, you don't look like a Charles."

He jerked his head up to glare at her. "That's what my mother always calls me."

"You look like a Charlie to me. Do you mind if I call you that?"

"I guess not," he said in a soft, sullen voice. He stared at the deer as though memorizing every detail. "Marjorie's still a dumb name."

"I named her after Marjorie Kinnan Rawlings."

"Who?"

"The woman who wrote *The Yearling*."

He shook his head. "Never read it."

"Too bad. It's wonderful."

The boy looked up at her again, one eyebrow raised in inquiry. "Any monsters in it?"

"Afraid not. No car chases or killer tornadoes, either. But there's a young boy in the story. He lives deep in the Florida woods with his family, and he finds a fawn, just like Marjorie here."

"Sounds exciting," Charlie commented with a

marked lack of enthusiasm. "When are you going to let her go?"

Nora frowned and looked down at the yellow paste in her hands. "Perhaps in a few days."

"You don't want to?"

"She has to be released," she replied, more for her own benefit than his. "She's probably stayed too long as it is."

Charlie straightened, and Nora was aware that he was suddenly watching her closely. For a kid, he seemed very intuitive. She had the strangest feeling that he knew exactly how much the mistake she'd made with Marjorie was costing her.

"You could lie," he said quietly and gave her a sly look, as though they were suddenly coconspirators. "Tell them you let her go, but keep her instead."

"I couldn't do that."

"Why not?" he asked. He seemed genuinely surprised by her answer. "'Cause you'd get caught?"

"No. Because then she'd be miserable instead of me. She's a wild animal who wouldn't be happy living in a pen."

He seemed to give this thought serious consideration for a long moment. Then his shoulders rose in an elaborate shrug. "You should just do what you want, and the heck with what anybody else thinks, including Marjorie."

"Surely your parents taught you that's not a very good way to live your life?" Nora said.

The boy actually stiffened. With a quaint and somehow heartrending dignity he said, "My mom taught me everything I need to know, and she did everything right.''

His eyes had taken on a militant sparkle, and Nora realized that he was waiting for her to dispute that statement. She didn't. Instead, she said lightly, ''Wow. A mom who doesn't make mistakes. I hope she's going to write a book on motherhood.''

''She's a famous model.'' Charlie's expression turned to one of pride. ''So famous that she doesn't even need her last name anymore. Her name's Thea. You've probably seen her. She was on two magazine covers last month.''

Nora never bothered to follow the news about the ''beautiful people,'' but even she'd heard of Thea. The woman—in her early thirties—was the latest darling of the photographers. Some perfume company—trying to woo the aging baby boomers—had just given her an ungodly amount of money to be the star of their multimedia ad campaign. There was some other reason Nora was familiar with the woman's name, but for the life of her, she couldn't put her finger on it.

She went to the sink and washed the spatula she'd used to stir Bandit's medicine. With her back to Charlie, she said, ''A mother who doesn't make mistakes and is a supermodel. Your dad must feel pretty lucky.''

''They're divorced. He hates her.''

She cocked her head in the boy's direction, not certain she'd heard correctly over the sound of running water from the tap. ''How do you know that?''

''He took me away from her. Just to make her mad.''

That statement carried such fury that Nora turned and looked sharply at the boy. She was about to engage Charlie in further discussion, but she became aware of Jake Burdette standing in the open doorway.

Hot blood surged into her cheeks, and she was glad for the late-afternoon light that gave everything in the rehab shed a mellow glow. She wondered if he had heard the last of his son's remarks. His face gave nothing away.

Charlie—obviously expecting her to react to his words—turned his head and caught sight of his father. His posture went from stiff to ramrod straight.

''Charles,'' Jake Burdette said mildly as he ducked his head under the low doorway and moved farther into the shed. ''You shouldn't have run off without telling me where you were going.''

An argument looked ready to drop from Charlie's lips, and Nora plunged in quickly. ''My fault,'' she offered in an effort to lighten the sudden tension between father and son. ''I'm always looking for someone to fetch and carry, and he was too nice to refuse.''

Jake gave her a vague smile, his attention still focused on Charlie. ''Get your things together from the car. We're checking in.'' He held up one of the Hideaway's large key rings. ''Cabin Two.''

''You're kidding.'' There was no mistaking Charlie's feelings about staying a night in one of the cabins.

When Jake ignored the comment, Charlie sighed heavily, snatched the key from his father's hand and stomped out of the shed without a look or word in her direction. Silently, the two adults watched him go.

"Thank you for keeping him occupied," Jake said eventually. "He didn't want to come on this trip, and he's been reminding me of that fact ever since we left Norfolk."

"No problem. He seems like a nice enough kid."

"Does he?" Jake replied with a surprised look and a light laugh. "I've yet to see much of that side of him. I've just recently gained custody, and our relationship is a little thorny."

"I'm sure he'll come around."

It was the kind of hope-filled comment all parents like to hear, and he gave her a small smile to indicate he knew that. Then he looked at her in such a calm, deliberate way that her pulse jumped. Before she knew it, he was taking her hand, as though meeting her for the first time. "I'm afraid we got off on the wrong foot. Isabel speaks very highly of you, and I know firsthand that you're very protective of her."

She dipped her head. "I'm rather embarrassed…"

"Don't be. Everyone should have a friend like you."

The words were low, but sounded so sincere that her pulse jumped again, even danced a little. Silly, she thought, and unexpected. Had it really been so long since a good-looking man had said nice things to her that she should react like a teenager on her first date? Jeckle began to screech unpleasantly, and Nora used the crow as an excuse to move away from Jake Burdette.

She removed the water bottle from Jeckle's cage. "So," she remarked in what she hoped was an off-handed way. "Isabel checked you in."

"We both felt we needed more time to talk. Do you object?"

She shrugged. "If Isabel doesn't mind, there's no reason for me to."

"How long have you known her?"

"Isabel answered an ad I'd placed for seasonal help three years ago. She's been coming every break from college since then." She looked up at him over the edge of Jeckle's cage. "Well, all except the holidays last year when she met your brother. Over the years we've developed quite a friendship. We're more like sisters now."

"I'm glad she had a good friend to turn to when she needed one."

"I'll do anything I can to help her."

He was quiet for a long moment, watching her replace the refilled water bottle into the crow's cage. Then he said in a tone that sounded almost sympathetic, "Does that include adopting her baby?"

She leveled a look at him. "You make it sound like I'm only doing it to help her out of a jam. I assure you it wasn't a quick decision."

"Isabel's very young. Probably confused about what she really wants—"

"She's not confused at all," Nora countered. "Perhaps she was at first, and certainly she was frightened, but she's very clear on what she wants now."

"So you had nothing to do with her plan to give you her baby?"

The conversation was deteriorating rapidly. "What are you suggesting?" she asked in what she meant to be a chilling voice.

"I'm not suggesting anything," he said. "I'm pretty much stating it up front. I think this decision to give her baby away is too hasty. Perhaps she saw it as the only way out of a difficult predicament."

"If she found herself in a difficult predicament, your brother was the one who helped put her there. He washed his hands of the problem and even suggested an abortion. Are you aware of that?"

He nodded. "I am. Isabel's telephone call threw him for quite a loop. That doesn't excuse him, but I do know that he came to regret that suggestion almost immediately after he made it."

"And yet you're the one who's come here, when it should be him—"

"My brother is dead, Miss Holloway. He died a few days after he received Isabel's phone call."

He said the words in such a matter-of-fact way that at first Nora thought she'd heard incorrectly. She looked at him, trying to gauge his feelings, but his features were expressionless. "I'm sorry. I didn't know."

His broad shoulders moved uneasily, and she suspected he wasn't comfortable with her sympathy. His hands roamed over a line of bottles and cans that sat upon the counter, as though he had real interest in containers of peroxide and liniment.

"He was working with me in Nigeria, building a bridge. A group of bandits attacked one of my field crews. Bobby hung on for a while, but…" He broke off, turning away from the counter suddenly. There was an odd twist to his mouth, as though he'd said too much and wished he could call back the words.

"Have you told Isabel?" Nora asked softly.

"Yes. She took it well, I think." He grimaced. "I know Bobby's initial reaction to her telephone call hurt her pretty badly. I don't believe she's been entertaining pleasant thoughts about him all these months."

"Still, I should go to her." Placing the last of the medicine in the refrigerator, Nora washed and dried her hands. She turned to face him suddenly. "You said Bobby came to regret his decision?"

"I sat by my brother's hospital bed for almost two days before he died. He wanted to come home, find Isabel and tell her he'd made a huge mistake. There's no doubt in my mind he would have married her and given his child a name." Jake expelled a long sigh. "Toward the end he knew he wasn't going to… He asked me to make sure she was all right. That she'd have enough money to support herself and the baby. That's why I'm here. Of course, everything's changed now."

Nora's heart cramped suddenly. "What do you mean?"

Jake gave her a hard, level look that didn't reassure her any. "I'm sorry, but I can't go along with what Isabel wants. I can't let you adopt my brother's child."

CHAPTER FOUR

IT WAS ABSOLUTELY as bad as she had feared. Her dream was disintegrating. A sudden weariness dropped over Nora like a second skin.

Please don't do this to me, she wanted to beg. Not again.

It was an effort to keep her lips from trembling, but somewhere in the past she'd learned the trick of shielding herself. Somehow she managed to find enough voice to say firmly, "The decision has been made."

Jake shrugged. "It can be unmade. I understand no adoption papers have been signed yet."

"They will be. Isabel is not going to change her mind."

"We'll see. I've asked her to give me a week to convince her otherwise."

"Mr. Burdette, did Isabel tell you about her plans for the future?"

"No. I suppose that's one of the things we'll need to discuss. We barely covered the basics. She told me the child was a boy, but little more than that."

Nora snorted in derision. "I'm afraid you're in

for quite a disappointment. Isabel may seem rather...scattered right now, but she has very specific goals for herself, and they don't include raising a child."

Her hands were shaking, and to find something for them to do she began reorganizing the items on the counter, tilting bottles this way and that as though they were intended for some sort of display.

Jake observed her silently for several long moments, then he reached over to place one hand on top of hers.

"Miss Holloway," he said in a surprisingly gentle tone. "Nora. I'm sorry. I'm sure you're a very nice person—"

She snatched her hands out from under his and jerked her head up to glare at him. "You don't even know me."

"By the end of the week I intend to know everything I need to know about you."

The sudden steely tone in his voice made her heart buck in rebellion. Her eyes narrowed. "Are you trying to intimidate me?"

"There's no need to be defensive."

She clamped her jaw around a few harsh words that came to mind. Giving him the same hard, level look he had given her only minutes ago, she said with biting courtesy, "Mr. Burdette, I've waited a long time to have a child. Now that it's about to become a reality, I'm not willing to just politely step aside. I want this baby. It's Isabel's intention that I have this baby. The wishes of the mother hold a considerable amount of sway in the eyes of the law.''

He appeared completely unperturbed. If anything, something in his stillness became more ominous. ''Yes, they do,'' he agreed in a quiet tone. He pushed away from the counter and headed toward the door. Before he left the room, he turned to look at her one last time. ''But I doubt very much that the courts would completely ignore the concerns of a blood relative.''

ISABEL PLEADED a headache when Nora returned to the lodge, and she allowed the girl to escape into her bedroom for the evening. Tomorrow was soon enough to find out if all her hopes and dreams for this baby had been for nothing.

But in the morning, Isabel was already gone when Nora woke. A note on the kitchen counter indicated she'd gone into town with Jake Burdette and would return by mid-morning. Instead of trying to drum up an appetite for breakfast, Nora began working on the baby's quilt the two of them had been piecing together. She wanted desperately to believe that one day her child would lie under it.

By ten o'clock, when she head the front lobby door of the lodge open and shut, her nerves were as tight as each stitch she had pulled through the pastel material.

Isabel came into the living room. Nora discovered that she couldn't look at her right away. She was afraid of what she'd see in the girl's eyes, afraid she wasn't strong enough yet to accept whatever cataclysmic decisions about her future had been decided over a simple breakfast.

"You got my note?" Isabel asked as she went into the kitchen.

"Yes."

That was the best response Nora could manage. Every breath she took seemed dangerous now. She heard the sound of Isabel cracking ice into a glass, and she thought, *Are you afraid to tell me, Izzie? Is it so bad that you have to build up your courage first?*

The fear of the unknown was like pain, swallowing her alive. She couldn't stand it any longer. If the baby was never to be hers, she had to know.

The moment Isabel appeared in the doorway between the kitchen and living room, Nora stopped stitching and looked up. Her eyes captured Isabel's.

"Do you want to talk about it?" she asked.

"Yes, I suppose we should," Isabel answered vaguely, then shook her head. "No. Not yet. Oh, Nora, why did he have to come here?"

"Please don't upset yourself. It isn't good for you or the baby."

Isabel settled on the couch, leaned forward as far as her burgeoning stomach would allow and placed her hand on Nora's shoulder. "You've been so good to me. You know I'd never want to see you hurt, don't you?"

The pain in Nora's chest became a vise. She pushed the fabric from her lap, wanting to rise, but she felt bowed by the kind of grief that would not let her stand straight. *I mustn't give in to it. I have to be strong.*

She twisted onto her knees so that she could face the girl. Isabel's fingers were clutched tightly around the glass of water. Nora took it out of her hand, set in on the coffee table, then took both Isabel's hands in her own.

"Izzie, it will be all right," she said softly. "Listen to me. There is nothing I want more than to raise your child as my own. But if you're trying to find some kind way to tell me…if Jake Burdette's coming here has made you change your mind about the adoption…I can accept it. I must."

Isabel gave her a surprised look. "No. Oh, no! I'm more determined than ever that you should have this baby."

Renewed hope fluttered in Nora's chest. "Do you mean that?"

"Absolutely."

Nora gave her a puzzled look. "Then what has you so upset?"

"It's him, Bobby's brother. I told him what I want to accomplish when I go back to Bosnia. I even showed him the letter I got from Blakely-Forbes. I asked him if he knew how few medical students ever get an opportunity to intern at the best hospital for reconstructive surgery in the world."

"What did he say to that?"

"He congratulated me."

"What's wrong with that?" Nora asked.

"Nothing, I suppose," Isabel said, chewing on her lower lip. "But I was very unnerved by his calm, quiet attitude. What if he tries to make things difficult for me?''

''What could he do?''

''Suppose he talks to someone at Blakely-Forbes? Would they want an intern who's had an illegitimate baby? I know he wants to convince me to keep the baby. But I won't do it. I won't.''

''Then how can he?'' Nora squeezed Isabel's hand to keep the girl's panic from spiraling out of control. ''Besides, do you really think I'll let him upset you? You know I'll protect you, Izzie. You know that, don't you?''

''Yes.''

''Then, why are you letting yourself get so worked up?''

''I'm not sure. The only time Jake showed any anger at all this morning was when he reminded me that the baby was a member of his family, too, and that he's not going to respect my decision to let you adopt this child.''

''He'll give up and go away once he sees that we're both determined. He doesn't know what a formidable duo we are.''

''Bobby told me once that Jake's very tough and stubborn. He brought the family business back from the edge of bankruptcy. He has…connections. He's smart. The night I met him he carried on our entire conversation in my native language. Dialect and all.''

''What's that got to do with anything?'' Nora asked with a light laugh.

''He speaks six languages and can do business

in all of them. A man that worldly isn't going to be intimidated by a couple of women."

"Isabel!" Nora scolded. "How can you say such a thing? You're a disgrace to American women everywhere."

"I'm not American," Isabel reminded her with a smile, clearly willing to be reassured and teased out of her worried state.

"You know what I mean. The truth is, honey, he can't make you keep this baby. So no matter what he thinks, Mr. Jake Burdette is about to hear the word *no*. In six different languages if necessary." Nora cocked her head at Isabel. "Why are you looking at me like that?"

"I don't think I've ever seen you this…intense before."

Nora placed her hand against the swell of Isabel's stomach. "That's because I've never wanted anything more in my life. And I'm willing to fight for it."

They spent the next two hours working on opposite ends of the quilt, involved in talk about the baby. Their laughter was a little too bright, their conversations a little too loud, but gradually the crinkle of nerves in the pit of Nora's stomach began to smooth out and disappear.

Around noon, Nora looked over at Isabel's needlework, then tossed her own section of the quilt away from her lap. "Oh, drat! Your stitches are perfectly uniform and mine go all over the place."

"It's all the practice I've had suturing in medical school."

"They're beautiful," Nora said as she leaned closer to inspect the girl's handiwork. She slipped an awed look upward. "You're going to make such a wonderful surgeon, Izzie."

Isabel stopped stitching and smiled at her. "Do you really think so? I want to be the best reconstructive surgeon my country has ever seen. Think what good I could do for bodies that have been destroyed by bombs and bullets. Oh, Nora, it will be like working magic, don't you think?"

Nora returned her friend's smile. In the months since Isabel had made the suggestion that Nora adopt her baby, there had been many times when she had wondered how the girl would be able to walk away from something as precious as her own child. But hearing her friend speak of her surgical future with such reverent hope, Nora knew nothing would stand in Isabel's way. She almost felt sorry for Jake Burdette.

Nora moved forward to give Isabel a swift hug. "You'll be awe-inspiring, Izzie. You really will." Slipping a book off the coffee table, she settled back against the couch. "Now, take pity on me. Fix the mess I've made on this square while I propose some more names for the baby."

"Oh, no, not again!" Isabel protested, but she picked up Nora's side of the quilt anyway. "We've been through all those names a dozen times."

"And still nothing jumps out at me. Which is why we have to go through them again." Nora riffled through the book. "How about Kevin?"

Isabel made a face. "Not Kevin. I dated a Kevin

in my first year of college. He had cold hands no matter what the temperature was. It was like being touched by a fish."

"How about this one? Ivan."

"As in 'The Terrible'? You wouldn't do that to a kid."

"What about Einion?"

"Onion?"

"Einion."

"You're making that up."

"I'm not," Nora said with a laugh, and flipped the book around so Isabel could read it herself. "Einion. It's Celtic."

"And it's horrible," Isabel said. "Keep looking."

The task quickly escalated into a silly game. Nora called out a few more names, each one more preposterous than the last. Isabel started to make up stories about the kinds of kids who would have such impossible names, and both women ended up laughing until they were crying, and Nora had to jump up to find them tissues.

Finally, with Isabel wiping tears from her eyes, Nora slapped the book back on the coffee table and shot mock daggers toward her friend. "You are not helping one bit. He can't stay Baby Boy Holloway forever. What are we going to name this kid?"

"How about Robert? After his father?" a voice cut through their laughter.

The fact that they were no longer alone startled both women, and they looked quickly toward the door that led to the registration desk. Jake Burdette stood in the opening. His presence silenced the sound of their amusement like someone snapping off a radio.

No one spoke for several awkward seconds. It annoyed Nora that Jake had barged into her private quarters to make a suggestion he knew she'd find upsetting. Deciding that the best way to handle his recommendation was to ignore it, she stood up.

"Did you need something?" she asked.

He motioned back toward the outer lobby. "Sorry to interrupt your fun, ladies. But I did ring the bell on the counter and no one came."

Nora hadn't seen him since he'd left her standing alone in the rehab shed yesterday. Cabin Two was angled in such a way that she could have a clear view from the front windows, but she'd stubbornly refused to show an interest in Burdette's comings and goings. If he and his son ate dinner out, or cooked something simple in the cabin's tiny kitchen, or sat on the front porch and watched the sun go down over the pines, she never knew.

What she did know was that he was just as attractive today as he had been yesterday. More so, if that was possible. He looked completely relaxed in jeans and a polo shirt of dark blue that made his body seem to be casually hung together and yet muscularly controlled all at the same time. His eyes, clear and level, with nothing shirked, nothing hidden, rolled over her. For just an instant, Nora felt flushed, tongue-tied. Then she pulled herself together.

"Did you need something, Mr. Burdette?" she

asked again, hiding behind the mask of polite disinterest while the tension within her stretched from
nerve ending to nerve ending.

"A wrench, if you've got one. And maybe a can
of WD-40."

The request caught her off guard. "I beg your
pardon?"

"The kitchen sink in the cabin is blocked. I tried
the plunger I found in the closet, but the clog won't
budge. I can fix it, but I'll need tools." He tilted
his head, giving her a look that indicated he thought
he might be dealing with someone completely inept. "You do have some, don't you?"

"Of course I do," she replied in a tone that was
sharp with annoyance. She stood quickly, pulling
down the hem of her shorts and tucking the tail of
her blouse into the waistband. "And I'm the one
who should fix it. I'll come right down."

"That really isn't necessary. I can handle it."

In a businesslike voice, Nora said, "I'll handle
it, Mr. Burdette. I don't ask my guests to do their
own maintenance." She looked at him suddenly,
giving him a false smile that would shame a shark.
"Besides, I wouldn't want your stay here to be unpleasant."

"No, not unpleasant." He returned her smile,
and something in the gleam of his eyes told her she
hadn't fooled him one bit. "Just short, I imagine."

SHE WAS TRUE to her word. Less than ten minutes
after Jake had returned to the cabin, he looked out
the screen door and saw Nora Holloway marching

down the driveway, toolbox in hand. With her long, shapely bare legs and swinging ponytail, she made the most attractive maintenance man he'd ever seen, and only the slight frown carved upon those delicate features ruined the appealing picture she presented.

A twist of amusement lifted his mouth. He had a pretty good idea just who was responsible for that frown. The woman had decided not to like him, and she wouldn't pretend to feel otherwise.

He scooped up the bag carrying the rest of the supplies he'd purchased in town and went to join Charlie on the front porch. The kid's grumbling had gotten louder in the last few minutes. Evidently he'd made no headway untangling line from the new spinning reel Jake had attached to one of two new rods.

The boy might be able to tell the difference between a Monet and a Matisse at twenty paces, but, in his hands, a simple rod and reel became a deadly weapon. Jake had spent an hour this morning teaching him to cast a line, and so far Charlie had managed to hook the cushions on the rocking chairs twice and poke a fair-size hole in Jake's favorite jeans.

"Got it untangled yet?" he asked his son as he rooted through one of the bags.

"No," Charlie said, stretching the word out for effect. He huffed noisily and stared at his father. "And I don't see why we have to do this. If you want fish for dinner, even a podunk town like this one has to have a supermarket."

"Have you ever had fresh fish?"

"Better, probably. Marisela, our housekeeper, was only allowed to shop in the best markets. She handpicked all our food because Mother has to be very careful what she eats."

Of course, Jake thought, and dropped his head to hide his wry smile.

"Let me amend that question," he said patiently. "Have you ever had fresh fish that you yourself have caught?"

The boy threw him a skeptical look over the knotted line in his lap. "No, but do I have to whack the cow myself before I can enjoy a steak? I don't see the difference."

"Let's give it a chance anyway."

The kid might have argued further, but in that moment he noticed Nora Holloway making her way toward them. Unexpectedly, his son's frown smoothed out, and his posture improved. Jake realized that, for all his disinterest in being here, evidently Charlie wasn't immune to the sight of a pretty woman, either.

Nora came up the steps slowly. Jake, with one hip and a leg hitched over the edge of the porch railing, gave her his best smile. She didn't return it.

He nodded toward the toolbox banging against her bare leg. "Seems like an awful lot of tools for such a small clog."

"Well, you never know what you'll find once you get in there."

Jake looked up from the lead weights he'd been

juggling in his hand. "I'd imagine there are a lot of problems in maintaining a place like this."

"None that I haven't been able to handle," she replied in her most efficient manner. She glanced over at Charlie, and Jake was annoyed that she could find a smile for the boy, but not for him. "Hi, Charlie."

"Hello."

"Going fishing?"

The kid grimaced and held up the knotted line. "Gee, what gave it away?"

Nora turned her glance back to Jake. Still absorbed by the fact that his son hadn't taken her head off for calling him Charlie instead of Charles, he almost missed her next words. "There's no fishing allowed in the spring pool, but you can pick a spot anywhere along the riverbank."

"Do you want to recommend any place in particular?" Jake asked.

She turned and took the weight off her arm by lifting the toolbox onto the railing beside him. After staring down the slope that led to the river for a few moments, she pointed toward a spot a good distance away from the spring. "I've always had luck over there. Where those trees sort of interlock overhead."

His gaze didn't follow her pointing finger.

He supposed he shouldn't have been surprised to discover that he was suddenly aware of her in a distinctly sexual way. The past few months had been time-consuming, demanding—his efforts to put a satisfactory end to the African job in spite of

Bobby's death, all the battling with Thea over Charlie. There hadn't been much time to think about women.

But suddenly here he was, feeling his body tighten in quick response to her proximity, noticing little things about her that he had no business noticing. Like the way the fine hairs at the base of her neck—too short for the ponytail—looked as though they'd feel like silk if he touched them. The way her nose tipped up at the end, just slightly, just enough to keep her profile from being too serious.

Only this wasn't the woman Jake should be taking an interest in. Since he and Isabel had talked this morning, he'd been thinking a lot about Bobby's child, sorting through several possibilities—none of them likely to make Nora Holloway feel kindly toward him.

His lack of response made Nora turn her head his way. Her expression was questioning, uneasy, and although she didn't say another word, he watched the slow slide of movement as her throat worked, and she swallowed. He would have bet the family business that she knew exactly what he was thinking.

Oh, hell, a little voice murmured in his head. Don't look at her.

He tried to recall exactly what the conversation had been about while he mastered his anatomy.

Something about fishing.

Yeah, that was it.

He swung his head toward the river, searching out the spot she'd suggested.

He had to smile when he realized the place she meant. Early this morning, too restless to sleep, he'd walked quite a stretch of the riverbank, and if there was ever an unlikely spot to cast a line, the place Nora Holloway suggested was it. It was so overgrown and muddy that access to the river would be nearly impossible. More important, the current took a sharp turn there, creating a still cove. The only thing likely to be biting would be mosquitoes.

He looked back at her. The beginnings of an innocent smile told Jake she'd be perfectly delighted to have him spend the entire day fishing and coming up empty-handed.

He shook his head, then turned his attention back to the river and pointed in an entirely different direction. "I was thinking there, where that overspill from the spring makes a small waterfall. Lots of aerated water at the base of it. Bound to be fish hanging around."

"I suppose," she agreed pleasantly, although she couldn't quite manage to keep the disappointment out of her voice. "You'll need bobbers, so your line doesn't drag bottom and snag on the rocks."

He held up a package of red-and-white floats. "Like these?"

Checkmated, her forehead settled into a frown for a moment, then she said levelly, "I'd better see to that clog."

Hiding a look of triumph, he watched as she slid the toolbox from the railing and banged through the screen door. There wasn't a doubt in his mind that she was cursing him all the way to the kitchen.

"What was that all about?" Charlie asked, rousing Jake from his reverie.

"What was what all about?"

"The two of you. You act like you're in some kind of competition. Don't you like her?"

"I haven't thought much about her one way or the other." Jake didn't elaborate. Instead, he slipped off the railing and removed the tangled reel from his son's hand. "I'll work on this," he said. "You go change into the clothes I bought."

Charlie rose from the rocker, the mulish tilt to his mouth once more in place. "I told you, I don't like jeans. They're sloppy-looking and they're—"

"Perfect for running around a place like this," Jake finished for him. He could see the battle brewing in Charlie's eyes and decided on a different approach. "You don't want to mess up all those fine clothes you brought with you, do you? Wear the jeans while we're here, then when we leave you can throw them in the trash if you want to."

"How long are we gonna be here?"

"A few days. Do we have a deal?"

"I suppose."

"Go on, then. I'll have this fixed in a minute, and you'll be all set to catch your supper."

"I don't want to fish."

Jake smiled brightly at his son, wondering just when it was that Charlie had stopped being a normal, fun-loving kid and turned into a rude, overbearing brat. "Well, we could sit around the cabin and just talk, if you'd rather."

That suggestion got the expected response. The kid snorted in disgust and made his way toward the door. "I'll get dressed." As he yanked open the screen, he shot a disgruntled glance toward his father. "Can I bring—"

"No," Jake interrupted without looking up from the reel in his hands. "No video games."

Charlie bore himself off like an offended prince, and Jake concentrated on the mess his son had made of the fishing equipment. He grimaced at the nest of knots. Was he pushing too hard by forcing the kid to go fishing with him?

Jake had always loved the long, languid hours he and his grandfather had spent at the lake. It hadn't been about the fish they caught—although it was always great to arrive triumphant in the kitchen with a creel full of fish. More than anything, it had been about time spent together—without Bobby, who was too young and restless to sit quietly for long, or his father, who saw every excursion on the water as an excuse to stock an ice chest with beer.

No, no outsiders. Just him and the old man.

And as the sweetness of a summer morning broke through, as the mists rose around their boat like ghosts meeting and embracing, they had fished and talked about every subject imaginable. Silly things. Important things. Those were wonderful hours when the world had telescoped down to just the two of them.

Jake glanced toward the river, thinking how

much his grandfather would have liked this place. He'd been gone fifteen years, and Jake still missed him. He wished the old man were here to help Jake find the best way to reach his son. Maybe the kind of relationship he'd had with his grandfather wasn't possible with Charlie, but damn it, Jake knew he could do better than his own father.

Samuel Burdette had been drunk most of the time and had run the family business into the ground. He'd never given his kids a second thought. As the oldest son, Jake had been the one to look after his younger brother. All things considered, he hadn't done such a bad job. So now he could do the same for his son.

Time and patience. That was all he needed. And a few lazy days of catching fish in the dappled sunlight of this peaceful place.

His gaze traveled over the grounds of Holloway's Hideaway. It was a beautiful piece of property, situated in a location that would be coveted by every developer in the state if they only knew it existed.

But anyone with a college degree in business could see that the Hideaway was a losing proposition. There were too few cabins to turn a real profit, and though they were functional and clean, he'd spotted more than one sign that the units needed renovation and a major infusion of cash. Asking the right questions of Isabel this morning had gained him the knowledge that money was one thing Nora Holloway didn't have much of, and he wondered how long she could hold on.

Not a very encouraging future. And not a very

stable environment in which to try to raise a child. Frowning, Jake leaned forward to run his hand along one of the porch struts. Dry rot was taking hold of the wood, and it would have to be replaced before too long.

Was he really willing to walk away and let Bobby's son be raised in this place, by a complete stranger with limited resources?

He still wasn't sure, but he knew he couldn't make a decision until he knew more about Nora Holloway. Until he knew just what kind of woman she was.

He straightened and went inside the cabin.

CHAPTER FIVE

THERE WAS a lot of banging coming from the direction of the cabin's kitchen, then a muffled curse. Jake smiled. Evidently, "I'll-handle-it" Holloway had run into a little trouble.

Charlie was still in the bedroom. Jake found Nora alone in the kitchen. The plunger was lying in the sink in a couple of inches of standing water, just the way he'd left it. Clearly she hadn't had any more luck breaking the clog loose than he'd had.

She was on her side, braced on one forearm, her attention focused on working a wrench around the exposed pipe under the sink. Occasionally she hit the wrench with a small hammer to try to work the P-trap nut loose. The unobstructed view he had of her legs was enough to make the trip in from the front porch worthwhile. All sculpted cream and silky skin. Damn, but the woman was put together nice!

He drew in a deep lungful of air and decided the only gentlemanly thing to do was to see if she could use a hand. He'd just have to make certain that she didn't bite it off.

He leaned against the small stove, determined not

to let the slightest hint of amusement slip into his voice. "Can I help?" he called out to her.

The banging ceased immediately, and it was dangerously quiet all of a sudden. She didn't emerge from under the sink or even turn her head his way. But her legs, which had previously been stretched out straight, drew up a little. "No," came her stubborn response.

"Is there a problem?"

"Nothing I can't handle."

"So you've said," he remarked in a mild tone.

He listened to her torture the pipe a little more while he slid a couple of sodas and a bag of chips into the backpack he'd bought this morning. She grunted and groaned over the recalcitrant nut. He could have told her she didn't have enough strength to work it loose, even with the wrench. The P-trap probably hadn't been taken apart in years.

Finally, he settled in front of her, sitting cross-legged on the worn linoleum. A few tendrils of dark hair had escaped her ponytail. They clung wetly to her temples and the base of her neck. Her lips were a tight line of frustration, matching the frown across her forehead, but she ignored him and kept working.

"Nut?"

She stopped immediately and looked at him, her gaze challenging and as sharp as a blade. "I beg your pardon?"

"I was asking if you'd like a nut."

He smiled and held out the container of mixed nuts he also planned to stow in the backpack. It took her a few seconds to focus her attention on the can. Then she gave him a small smile in return, moved into a sitting position and plucked out a cashew.

"You know," he remarked quietly, "there's nothing wrong with asking for help."

She popped the nut into her mouth. The large wrench lay across her lap. Her fingers played along the dial that adjusted the tool's jaws. "I never said there was. But I'm perfectly capable of fixing the problem. I've been doing this sort of thing for years."

"No maintenance man?"

She offered a little shrug, and he was pleased to see that some of the tension seemed to have left her. "Too expensive to keep one on staff. My brother, Trip, is pretty handy. But he's off on some grand quest for adventure."

Her tone of voice and the way she rolled her eyes told him just what she thought of that idea.

Jake pushed a finger through the nuts, in search of his favorite. "A little resentful about that, I gather."

"No," Nora said succinctly. Then with a grin, she ducked her head and confessed, "Yes. But only on days when I can't get a stupid pipe to cooperate."

To emphasize her point, she lifted the wrench and banged lightly on the plumbing. He said nothing for a few moments, just watched her frown as if by sheer will she could make the metal coupling loosen.

She wore a pale blue cotton blouse, collar open, and he found himself noticing the base of her throat, where her skin gleamed under a light sheen of perspiration. To distract himself, he shook the can of nuts, drawing her attention.

"Trade with me," he said, indicating the wrench. "I promise not to tell anyone you couldn't get it to budge."

Maybe she decided it wasn't worth an argument, or maybe she'd come to realize that this fix-it job needed more strength than she had. Whatever the reason, she didn't protest further. She took the can of nuts out of his hand, replacing it with the wrench as though she were a nurse passing surgical instruments to a doctor.

He repositioned himself closer to the P-trap. Readjusting the wrench's jaws, he leaned into it, and in another minute, the nut was coming loose.

In spite of the fact that she'd made no headway in loosing the nut, she really was pretty knowledgeable. Before he even made the suggestion, Nora had positioned a bucket under the drain to catch the water that had pooled in the sink. After he ran more water through the trap, he checked the opening to make sure nothing else blocked the flow. His wiggling fingers encountered a hard barrier, and a moment later, two objects rolled down his palm and dropped into the bucket Nora held.

She plucked one out and held it up. It was a green plastic toy soldier, obviously the lost warrior of some previous young guest.

"There's your culprit, " Jake said, noticing the

battered edges of the soldier's figure. "Poor guy looks like he's ready for a military discharge with honors."

"I'll retire him to the rest of our lost-and-found regiment," Nora replied. She gave the soldier a quick salute, then flicked him into the toolbox.

"What else do you have?" Jake asked, mildly curious to see what the second object had been.

Nora peered down into the bucket, then gasped. "Oh my gosh!"

Jake stopped retightening the nut and stared at her. "What's the matter?"

"Do you know what this is?" Nora exclaimed as she shook her hand free of the water and held up the other obstacle, captured between two fingers.

It was a gold ring, with a trio of tiny diamonds across the top. Because it was wet it sparkled prettily, but didn't look particularly impressive. Jake shrugged. "My guess is that it's not the Hope diamond."

"It's Becky Fuller's wedding ring."

"Should I know who Becky Fuller is?"

"No," she replied, shaking her head. Her attention was still focused on the ring. "I'm sorry. It's just so unexpected. Becky and Harold Fuller came here as honeymooners. They stayed in this cabin a year ago."

"And the new Mrs. Fuller lost her ring down the sink."

"Not exactly." Nora's gaze met his, and her features were suddenly very earnest. "She threw it down the drain. She and Harold had a huge quarrel.

Everyone who was staying here at the time heard all the yelling and crying. The Fullers cut their honeymoon short. She took the car and roared out of here in the middle of the night, and he had to take a bus home. I called her two weeks later, and she said they were getting an annulment. Since then…"

"Since then, what?"

"Since then we've considered this cabin sort of haunted."

"Haunted," he repeated, the beginnings of a grin starting to stretch across his features. "As in ghosts?"

"No…not really. Just little things, like plumbing problems, a blocked chimney, leaks in the roof. Once we had an infestation of bats in the attic."

"And you think those things are a result of bad karma from the Fullers' honeymoon? Not just a lack of preventive maintenance."

She grimaced as if he'd touched a nerve. "I shouldn't have said anything. It's just that we've never had newlyweds who weren't crazy about this place, who weren't affected in a positive way. The Hideaway knows how to treat young lovers. You can see, can't you, how romantic it could be to two people in love?"

He looked around the room, offering a tentative nod. "I can see the potential."

"Potential!" she refuted with a hint of indignation. "It's more than that. It has atmosphere, intimacy. There's peace and quiet. And the beauty of nature all around you." She'd been drying the ring vigorously on a clean rag that lay in the toolbox.

She stopped, looking at him closely. "You should see the way the light sparkles on the spring pool when there's a full moon. It's almost magical."

Her words were hushed, lovingly reverent. For a split second, for as long as her soft, brown eyes locked with his, he wanted to kiss her. It was a crazy idea that came out of nowhere, and as he watched her drop her gaze, he wondered if she'd felt it, too—that first, unexpected, exciting flash between two people.

"Maybe you can show it to me some night," he said softly, feeling her nearness like a tingling in his fingertips.

She looked a little stunned. Her mouth parted, and the pulse at her throat was fluttering wildly. Damn fool that he was, he wanted to put his lips to it, feel her flesh tremble against his tongue.

"I don't think there's a full moon anytime soon," she said quietly, and then she was suddenly concentrating on rearranging the tools in the box, finding a safe place to store the ring—and the conversation.

The golden moment was gone, but it was replaced by the realization that this woman genuinely loved it here. In spite of every demand the Hideaway might make of her. He admired that kind of commitment, that kind of dedication. To draw her attention, he touched her arm. Her eyes flew to his, looking startled. "The Hideaway means a lot to you, doesn't it?"

"Four generations of Holloways have lived here. My great-grandparents built the main lodge when there was no reason for anyone to come to Florida. My grandparents added the cabins. It's the only home I've ever known. Or wanted.'' She gave a little snort of self-deprecation. ''You probably think I sound like a hick.''

''I don't think that at all. I think you're lucky to have found a place you can envision spending the rest of your life. Not everyone does, you know?''

''My brother, Trip, thinks we ought to sell it now that Mom and Dad are gone.''

''But you don't agree.''

''Right now it's not a consideration.'' She stared down at the ring in her palm and shook her head disbelievingly. ''Imagine a woman throwing her wedding ring down the drain.''

Jake laughed. ''I'd hate to think where my ex-wife put hers.''

Frowning, she cocked her head at him. ''Not an amicable divorce?''

He lifted the wrench to the nut again, tightening it back into place. ''Not exactly. Thea would have my heart served at her next party if she thought the cops wouldn't show up at her door.'' Grimacing, he shook his head. ''At first, we kept it pretty civil. But in the five years since then, the relationship has deteriorated considerably. Earlier this year, when I got back from the job in Africa, I had to threaten to take her back to court in order to get permanent custody of Charlie.''

''I'm sorry.''

''So am I. Not for me, but for what it's done to Charlie's attitude. The hostility you witnessed yesterday is pretty much standard operating procedure for him.''

''Perhaps he just needs a little time to adjust.''

The gentle sympathy in her voice made him look at her. He didn't know why he was telling her about his personal problems; he was closemouthed by nature. But it felt good to tell someone, and she seemed to understand so much more than he was able to articulate.

Feeling suddenly uncomfortable, he said, ''Tell me something, Nora. Do you think the Hideaway can work a little magic for Charlie and me? Or is that just reserved for honeymooners?''

He never found out the answer to that question. Charlie appeared in the kitchen doorway, dressed in his new jeans and T-shirt. ''So are we going fishing or what?'' he asked.

THE FISHING TRIP was hardly what anyone would consider a success.

Although Jake and Charlie spent the better part of the afternoon at the river, they did not catch a single fish. Charlie snagged his line on some obstruction, and Jake's attempt to work it free failed completely, so he was forced to cut it—losing hook, line and sinker to the river bottom. Charlie didn't even pretend to be disappointed.

More importantly, the camaraderie Jake had hoped would spring up between the two of them did not happen. There were lots of impatient, heavy sighs from Charlie, and Jake's attempts to jump-start conversation—any conversation—was met with monosyllabic responses. Every topic of discussion petered away quickly, until Jake was so frustrated he wanted to throttle the boy and throw him into the slow-moving current along with the lost tackle.

It was a silent pair that trudged their way up the bank and back to their cabin.

"What now?" Charlie asked his father as they stacked the fishing equipment in a corner of the porch. His expression indicated he'd been indulgent thus far, but had clearly run out of patience.

"I saw a steak house when we got off the interstate. Let's wash up, grab dinner there and then stop at the grocery store. We'll need food for tomorrow."

"What? You don't want to try to catch our breakfast? Maybe there are a couple of chickens around here we can run down for eggs."

"Just get cleaned up," Jake replied, giving his son a look meant to convey that he was in no mood for sarcasm.

There was only one bathroom in the cabin, and while Charlie took a shower, Jake decided to wait his turn by outfitting the boy's rod with a new line. He settled in one of the porch rockers, placed the tackle box on his lap and began poking through the few items he'd bought.

All things considered, the fishing outing hadn't been a complete disaster. At least the hours on the riverbank had given Jake enough quiet time to think about the future of Bobby's child.

After his conversation with Isabel this morning,

he'd realized that there was very little chance he could persuade the woman to change her mind about giving up the baby. She seemed determined to follow through with her career goals, and had the circumstances not involved his own nephew, Jake might have admired that sort of commitment.

But Nora Holloway as a single parent to his brother's child? It was possible, he supposed, to leave this place and feel fairly comfortable that the baby would have a good home with her. But he still wasn't sold on the idea of turning Bobby's only offspring over to a stranger, especially someone who'd never even known Bobby.

After his initial shock at Isabel's news, Bobby had quickly warmed to the idea of becoming a father. Only the cruelest hand of fate had kept him from returning to the United States and making things right with Isabel.

Fate, and my own poor judgment.

Jake slammed the door shut on those thoughts and forced his mind back to the problem at hand.

No, Bobby couldn't come back and make things right.

But Jake could.

It wasn't too late for him to see to it that Bobby's son grew up knowing who his father had been, what kind of family he came from. If he let the Holloway woman adopt the baby, if Jake just hopped on the next plane back to Virginia and disappeared, who would make sure that happened?

Who would tell the kid that his father had been so bright, such a whiz in school, that he'd won a scholarship to the best architectural college in the country—won it and refused it—so that he could go to his brother's alma mater instead? How would the boy ever know that Bobby had been the center of every party, every family reunion? The one who could be counted on to tell the funniest jokes, the scariest ghost stories. Did Nora Holloway know that Bobby had been a track star in high school, or that as a kid he'd wanted to be a magician and had actually once made Aunt Clarissa's cat disappear before the eyes of the entire family?

Those were fragments of a life cut too short, too soon, and the kinds of things a child ought to know about his father. Didn't Jake owe it to Bobby to see to it that his kid remembered him as more than just a name on a birth certificate?

I can do it, he thought. I could become this child's father.

JOHN FORRESTER, Nora's lawyer and a family friend since high school, called early the next morning, asking that Nora and Isabel meet him in his office in town at eleven o'clock. He remained mysteriously and annoyingly unforthcoming about the reason for the meeting, simply stating that it involved their adoption plans and that he'd rather discuss the issue with them in person.

Isabel had an appointment with Dr. Brewster at nine-thirty. Her bouts of violent nausea were still a worry, and the doctor didn't want to take any chances with her health. After a few tests, the man who had delivered most of the babies in the county pronounced the baby in fine shape, but he cautioned Isabel about too much stress and emphasized the need to make concessions in her life for the baby's sake.

With a list of new instructions from Dr. Brewster and an I-told-you-so look in Isabel's direction, Nora led her out of the obstetrician's waiting room and across the street to John Forrester's law office.

The two women had no more than settled into the cold, hard chairs in John's office, when he got right to the point. "I've been contacted by an attorney representing a Jake Burdette. He claims to be your baby's uncle, Isabel. Do you know him?"

"He showed up at the Hideaway the day before yesterday. He wants me to reconsider our plans for the adoption."

"As I understand it from the attorney, Mr. Sanstrom, Jake Burdette wants to adopt his brother's child."

His words, quiet and succinct, pulled a gasp from Isabel and made the blood run faint in Nora's veins. She shook her head at him slowly. "If this is your idea of a joke, John, it's not a very funny one."

He met her eyes levelly. It was one of the things she had always liked about John. He never ran away from unpleasantness. "I wouldn't joke about a thing like this, Nora. I know how serious you are about adopting the baby. Have you spoken to this man, Isabel?"

"Yes. But this can't be right. It's impossible."

"I'm afraid it's not impossible at all."

Nora's thoughts were still reeling. "Jake Burdette wants to raise Isabel's child as his own?'' she repeated.

''It seems so. His attorney called me this morning to discuss whether you were seriously intent on the adoption.''

A hot, drenching surge of anger rose within her. ''Seriously intent? I hope you set him straight.'' She turned toward Isabel, who had begun to cry the moment John had informed them of this latest development and showed no signs of stopping anytime soon. Grabbing a tissue out of the box on John's desk, Nora wedged it into the girl's hands. ''Stop crying, Izzie,'' she said, struggling to control her own emotions. ''Upsetting yourself won't help matters one bit.''

''I can't help it,'' Isabel sniffed. ''All I seem to be able to do lately is cry. Oh, I can't believe he'd do this. Especially after I told him to let things be.''

Nora felt her cheeks go hotter. ''He's already discussed this with you?''

Isabel nodded, looking more miserable by the second.

''When?''

''Yesterday. While you were at the vet's office.''

''Why didn't you tell me?''

''I didn't want to upset you. And I told him no. I thought he understood that it isn't what I want.'' Isabel turned her head toward John, favoring him with a sullen, angry look. ''I'm this baby's mother. Doesn't what I want matter at all?''

''Of course it does, Isabel,'' John said softly. ''But—''

"Well, what I want is to have Nora adopt this child. It's as simple as that."

John shook his head. "I'm afraid it may not be that simple."

Nora's head snapped around. Before she could speak, she had to take a deep breath to ease the tightness in her chest. "Can he really keep me from adopting the baby?"

"It's possible. If he decides to go to court. He can try to prove he can provide a better home for the child, or that you would be an unfit mother."

"He'd have a hard time proving that," Isabel interjected with the first real show of spirit.

"I don't doubt that for a minute," John agreed with a smile. "But he is blood kin to the baby, which would definitely be a consideration for a judge. Whenever possible, the courts like to keep families together."

Nora's throat was so tight she had to force the words out. "I'm not going to give up without a fight. What can we do to stop him?"

"I'm afraid you can't stop him from petitioning the judge. Between now and the time the baby is born, all we can do is try to convince him that a lengthy court battle would be in no one's best interest. Least of all the child's."

Nora nodded vaguely, although it frightened her to think how costly this fight might be—and in more ways than just financial.

"I've done some checking," John went on. "I think I should warn you, Burdette has one of the best attorneys in the country. Gregg Sanstrom is a shark. He headed up the man's custody case against his ex-wife. And it never even went to court.''

Charlie's claim in the rehab shed suddenly came back to Nora. ''He took me away from her. Just to make her mad.'' Could Jake Burdette really be so insensitive, so cruel that he would do such a thing? She remembered now why Thea's name had sounded familiar to her. Nora had read that, in addition to commanding a record-setting salary from the cosmetics line, the woman had been embroiled in ugly legal wranglings with her ex-husband and had unexpectedly conceded defeat just before the case went before a judge. Surely Thea, a public figure with numerous resources available to her, would not have given up custody of her son unless Jake Burdette and his legal team had been ruthless, unstoppable.

''If you wish to consider hiring another lawyer...'' John cut across her thoughts. ''Someone more experienced...''

She rose suddenly, shaking her head vehemently. ''I have faith in you, John. Please. Will you help me get through this?''

John had risen as well, and he came around the desk, his arms outstretched to encompass her. He had always been a good friend, and she suddenly wished that years ago, when they had dated, there had been some spark between them.

He gave her an encouraging smile. ''Of course I will, Nora.''

''I won't give up,'' Nora repeated, more for her own benefit than his.

He gripped her hands in his. "I'll do my best," he replied. "Now, why don't you two leave this matter to me for a few days? Perhaps I can make Mr. Burdette see reason."

"I'll make him see reason," Isabel said, wiping away the last of her tears. "Just wait until I get back to the Hideaway. He'll wish he'd never heard of me."

John looked at Nora uncertainly, and she shook her head. "You'll do nothing of the kind. I told you I wouldn't allow him to upset you or the baby, and I meant it. Remember what Dr. Brewster said? No stress, and lots of rest. When we get home, you're going to put your feet up in a dark room, and I'm going to make you some of that tea you like so much."

"But somebody needs to set that man straight."

"Don't worry," Nora said with a grim smile. "Somebody will."

CHAPTER SIX

As PROMISED, Nora saw Isabel settled in her bedroom with her feet up and a cup of herbal tea at her elbow as soon as they returned home. Then she headed straight for Cabin Two.

Memorial Day weekend, the official opening of the Hideaway's summer season, was only two weeks away and already the sun's intoxicating heat lay warm upon the back of Nora's blouse. She hardly noticed it as she strode down the pathway that connected the cabins.

From the corner of her eye she spotted movement in the direction of the spring pool. She realized that it was Jake and his son, coming up the railway-tie steps. She detoured in that direction and met them halfway on the shady path.

They wore bathing trunks and towels draped around their necks. The clear springwater dripping from their bodies pooled at their feet as they came to a halt in front of her.

Jake gave her a friendly smile. "You should have warned us that the water's so cold," he said. "We've got goose bumps on top of our goose bumps."

That might have been true for Charlie, whose pasty white body didn't look as though it saw much exercise or sun, but it was completely inaccurate for Jake Burdette. In spite of her anger, Nora noticed that he had muscles on top of muscles—not goose bumps. His bare chest, broad and lightly covered with wet hair, created a tingling in the pit of her stomach.

The fact that he was in good shape didn't really surprise her. The fact that she could be so furious with him and still *notice* how great-looking he was did.

"I'd like to speak to you, Mr. Burdette," she said.

"Don't tell me our swim has violated some kind of Hideaway rule?" When her only response was silence, one of his eyebrows lifted slightly. He looked toward his son. "Charles, how about making us some lunch while I stay here and try to figure out what has Miss Holloway looking so annoyed?"

The boy grumbled something under his breath and continued up the steps.

When he was out of earshot, Nora turned her attention back to Jake. "Mr. Burdette—"

"Make it Jake, or we're not having this conversation," the man said, holding a hand up in front of her. "And can we talk in the sun, or is it your intention that I freeze to death?"

The tingling in her stomach had disappeared, thank heaven, allowing her to maintain some control of her thoughts. Abruptly she turned away and headed toward the small, sunny observation deck that jutted out over the slope.

While she sat down on one of the wooden benches, he moved across the deck to the railing's edge, leaning back against it as if he didn't have a care in the world. "Now then," he said, tilting his head in her direction. "What's the problem? Another drain need fixing?"

"You can drop the innocent act, Mr. Burdette...Jake. It doesn't work."

"I beg your pardon?"

His attitude rankled. "Don't pretend you don't know what I'm talking about. All I want to know now is, what do you think you're doing?"

"I'm trying to make conversation with a very hostile lady. And not succeeding, by the looks of that frown."

She stood, approaching him with her head thrown back. "Isabel and I have just returned from my lawyer's office. He's told me what you're trying to do."

He scowled and pursed his lips thoughtfully. After an extended silence, he said, "I apologize. I didn't realize that Gregg—my attorney—would be in touch with your attorney so quickly. I wanted to talk to you first. I spoke to Isabel yesterday, and I was hoping to speak to both of you sometime today. Together."

"I doubt that will be possible. Isabel's so upset by your plans she's practically incoherent."

Idly, he plucked a dead leaf from the railing and twirled it in his hands. "It wasn't my intention to upset her. Or you. I would like for us to discuss the future of Bobby's child in a calm, constructive manner.''

"There's nothing to discuss. What you want is out of the question.''

He tossed the leaf away and looked at her severely. "Is it?''

"Let me ask you something. Did you come here with the idea of adopting Isabel's baby?''

"Not just Isabel's baby. My brother's as well.''

"Just answer the question.''

"You know I didn't.''

"So am I to believe that in the course of forty-eight hours, you've suddenly decided that fatherhood is absolutely essential to your future happiness?''

"I'm already a father.''

"Yes, you are. And from what I've seen of your relationship with Charlie, I'd say your success there is debatable,'' she said in a cold, curt tone.

He stiffened, and his features went so dark that she feared for one moment he might walk off. Instead, he said quietly, "Nora, I'm going to overlook that remark because I know you're angry with me. But let's keep this discussion civil, or from now on all our conversations will have to take place in the presence of our attorneys. Agreed?''

She drew in a deep, calming breath. "I'm sorry,'' she said. "That comment was unfair and out of line.''

She moved away from him, returning to the wooden bench. "But I can't let you have this baby," she said in a voice so soft it was almost a whisper.

He jerked the towel from around his neck. "What's so important about this particular child? Why don't you have a child of your own? You're young and attractive. You seem in good health—"

"Oh, thank you very much!" she exclaimed with an indrawn breath of pure outrage. "Would you like to check my teeth as well?"

He scowled. "I only meant that there's no reason to think that you'll never get married and have children of your own. But if you're determined to adopt a baby, surely there are others whose families—"

"For heaven's sake, we're not talking about peaches at a produce stand!" She gritted her teeth, knowing that if she didn't hang on to her temper, she would never be able to convince this man of anything. "Isabel and I came to this decision months ago. But even before that, I've spent every waking moment planning for this baby's arrival, carefully guarding his development, making sure Isabel does everything she needs to in order to deliver a healthy child. And now you expect me to step aside and allow you to take him away?" She shook her head at him. "Tell me why I should, especially considering that Isabel herself wants me to adopt her baby."

He crossed the distance between them and settled beside her on the bench. She didn't look at him, and unexpectedly, he took her hand in his. His grip was strong and warm, but her thoughts were jostling together in a dark, fathomless flood of fear and hurt, so that she was hardly aware of the contact. Feeling as trapped as the caged eagle she had transported to her rehab shed the day before, she turned to look at him.

He grimaced. "I don't doubt the love and care you've given this baby, Nora. But for all that, you can't give the child a sense of who he is, where he comes from. This child is my family. He's the only offspring that will ever bear my brother's blood. I'm not sure I even understand all the reasons it's important to me, but I can't let Bobby's child slip away to be raised by a stranger. No matter how well intentioned you might be."

"Will knowing his place on the Burdette family tree be more important than the love I can give him?"

"Do you think I won't love him as my own?"

"I think you feel it's your duty. Something you owe to your brother's memory."

"You're wrong. It's much more than that."

"Can you deny that right now you're a man struggling to reach your own son? How will it help to have a newborn baby to look after as well? And what about your work? How will you raise two children when you're halfway around the world building bridges?"

"That's no longer an issue. Part of the reason I couldn't come here sooner was that I've spent the last few months reorganizing my life. I no longer have to make extended trips overseas. After Bobby..." He frowned and looked away for a moment. Then he began again. "I'm ready to settle down."

She gave him a skeptical look. "As a single father with an armload of responsibilities?"

"Is that any different from being a single mother with an armload of responsibilities?" He glanced down at their hands. When he lifted his eyes to her again, they were speculative, glittering, so that he seemed to have the sunlight inside him. "Perhaps we should pool our talents and raise the boys together."

He completed that suggestion with a wry smile, and if the sunshine did something intriguing to his eyes, Jake Burdette's compelling, male nearness did something even more interesting to her insides. Sitting there, in the warm, golden stillness, Nora's heart gave a little thump. She hated that he could have that effect on her.

She pulled her hand out of his grasp. Taking a moment to modulate her voice, she said at last, "I want this baby, Jake. Isabel wants me to have this baby. I won't give up without a fight."

She watched his jaw tighten. "I don't want it to come to that," he said softly.

"Perhaps there's no other way." She ran her tongue over suddenly dry lips. Drawing a deep breath, she looked him hard in the eyes. "My attorney has already warned me what to expect. I'm afraid you'll have a difficult time proving that I'd be an unfit mother. Nothing much happens in Blue Devil Springs. There's nothing in my past that a judge would find unacceptable. Can the same be said for yours?''

Jake's lips flattened. ''Does it really have to get so ugly between us?''

''That's up to you, I suppose.''

He looked down, silent and pensive. When he finally looked up at her, his eyes were filled with kindness, and a pity that she found almost unbearable. ''You can't win this, Nora,'' he said gently. ''Let it go.''

Her heart spasmed as she tried to dismiss the gnawing fear that he was right. ''I can't.''

Fighting the tears that threatened to obscure her vision, she stood and moved away from him. She leaned on the railing. A few feet below and fifty yards away, she could see the bubbling eruption where the headwaters of the spring found the surface of the Hideaway's natural pool. *Concentrate on that,* she told herself. *Don't think about anything else.*

''I'm sorry,'' she heard him say. ''I wish it could be different. In another time, another place—''

''I think we understand each other.''

''I plan to stay in Blue Devil Springs for a little while. Charlie is through with school for the summer, and we can use the time together. If you'd like me to find other accommodations...''

She swung around, giving him the impersonal innkeeper's smile. ''That won't be necessary. Whether you remain or not makes no difference to me, as long as you pay the bill. All I ask is that you refrain from upsetting Isabel any more than you already have.''

He nodded, and Nora strode off the deck and back onto the path. She sensed him following a short distance behind her, but she didn't look back.

By the time she reached the top of the slope, every painful heartbeat was zigzagging in her breast, but she felt surprisingly calmer for having released some of her anger and frustration. She felt stronger, more focused. There might be a heck of a fight ahead of her, but Jake Burdette hadn't won yet.

Larry came to meet her barking and running in circles excitedly. The dog rarely acted this way toward anyone. Only her brother could make him—

It couldn't be. Nora lifted her head quickly toward the main lodge. Standing at the bottom of the steps, backpack at his feet, the slight breeze lifting the unruly tangle of dark hair off his shoulders, was Trip.

He spotted her, and his long legs ate up the distance between them. Nora returned his broad smile. Her spirits lifted a little. She loved her brother, and right now she was damn glad to see him.

He pulled her into his arms, lifting her clear off the ground. She kissed him soundly, and when he turned her loose, she rushed into speech, her head full of a million questions.

''What are you doing here?'' she asked first. ''I wasn't expecting you back for months. How did you get here?''

''I hopped a bus from New York to Tallahassee

and hitched the rest of the way. I came back because I missed you, silly.''

Nora tucked her chin, giving him a suspicious look. ''You ran out of money.''

He laughed. ''I never can fool you, can I? Yeah, I ran out of money—because the thieves who ransacked my campsite took everything. Even my extra set of clothes. The Outback of Australia might be a cheap place to live, but everyone wants your stuff.''

''Thieves? Did they hurt you?'' Nora asked, running a concerned hand down the side of Trip's face where a trio of tiny new scars marred the corner of his chin.

''Nah.'' He fingered the half-healed marks. ''A bunch of rocks on the river bottom tried to break my face when I got dumped on the Sacrament. That river was one hell of a challenge, sis. Tore up two kayaks before I got down it completely on the third try. I have to admit, even I was thinking this adventuring thing might have been a huge mistake.''

''But now you're back, and I'm so glad to see you.''

''We have to talk.''

She knew what that meant. Money. But not yet. She leaned into her brother's arms again, and this time she was the one hugging him as tightly as she could.

''Who's that?'' Trip asked over the top of her head. ''Don't tell me we've got paying guests?''

Without lifting her head, Nora glanced to the side to see Jake Burdette coming toward them. ''I guess you can call him a guest," she muttered. "Let's just say that while you've been in the Outback meeting your challenge, I've been here...meeting mine."

IT ANNOYED Jake that he was so interested in the newcomer who now held Nora Holloway tightly in his arms. Boyfriend? Ex-husband?

What did it matter who the guy was? Considering the conversation he and Nora had just had, he should make a beeline for his cabin.

Instead, he let himself catch the man's eye, nodding to acknowledge the fellow's friendly interest, then strode toward the couple.

He saw the change in Nora's face as she realized he intended to join them. Her mouth tightened, and her eyebrows were drawn as though she were in pain. Even from a distance—and in spite of the fact that her head was practically buried in the man's chest—he could see pink along the rise of her cheekbones.

"I'm Trip," the man said as Jake reached them. "Are you a guest here?"

Jake took the man's hand. "My son and I checked in the day before yesterday."

"Great! Glad to have you here." He glanced down, offering a teasing smile to Nora. "My sister treating you all right?"

Sister, huh? That information pleased Jake more than it should, and he was turning the reasons for that around in his head even as he heard himself reply, "I can't remember when I've received such a welcome."

"I see you've been brave enough to try the springs. There's a lot to do in the area, particularly if you like water. I'm sure Nora's filled you in."

"As I said, your sister's been very hospitable," Jake stated, then had to work to hide a smile as he watched the annoyed flush spread across Nora's creamy complexion. "And I'll bet she's full of suggestions on what I can do...with my time."

"Will you and your son be here over Memorial Day weekend?" Trip said. "You should plan to stay at least that long."

Nora stopped just short of jumping visibly at that suggestion. "Mr. Burdette has quite a demanding schedule. I doubt if he can spare—"

"Actually, I've been thinking I deserve a little time off." He turned his attention back to Trip Holloway. "What happens Memorial Day weekend?"

"The Springs incorporates the annual Founder's Day celebration into the holiday. This place should be jumping by then—10K runs, all kinds of contests and kids' activities, the best food in the South. Oh, and you don't want to miss Blue Devil's Bash and Dash Boat Race. Best part of the whole weekend."

"A boat race?"

"Not a real one—at least, not anything that uses what you'd consider an actual boat. Anything that floats qualifies. You'd be surprised at some of the contraptions people think will get them down the river. Last year's winner was a guy who strapped two coolers to his feet and used them as floating shoes. This year I was thinking of making some kind of raft with inner tubes." He looked at Nora. "What do you think, sis?"

"I think I'll be fishing you out of the river again."

Her brother laughed, a hardy sound that took no offense. "Wouldn't be the first time. How about it, Mr. Burdette? You think you're up to the challenge?"

Jake watched the emotions that warred in Nora's expression. Clearly she was indulgent with her brother, who seemed to be the kind of fellow who'd never met a stranger. It was also quite plain that she hoped Trip wouldn't encourage Jake's participation. He made the decision quickly and told himself it was for Charlie's sake.

"I think I could do better than a couple of boards and inner tubes," Jake promised. "And it sounds like fun—something that my son and I could do together."

"Great," Trip said enthusiastically. "I'll pick up entry forms and a list of rules the next time I'm in town. As long as you don't use anything that comes directly off a boat, you can build whatever you want. We've always got scraps around here that you can help yourself to. We don't mind, do we, Nora?"

He smiled again at his sister, and Jake wondered if the man was myopic, because anyone could see that Nora Holloway minded very much.

FROM HIS PLACE on the couch, Charlie looked up at his father as if he'd lost his mind. "Build a boat?'' he repeated to make sure he'd heard right. ''Out of scraps?''

''Why not?'' his father asked, and he had on his patient-parent face now, the one Charlie had grown to hate. ''Don't you think we can do it?''

''Yeah, we can do it. But why would we? I mean, really. Why?''

''Because I think it would be fun.''

''No, you don't. You think if we work on this together it'll make everything all right. It won't. Not ever.''

He turned away quickly, because his throat was full of tears all of a sudden. He didn't want to cry. He didn't know how his father felt, but his mother hated crybabies.

Behind him, his father sighed wearily. ''Charles, I know you'd rather be with your mother. But what's done is done. Now, you can spend your time trying to shut me out, or we meet each other half-way. What do you say?''

He could think of a few things to say, things he'd heard in his mother's apartment from people who never remembered that there was a kid present. Charlie didn't dare say any of those things. His father didn't seem to have a sense of humor when it came to kids and bad language.

He settled for glaring over his shoulder and burying his chin in the pillow that he clutched against his chest. ''Leave me alone.''

''Come on, Charles. You're too bright to spend so much time sulking over things you can't change.''

Throwing the pillow across the room, Charlie faced his father. "My mother will change things. Any day now you'll be hearing from her lawyer. You probably would've already if this stupid place had a phone."

"Is that what Thea told you?"

"She didn't have to."

"That's because she knows she has to accept what the courts—"

"She doesn't care what the courts say. She's famous, and people listen to her. She's just busy right now, so she can't fix things so fast."

His father shook his head. "Not this time. I'm afraid you're stuck with me, pal."

Charlie focused on a spot over his father's shoulder and tried to ignore the queasy feeling in his stomach that told him he was probably hearing the truth. He wondered what his father would say if he admitted what he'd done yesterday while his dad was in the grocery store, the collect telephone call he'd made just because he couldn't stand it any longer.

There was an extended, uncomfortable silence that neither of them tried to fill. Finally Charlie said sarcastically, "Is it all right if I take a walk, or do you want me to stay where you can keep an eye on me?"

His father frowned but nodded slowly, and Charlie didn't wait for any further permission. He banged through the screen door and didn't slow his stride until he'd nearly reached the main lodge.

Tears started to cloud his eyes. He knuckled them away with his fists, knowing that they were useless. Why didn't his father understand that Thea needed her son? She was a beautiful woman, but she didn't always take care of herself. Sometimes she seemed like a little girl looking for attention. And when that happened, Charlie had always been there for her. What would she do now? Who would look after her?

With no answer to those questions, Charlie detoured around the lodge and headed for the rehab shed. At least being close to actual wild animals wasn't completely a yawner, and if Nora was there, he didn't mind keeping her company. She seemed kind of nice, and not too pushy if you didn't feel like talking. Which he didn't.

As soon as he opened the door, the animals inside the shed started making a fuss, as though they'd been waiting for him. His spirits lifted a little. In New York he hadn't been allowed to keep a pet. His mother was allergic, and even if she hadn't been, she wasn't an animal person. Not that there was anything wrong with that, but it would have been nice to have had a pet.

In one corner of the room was a huge cage that hadn't been there yesterday morning. The biggest bird Charlie'd ever seen eyeballed him as though it had spotted its next meal. Charlie guessed it was a bald eagle, although it didn't look very proud. Just kind of sad, with one of its wings hanging at an odd angle, and its cap of white feathers rumpled and dingy-looking.

There was a rustle of hay, and Charlie turned his attention toward the deer pen. Marjorie had come forward to rub her body against the wire. Charlie almost reached over the edge of the pen to pet the deer, then remembered what Nora had said.

"Sorry, Marj," he told her. "You gotta stay wild."

Marjorie's liquid brown eyes looked up at him pleadingly, and Charlie plunged his hands into his back pockets to keep temptation from overtaking him.

"You've got a rehabber's natural instincts," a voice said from the door.

He whirled to find Nora there. "I was just looking," he said quickly. "I didn't touch anything."

Nora smiled and came farther into the room. "I know. I wouldn't have put you to work helping me if I didn't think I could trust you."

The comment made him feel kind of good inside, even though he could also feel his face growing hotter and hotter. As a distraction, he moved toward the eagle's cage.

"I haven't named him yet," Nora remarked, joining him. "I was thinking Baldy."

Charlie made a face at her. "Baldy? That's probably what every bald eagle gets named. What about Leo?"

"Why Leo?"

"'Cause nobody would name a bird that. And 'cause he's got a nose like a guy that used to date my mom. Kinda hooked on the end." He nodded as the decision took hold in his brain. "Yeah. Leo."

"I guess I can live with that."

Nora moved away to rummage through a cabinet filled with the kinds of things Marisela kept in the kitchen drawer at home: string, half-burned candles, adhesive tape, scissors. Finally she pulled out a wide roll of duct tape.

"What are you going to do with that?" Charlie asked.

"I've found a better branch for his perch, but it has to be wrapped so that the rough edges of the wood can't hurt him. Want to help?"

"Sure. What's wrong with him?"

"He broke his wing when he ran into some wire and he hasn't been able to hunt for food, but as soon as the vet's splint takes hold and we put some meat on him, he'll be okay."

From the worktable Nora picked up a thick branch that was long enough to fit across the width of the eagle's cage. She handed it to him, positioning his hands at each end of the wood.

"Hold this out in front of you while I wrap it. All right?"

He nodded.

Starting at his left hand, Nora slowly began winding the silver tape around the branch, smoothing down the edges as she went so that the seams of the tape seemed to disappear. The wood, crooked and narrow in some places, felt stronger with every turn she made.

Concentrating on holding the branch steady,

Charlie asked, "You know that book you were telling me about? The one with the deer?"

"The Yearling?" Nora replied. "What about it?"

"Is there a library I can borrow it from? I mean, there's not much to do around here, so I figure I might as well read something."

Smiling, she looked away from the tape for a moment, and he had the feeling that he had pleased her somehow. "As a matter of fact, it's in the Hideaway's library up at the main lodge. Check the bookshelf nearest the fireplace."

"I don't know if I'll finish it," he hedged. "I might not like it."

"But then again, you might."

"We'll see."

"You know, Charlie..." She inclined her head toward the deer pen. "I'm planning to release Marjorie in a couple of days. Would you like to come along and help? I could pack a picnic lunch."

"I guess. Nothing better to do. Unless my dad starts making me build this stupid boat he wants me to help him with."

"For the boat race," she stated, and her voice sounded flat.

"I'll bet he thinks it will make me like him better."

Her eyes lifted to meet his. "You don't like your father?"

"He's all right, I guess. I mean, he doesn't beat me or anything."

"Well, that's a plus," she said with a grin. "Move your hands in so I can do the ends."

He did as she asked. "It's just that he doesn't understand. My mother needs me. He doesn't."

"Why would you think that?" She sounded surprised.

"He was gone for five years after they got a divorce. It didn't bother him then that he only saw me for a couple of weeks a year. Now, all of a sudden, he wants to be Superdad. My mom says he only wanted custody so he could make her look bad in public. So that people will hate her."

Nora stopped winding the tape and snipped off the end. "He doesn't seem like that kind of person."

Charlie frowned. "My mom said it. So it's true."

"Maybe your mother was just angry with him. What was your father like before your parents divorced? Do you remember?"

"Not really," he said, but even as he spoke, he knew it was a lie.

He did remember. Some things real clear.

Ice-cream cones shared in the car. The two of them sailing toy boats in a pond. The soft rumble of his father's chest against his ear when he read stories aloud. In spite of Charlie's determination not to remember the good times with his father, he found the pictures flipping through his head anyway.

Nora was watching him closely now, and he had the feeling she was very interested in his answer, though he couldn't figure out why. He handed her the branch, now completely covered in silver tape.

"He used to take me to football games," he said, and even though he didn't intend it to come out that way, he found himself adding enthusiastically, "And once we went to a basketball game and sat right behind the players."

"You like sports?"

"Not anymore. My mother says contact sports are for people who haven't realized that we've evolved from rock-throwing cave dwellers."

"That seems a little harsh."

"My mother's really smart, and if she says it—"

"Then it must be true?" Nora finished for him.

"Yeah."

"Is it possible that your mother's wrong sometimes?"

He scowled, not happy that someone he'd begun to like should question his mother. "No."

She lifted her hands in mock surrender. "Hey, I was just asking."

"You're on the same side as my father."

Charlie could tell she didn't like that idea. She made a small sound of disagreement and swung away from him to toss the branch on the worktable. "No," she said very firmly. "I'm definitely not on your father's side."

"Well, that's good, 'cause you just ask my mom. He only likes to hurt people."

Nora turned back to face him, and he was surprised how upset she looked. "I sure hope you're wrong about that, Charlie."

CHAPTER SEVEN

ON MONDAY, in spite of the fact that the time she'd been dreading for ages had finally come, Nora was almost relieved at the thought of today's trip. Releasing Marjorie back to the forest would be painful, heart-wrenching, but Nora would welcome any excuse to be away from the Hideaway—and Jake Burdette—for a little while.

As she slid containers of fried chicken and coleslaw into the picnic hamper, she smiled grimly. For today at least, she and Charlie would escape.

When she had the truck packed with her art supplies, the cooler and a blanket, she walked down to Cabin Two.

Actually, she was looking forward to spending time with Charlie. He wasn't a bad kid, just a little arrogant and a lot spoiled. But he was bright and inquisitive, and it was fun to catch glimpses of the boy he could be, to see him shed that veneer of sophistication he'd adopted from years of living with his mother in New York.

Before she could reach the cabin, Charlie came rushing out the front door to meet her. She thought at first he was just excited, but as she got closer, his expression reminded her of the expendable teen-ager in the first ten minutes of a horror film.

She raised her eyebrows at him. "What's the matter?"

"You're not going to believe it," the boy said in a solemn undertone.

They had reached the porch, and just then the screen door squealed open. When Nora looked up, she saw that Jake stood at the top of the porch steps, dressed in khaki shorts and a T-shirt. "Good morning," he greeted warmly.

"Good morning," Nora returned in a wary voice. "Did Charlie tell you where we were heading today?"

"Yes, he did," he said, rubbing his hands together. "I can't wait to get there and check out the fishing."

"I beg your pardon?" Beside her Charlie made a sound of complete disgust.

"I'm going with you," Jake replied.

"No, you're not." The words popped out before she could stop them.

"Sorry. It's a package deal. Both of us, or nothing."

"Why?"

He didn't look in the least offended by her abruptness. "I don't know anything about this place you're going to. Charles is my responsibility, and I can't just send him off with you and hope you know what you're doing. It's too dangerous."

"Dangerous?" Nora parroted. She made no effort to hide the fact that she found that excuse ludicrous. "It's a national forest. It's visited by millions of tourists every year."

"Are there snakes?"

"Yes, but—"

"Bears?"

"Some, but they're not like the ones in Yellowstone. They stay away—"

"Charles is a city kid, Nora. He's not used to being out in the wilderness. Suppose he gets lost?"

"Dad!" Charlie exclaimed, obviously embarrassed.

Nora narrowed her eyes. Surely Jake wasn't just being difficult because they had parted on less than friendly terms the other day. Even he must be able to see how eager Charlie was to take this trip.

"I'm not in the habit of losing people," she said, striving for patience. "The place I intend to release Marjorie is one of my favorites. I've led hiking trips out there for years. I know it like I know every blade of grass here at the Hideaway."

"Sorry. That's not good enough."

"Dad…"

Nora placed a calming hand on Charlie's shoulder. The boy's father saw it and tilted a glance at his son. "I thought you didn't want to have anything to do with this place," he said.

Charlie looked down, biting his bottom lip. "Nora needs my help," he muttered.

Jake's eyes slipped back to Nora. She thought she saw a spark of something in his soft brown gaze, but she couldn't be sure what it was. His eyebrow lifted. "Is that true?"

"Yes."

"Fine. I won't get in your way. You won't even know I'm there."

Oh yes I will!

"No," she said, hoping to bluff him into conceding defeat.

Charlie turned a desperate, pleading glance toward Nora as his father opened the screen door and started to head back into the cabin. She was furious with the man, suspecting that he knew perfectly well she would have to call him back. No matter how much she wanted to avoid Jake Burdette, how could she disappoint Charlie? If she didn't agree quickly—

"Mr. Burdette," she called up the steps before he could disappear inside. "Jake."

He turned. "Yes."

"You can come," she agreed slowly, trying unsuccessfully to keep grudging acceptance out of her voice.

"Great. I'll get my tackle box and poles," he said with a broad smile.

He reappeared in such a short time that Nora knew he'd had his gear waiting just behind the door. She stowed it behind the driver's seat with her art supplies. Without a word passing between them, they headed for the rehab shed.

Tail swishing, ears up, Marjorie stood in the middle of the pen as though she knew something important was about to take place. Jake and Charlie watched while Nora removed a vial of medicine from the small refrigerator. Shaking the bottle, she rummaged through a drawer until she found what she was looking for—a clean syringe the vet had given her to use when this time came.

"I'm going to give her a light sedative so we can get her in and out of the truck without upsetting her," Nora explained as she inserted the needle into the bottle. She motioned her head toward the deer pen. "Charlie, will you take some of that hay and make a nice, soft bed in the back of the truck? Up near the cab."

The boy nodded and moved cautiously toward the pen. Marjorie sidled away as he slipped the latch and entered. Scooping large handfuls of straw, he began making the first of several trips to the truck.

"Can I do anything to help?" Jake asked as Nora placed the vial back in the fridge.

She gave him a sidelong glance. "Just stay out of the way."

Jake smiled at her. "Why do I get the feeling that you mean all the time, and not just right now?"

She swung to face him just before she entered the pen. With a glance out the window to make sure Charlie was out of earshot, she said, "Look, you manipulated your way into this trip, but that doesn't mean I have to like it."

"I have good reasons for coming along."

"I don't doubt it. You wouldn't want to miss an opportunity to make my life miserable."

"That's not what I had in mind."

"Then, what?"

"I know Charlie has been spending a lot of time

with you in here, and I haven't minded because I figured it would keep him from complaining about having nothing to do. But when he came into the cabin last night after being with you, he was more animated than I can ever remember seeing him. He'd never admit it, but something about this place is starting to grow on him. He was actually civil to me this morning at breakfast. Whatever's caused that, I want to be part of it. This little excursion today—anything we can do together—can only help to build our relationship."

She looked at him accusingly. "You knew I wouldn't stop you from joining us if it meant he couldn't come, didn't you?"

He conceded that fact with a tentative smile. "I was hoping you'd put aside your personal dislike for me for his sake."

She snorted. "If this is where you think I'll say I don't dislike you, you're wasting your time." Through the window she could see Charlie coming back up the path. She jerked her head toward the boy. "Him, I like."

Jake laughed. "Refreshingly honest. No wonder my son enjoys your company."

"He's probably just killing time."

"Maybe. But are you aware that he went up to the lodge the other day and came back with a book? Said you recommended it."

Surprised, Nora pivoted. "I did. But I wasn't sure—"

"He was up late reading it, too. It was the first time I've seen him spend time concentrating on anything besides video games. You seem to have a good influence on him.''

She lifted her eyebrows and gave him a smile. ''That's one of the reasons why I'll make a great mother.''

If he intended to refute that or make any other comment, he didn't get the chance. Charlie had returned and, by some unspoken agreement, neither Jake or Nora wanted to discuss the possibility of a legal battle in front of the boy.

While Jake and Charlie watched outside the pen, Nora moved forward slowly. ''Come on, Marjorie,'' she called in a soft, reassuring tone. The deer jerked a few times, snorted loudly, but eventually took cautious steps in Nora's direction. Nora put out her hand, and the deer allowed her to stroke its neck. ''Last time, little girl. You're going home.''

She slid the needle into the deer's hide. Marjorie hardly seemed to notice.

The animal's legs buckled in no time. Kneeling, Nora caught her as she fell and eased her over on her side. Stroking the deer's head, she said, ''Come on in, Charlie. Now's your chance.''

Charlie rushed into the stall. Jake was right behind him. The boy knelt and ran his hand down Marjorie's neck. ''Are you sure she can make it on her own? She doesn't look very big or strong.''

''She'll be fine,'' Nora assured him.

Opening Marjorie's mouth, she pulled the deer's tongue forward, then slipped it sideways so that it protruded between her teeth. ''We don't want her swallowing her tongue while she's out, or have it obstruct her airway,'' Nora told him. ''Can I count on you to make sure it stays there?''

Charlie made a face. Then he nodded and grinned. ''She looks goofy. Like a drunk in the cartoons.''

''You ought to see what you look like when you're asleep,'' Jake said behind him.

The boy laughed at that, and Nora could tell that the reaction surprised Jake.

When she was certain that the deer was fully sedated, Nora slipped her arms under Marjorie's body, preparing to carry her to the truck. The animal wasn't very big, but the dead weight made her seem inordinately heavy.

''I'll do that,'' Jake said, beside her now, nudging her out of the way.

''No. She's my responsibility.''

''Yes, I know.'' He winked at her. ''Pretend she's a rusty faucet that needs fixing.''

She wanted to protest further, but it seemed silly to take such a stand when he obviously could make a quicker job of it. Besides, suppose she ended up dropping the animal? If poor Marjorie ended up with a concussion, she wouldn't care one bit that Nora's pride had remained intact.

As though they knew she wouldn't be returning, the other animals in the rehab shed began making a horrible racket as Jake carried the deer to the truck. Nora and Charlie kept pace with him so that they could guard her limp head while he maneuvered her into place. Charlie begged to ride in the back, and Jake agreed, as long as the boy promised not to move around. With a whoop of delighted excitement, Charlie bounded into the truck.

As for Nora, she found herself sitting up front with Jake, in what suddenly seemed to be an excruciatingly small space. Neither one of them said a word. Bumping slowly onto the main highway, she wondered how long she could pretend she was completely alone.

Evidently not long.

Jake had been slipping occasional looks back through the rear window of the truck cab, and now he looked at her and shook his head. "You know, if you'd have asked me a week ago if I thought my son would ever willingly ride in the back of an open truck, I'd have called you crazy."

"Maybe you just don't know him as well as you think you do."

He shook his head. "I don't feel I know him at all anymore. But I'm trying to change that. If he would just meet me halfway," he muttered almost to himself.

Before she could think about whether she was prying, Nora asked, "What was your ex-wife like, before she became so famous?"

He frowned. "She was always exceptionally beautiful, so she was terribly spoiled by everyone. Her parents. Me, at first. She never liked to be told no, I remember that well enough. Maybe that's where Charlie gets his stubbornness."

"How did you meet?"

"I went to college in Virginia. During my last

summer break I worked as an aide to a senator. He took me to an embassy cocktail party one night because I have a pretty good ear for languages. Thea was there with her father.''

"And it was love at first sight.''

"We got married two weeks later. Thea had already been modeling for a few years by then—teen-magazine stuff, clothing catalogs, that sort of thing. The following year I took over the family business from my father, and by then she was pregnant with Charlie. Thea agreed to stay home with the baby. That took quite a toll on the marriage. She loved modeling, and I don't think she ever stopped blaming me for halting her career in its tracks.''

The note of regret in his voice surprised her a little. Charlie's claim that his father hated his mother enough to make her life miserable suddenly didn't wash.

Nora peered out the windshield with all the intensity of a race car driver. She was very conscious of the man sitting next to her: the crisp, clean scent of the aftershave he used, his long fingers resting against his thigh, the shift of muscles as he moved in his seat.

"You're too quiet,'' he said suddenly. "What are you thinking? That I made a lousy husband?''

She turned her head to meet his self-deprecating smile. She realized quickly that the last thing she wanted to do was tell him where her thoughts had taken her.

"No, I wasn't thinking that at all,'' she replied. "I was just thinking that sometimes people make the wrong choices in life, and they end by twisting themselves in knots, trying to make up for them.''

Their eyes met, held no more than a heartbeat, really, but a shudder of pleasure went through Nora. She didn't like it. This man could keep her from realizing the most important dream in her life, and she'd do well to keep that in mind.

She cleared her throat, determined to keep the conversation and her thoughts calm, composed and dispassionate. ''Well, at least Thea managed to revive her career.''

''The ingenue jobs are beyond her now, of course. But she's found her niche. Thea was always very resourceful.''

''Her picture seems to be everywhere now that she's a spokesperson for La Paloma Cosmetics.''

''Yeah. A real celebrity.''

''Maybe I shouldn't say this, but I think part of the problem with Charlie is that he honestly believes you hate his mother.''

''I don't. I just don't want her raising my son anymore.''

''And yet you found no fault with it for five years after the divorce.''

Jake arched a glance her way. ''He told you that, did he? Well, he's partially right. I should have spent less time out of the country. Maybe I would've noticed that Thea was turning him into something I didn't like, but I never imagined...well, let's say I waited longer than I should have to take action.''

He sighed heavily and fixed his gaze out the window. Jake was quiet, reflective, and something in the way his jaw tightened suggested to Nora that he wasn't seeing the scenery.

Before the silence could stretch any longer, she said, "You know, raising a second child isn't going to be any easier than the first."

"No, but I've learned a few things with Charlie, and I don't intend to make the same mistakes twice."

"A judge may not give you that chance."

He smiled at her. "How about we agree not to talk about the adoption today? I'm feeling too encouraged about Charlie to fight with you." He held out his hand. "Deal?"

She was proud of the way she managed to keep from hesitating. She took one hand off the steering wheel and shook his firmly. "Deal," she said, feeling much more in control. "Now tell me how you ended up building bridges halfway around the world."

JAKE DIDN'T LIKE the way she made him feel.

Hot.

Light-headed.

Horny.

What the hell was wrong with him? This wasn't the way he was supposed to be handling this.

Since he'd actually made the decision to raise Bobby's baby as his own, he'd known it would be his job to make sure this woman didn't succeed in that same quest. He should be finding fault with everything Nora Holloway did, everything she said, everything she was. Mentally filing away her flaws so that Gregg Sanstrom could find something to get his teeth into if a court battle became necessary.

Instead, he was bumping along beside her in a truck, hauling Bambi back to paradise, planning to top off this bucolic adventure with a picnic. A picnic, for God's sake! Gregg probably wouldn't have minded that Jake was keeping a close eye on the woman, but he was damn sure he wasn't supposed to be liking this so much.

He was relieved when they reached the entrance to the national forest. He'd been talking nonstop for about the last five minutes, replaying parts of his past as if he was on one of those daytime-television talk shows. When had he gotten so loose-lipped? When had his past problems with Thea been open for discussion?

He told himself it was for Charlie's sake. Whatever Nora's failings might be—and God, he hoped she had some—she had a knack for reaching his son in ways he could only dream of right now. Around her, Charlie seemed less prickly, more cooperative, and sometimes he even forgot to be surly with Jake.

He twisted in his seat and rapped on the back window to draw Charlie's attention. "Everything all right?" he shouted.

The boy gave him a thumbs-up signal and actually smiled. Jake nodded and turned around. Yeah, he thought. Yeah. Charlie is the reason I should be here.

As though he'd spoken aloud, he was aware of

ANN EVANS   141

Nora turning her head to look at him. His eyes met
hers, and she gave him a reassuring smile. It was
sweet, lovely, and the taut, tense feel of frustrated
arousal hit him. He swung a glance out the side
window, clamping down hard on his libido, but it
only bloomed with fresh gusto.

God, he prayed silently, get me out of this truck
before I make a fool of myself.

Evidently God decided to take pity on him. They
had bumped onto a dirt path, and now Nora pulled
the truck to a halt in front of a flat, grassy knoll.

There wasn't another soul in sight. Tall pines
whispered in a slight breeze, creaking with the
weight of years. Sunlight danced on the ribbon of
river that stretched as far as he could see, so bright
Jake could only bear to look at the water for a heartbeat. Beautiful. Peaceful. Perfect.

He joined Nora at the back of the truck. Charlie
was already sliding out of the bed. Jake picked up
the still-sedated deer and Nora led him to a spot in
the open where the grass grew tall and lush. He
settled the animal gently on the ground.

Nora and Charlie knelt beside Marjorie. Nora
lifted one of the deer's eyelids.

His hand stroking down the animal's neck, Charlie looked over at Nora. "Now what?"

"Now we just leave her alone, let her wake up
naturally." Nora lifted her chin to motion toward a
stand of tall pines and thick undergrowth. "Hopefully she'll get up and head into those woods. This
area's protected from hunters. She'll have about

fifty thousand acres to play in, and no one to hurt her."

"Sounds like deer heaven," Jake said from behind her.

"What if she won't go away?" Charlie's voice was worried.

"Then I'll have to scare her off. We can shout and wave the blanket at her, but I hope it doesn't come to that."

"Are you going to miss her?" Charlie asked.

"Very much," Nora said in a soft voice. She angled a look down at the deer, lightly running her fingers along the side of Marjorie's face. "But she was never mine, really."

This was tough for her. Jake could hear the dread in her voice, and her movements were wooden, as if she held herself tightly.

"Charles," Jake said, eager to capture the boy's attention, yet attempting to sound casual at the same time. "Why don't you say goodbye now, and then we'll break out the food and our fishing gear?"

"I don't—" Charlie began the protest with a frown, then stopped when Jake jerked his head toward Nora behind her back.

Give her some time alone, he telegraphed to his son, and surprisingly, Charlie was quick to interpret the message.

"Okay, sure," he said. In another moment, he had whispered a last goodbye to Marjorie, slipped off his knees and started loping toward the truck.

"I'd better help him out," Jake said.

He turned to follow after Charlie.

"Jake?" Nora's voice stopped him, and he swung back to face her.

"Yeah?"

"Thanks."

"No problem."

She stayed with the deer a long time. Jake and Charlie managed to set a pretty fine picnic under the trees, quite a distance away. Charlie kept glancing over to where Nora still knelt in the tall grass.

"Do you think she's all right?" his son asked. "Should we take her a glass of lemonade?"

It pleased Jake that the boy showed such concern. Evidently Charlie hadn't completely forgotten what it was like to care about someone else's feelings.

Eventually Nora joined them. She and Charlie were too tense and watchful of Marjorie to offer much in the way of conversation. But the food was good, the lemonade cold and tart. The warm sun filtering through the canopy of trees overhead reminded Jake how much he enjoyed being outdoors.

Toward the end of the meal Marjorie woke up and staggered to her feet. Nora and Charlie went still, and even Jake found himself holding his breath. The deer sniffed the air, then took a few tentative steps toward them.

"No...no," Nora whispered. "Go on, Marj. You know where you belong."

Unexpectedly, Marjorie stopped. She stood there a very long time, head up, ears twitching, as if enraptured by the stillness of her surroundings. A shaft of sunlight suddenly pierced the clouds and found the animal, brushing its keen head and lean flank with gold.

Then, inexplicably startled, Marjorie turned and leaped toward the woods on the far side of the glade. Her tail went up like a salute, her long legs gathered speed, although she had no reason to run except for pleasure's sake. Then she was gone— into the underbrush without a backward look or thank-you.

Beside him, Jake heard his son's excited gasp and Nora's slow release of breath.

"I like this ending better than the one in *The Yearling*," Charlie said.

"Me, too," Nora agreed, but Jake heard the tiny note of sorrow in her voice.

After that, the afternoon seemed anticlimactic. Jake collected the fishing equipment, and he and Charlie headed down to the riverbank. Loaded down with art supplies, Nora set up her easel and paints not too far away.

From his spot on the bank Jake watched her out of the corner of one eye. He couldn't see the picture she labored over, but she applied paint liberally, with broad strokes, and the only thing he could think was that he had never seen a woman who could manage to look so energetic and elegant all at the same time.

The fish were biting. Charlie reeled in three striped bass, one after the other. One slithered away before he had a firm grasp on it, splashing back into the current, but he didn't seem to mind, and surprised Jake by immediately insisting that he be baited up again.

The afternoon wore on until there was more shade than sunlight. Jake was sorry to see the day end, and he would have bet Charlie felt the same way. Freckles had popped out across the boy's nose and cheeks, his hair was no more than a tumbled haystack, but he was grinning, and he'd actually managed to participate in more than one conversation with Jake.

They walked back from the riverbank, heading for the truck where Nora was already stowing her paints behind the seat.

"Can we come back here?" Charlie asked.

"Sure," Jake replied, feeling a kernel of hope take hold within him. "Any particular reason why?"

"It's pretty and quiet," the boy said with a shrug of nonchalance. "And who knows? Marjorie might come back for a visit."

As they passed Nora's easel still standing in the grass, they both stopped. They were silent as they surveyed the small canvas she'd been working on, and they tilted their heads this way and that to get the right perspective.

It took some doing. Nora's half-finished depiction of a lone deer standing in the high grass was...well...a stretch for the imagination. The trees were somewhat recognizable, as was the winding current of the river in the background, but Marjorie...poor Marj couldn't have looked worse if she'd been a hood ornament on some hunter's front fender.

"I like Nora, but she's really a bad artist, isn't she?" Charlie commented under his breath.

"Pretty awful."

"What should we say if she asks us what we think?"

"What do you want to say?"

He gave Jake a speculative glance. "Mother says it's all right to lie if you don't want to hurt somebody's feelings."

"In this case, I think she's right. Besides, if we tell Nora the truth, we could end up walking back to the cabin. She's got the only vehicle out of here."

"She sure took a pretty place and made it ugly," Charlie said with a shake of his head.

"Yep," Jake agreed. "But this can be our little secret."

Charlie seemed to like that idea. His eyes sparkled. "Yeah, I'm cool with it."

With that pact made between them, Jake sent Charlie over to pick up the blanket and picnic supplies while he carried the fishing gear to the truck. Nora's back was to him, and as he approached, she didn't turn around. She seemed completely absorbed in something on the front seat of the truck, and when he was right behind her he saw that her paint box lay open in front of her. From it she had removed a dog-eared, paint-spattered picture of Marjorie that she had evidently been using as a guide in her latest work. Lovingly, she ran her finger across the face of it. Jake set the fishing equipment on the ground.

She must have sensed his presence, because she stiffened and began to turn around.

"You all right?" he asked her gently.

She wasn't. He could see the dark hurt in her eyes, and she had to swallow hard a couple of times.

"Nora...?"

Tears spilled from her lashes as she blinked. She raised shaking fingers to wipe them away, pink with embarrassment. "I feel so stupid," she said in a rush to explain. "She's just a deer. I don't usually—"

The sob she'd evidently been holding in check broke free. She gave him a wobbly smile, and there was nothing left for him to do but gather her in, pulling her into the comfort of his embrace.

"Shh," he said softly, running his hand along the curve of her spine. "It's all right. I'll bet she's already found some great stud of a buck to look after her."

"I hope not," she replied with a shaky laugh. Her hands were splayed against his shirt, a delicate warmth. "I want her to be independent."

His chin rested against the top of her head. Her hair was warm from the sun, and he caught the fragrance of its shining mass, a scent he suspected no perfumerie could duplicate. Without really giving it much thought, he pressed his lips against her temple.

The forbidden thrill of what he'd just done took

hold of him, and he went very still. He had no right to touch her like this. He should turn her loose.

He couldn't.

Nora drew a deep, ragged breath, tilting her head back to look up at him. "It's those big brown eyes. They get to you."

He didn't take his gaze from her. Instead, he touched the back of his hand to the wetness of tears against her cheek. "Yes. I know."

Her dazed senses seemed to recognize his nearness at last. She looked at him in almost quiet fascination. Her mouth parted on a little gasp of sound, but she made no move to pull away, no effort to stop what now seemed inevitable to Jake. His mind no longer functioned; his body seemed driven by instinct alone. It came as pure feeling—that need to touch her, to hold her, to see if her flesh was as soft and silken as he imagined it to be. He had to find out.

He lowered his head, letting his mouth graze her cheek. The taste of her tears was on his lips, warm and salty, and her skin felt like velvet. Beneath his hands he felt her body trembling, and yet she seemed utterly still, as though she was afraid to move, afraid to breathe.

His mouth hovered over hers, eager to touch and taste. He would have kissed her then. He needed to kiss her. If only once...

And then his peripheral vision caught sight of Charlie, coming toward them awkwardly with his arms piled high with supplies, and his vision—

thank God—obscured by the blanket they'd used for their picnic.

With a muffled curse Jake set Nora away from him. The last thing he needed was to confuse his son any further. Nora followed his lead, putting distance between them, brushing a distracted hand through her hair and across her face. She concentrated on snapping the lid of her paint box shut, and he noticed that she wouldn't meet his eyes.

The ride back was uncomfortable. Charlie rode in the truck bed again, but although they were alone once more in the cab, neither Jake or Nora mentioned what had almost happened back there in the glade.

By the time they reached the Hideaway's front driveway, the sky looked dark and threatening, and Jake could almost believe he had imagined the whole episode.

CHAPTER EIGHT

IT RAINED by early evening, a steady downpour that sent dark, swollen clouds boiling across an ominous sky. Jake stood behind the screen door of Cabin Two and watched lightning outline the treetops on the horizon.

Turning his head, he smiled at Charlie's valiant attempts to keep his eyes open. After the trip to the national forest and a grilled-cheese sandwich for dinner, the boy had slouched in front of the television, and was now half-asleep.

Jake, however, was restless, and whether because of the rain or the events of the day, he felt unable to follow his son's example.

It was too soon for bed. And even if he did crawl between the sheets, Jake reasoned, he'd only toss and turn, wondering how he could have come so close to kissing Nora Holloway today, wondering why he would want to kiss a woman whom he might very well have to face down in a court of law.

It was one thing to offer solace to a person in need, but what he'd done today had been unexpected, confusing and, reluctant as he was to admit it, downright exciting.

He wondered if Nora had felt the same way. He thought he had glimpsed a similarity between her face and his feelings. But he couldn't be sure. His body had been reacting with such lusty sexual need that he might have completely misinterpreted her response.

They should talk. He didn't want her to get the wrong idea. He certainly couldn't afford to get involved with her. Not with the decision about Bobby's baby still unresolved.

The rain had stopped.

He slipped into his jacket, tucking the copy of *The Yearling* into one of the pockets. Might as well take the book back to the lodge tonight. Besides, it offered him an excuse to seek out Nora. He slipped out of the cabin quietly, leaving his son emitting soft snores from the couch.

When he entered the main lodge, he saw that the registration desk was closed for the night. The service bell was on the counter, and only one small light in the corner of the room burned a mellow glow, giving the massive stone-and-timber lobby a dark, mysterious appeal.

Perhaps he should wait until morning. It wouldn't help to discuss the incident with Nora if she was too tired and ready to turn in for the night.

Before he could make that decision, he heard loud, sharp voices, both male and female, coming from the Holloways' private quarters. It could have been a television; the prime-time shows would have begun their assault by now. He strode over to the bookcase near the fireplace.

He had just returned *The Yearling* to the shelf and was running a hand over the rest of the selection the resort offered, when he heard the voices draw nearer. Before he knew it, Nora appeared in the registration doorway. She didn't see him. Her attention was fully fixed on someone on the other side of the door she'd just come through, and there was no opportunity for Jake to announce his presence.

"I'm going for a walk," she announced curtly.

"Damn it, Nora, we have to talk about this." The voice belonged to Trip Holloway. He sounded frustrated and angry.

"We *have* talked about it. And the answer is still no."

"You can't ignore our finances forever. We have responsibilities—"

She had been striding toward the front entrance, but now she swung around to face her brother, who had appeared in the doorway. "Don't you dare talk to me about responsibilities, Trip Holloway. I have a huge emotional investment in this place. I've spent every waking moment for years taking care of it, meeting my responsibilities, while you've been gallivanting around the globe."

"Then don't do it anymore. Let's sell and be done with it."

"No."

Trip slapped his hand down on the registration desk. "Why can't you be reasonable about this?"

"You don't want me to be reasonable. You just want your own way. You agreed that monthly payments for your half would be fine. Now you expect me to come up with a payoff amount? You know I can't."

"You deserve better than this, Nora."

"Don't pretend this has anything to do with what I want or need. Admit it. The money's all you care about. You don't care what we'd be losing if we sell this place."

Her brother threw his arms wide. "All right, so I've never felt the same way about the Hideaway that you do. But what would you be losing, Nora? You've been stuck in the past ever since the accident—"

Nora pivoted to continue her exit out the front door. "You don't know what you're talking about," Jake heard her snap.

Trip came around the registration desk, following in her footsteps.

She banged through the door, leaving her brother to catch the door after her. "Nora!" he shouted into the darkness. "Damn it, Nora. Come back here!"

He swore viciously and stalked back to the registration desk. Even across the distance of the room and in the poor light, Jake could see veins standing out on the young man's neck. Jake decided it was well past time to make his presence known.

He cleared his throat, and Trip's head swung in his direction immediately.

"I'm sorry," Jake said. "I was just returning a

book. I didn't intend to overhear that conversation.''

The man's frown deepened. ''Ah, hell, now we're arguing in front of the guests. Although, I suppose in a way, you're not really a guest, are you? Nora's told me why you're here. It looks like neither one of us is going to get what we want from Nora.''

There was no clue in his voice or features as to how Nora's brother felt about the adoption. Was he in favor of it? Jake wondered. This seemed like the perfect opportunity to find out.

''Your sister strikes me as someone who can be very determined,'' Jake stated in an offhanded way.

''Determined? Impossible is more like it.'' The younger man's mouth twisted into a slash of displeasure. ''You'll find out for yourself if you have to take her to court over this baby thing. And you will, unless Nora can be made to see reason.''

''You don't support her decision to adopt Isabel's child?''

''Hell, no!'' Trip said. He glanced back over his shoulder, as though he expected someone—Isabel, perhaps—to come out of the private quarters behind him. Then he came around the desk and strode across the room to face Jake. In a low, mean voice, he said, ''Adopting this baby is just one more way Nora likes to stick her head in the sand.''

Jake didn't understand that comment, but he could see that Trip was still furious. ''You know,'' Jake suggested, ''you may be underestimating her. Nora might be stubborn, but I suspect she's a very sensible person, too. Sentimental, perhaps, but completely capable of deciding what's best for herself.''

Trip glared at Jake. "You think so?" Unexpectedly, he moved to the bookcase, pulling out several books to look behind them, as though searching for something. Finally he found what he was looking for—a thin book with no markings on the front cover. He tossed it to Jake, who caught it with one hand.

"Take a look at that," Trip said. "Then tell me my sister doesn't need to get away from here and start a new life. Tell me she'd make a good parent for Izzie's child."

"I'm afraid I don't understand."

"She lost her husband and a kid a few years back in an accident. She hasn't been the same since."

This was the first Jake had heard about an accident; even Isabel hadn't mentioned it. He felt a familiar stab of pain somewhere in the region of his gut as he imagined the hurt that Nora had suffered. He knew all about loss, too.

But another part of Trip's comments made Jake uneasy and curious. Was there something about Nora's mental state he should be concerned about for the baby's sake? What had her brother meant? Only one way to find out, and the young man was angry enough not to hold back anything.

"What makes you think your sister wouldn't be a good parent?"

Trip didn't hesitate. "She's too serious. Too

quiet. She used to be the life of the party—my fun-loving sis. But I hardly recognize her anymore.''

Jake barely held back an incredulous snort of derision. It sounded to him as though Nora Holloway had done something her brother had not—grown up. He struggled to keep from giving Trip Holloway a lecture and settled on, ''I've heard your sister talk about the Hideaway. She places a great deal of value on keeping your family's legacy here alive. She seems very much in tune with its history, the traditions that began several generations ago. Perhaps that's what makes her seem so serious to you.''

Trip moved restlessly to glance out the wide picture window. He looked back at Jake over his shoulder. ''It's just wood and nails and shingles. Nora's a fool to let it run her life.''

Jake had a pretty good idea who the fool here was, and it wasn't Nora Holloway. But he could see Trip wouldn't listen, and even though he was no longer visibly angry, it was still there, just beneath the surface, waiting for a reason to strike out at someone. Jake wouldn't give him that reason.

Instead, while the young man continued to scowl out the window, Jake opened the book in his hands. It was obviously some sort of journal, covering a period of time five years ago. The handwriting was slashing and jerky, and there were numerous splotches of ink, as though the writer had suddenly stopped and started dozens of times. His eyes picked out a line here and there as he flipped through the book.

I don't know how I can go on...

...think about my baby all the time, wondering...

I wish it had been me instead—

He closed the book with a snap. He didn't need to read any further. The volume was full of Nora's private pain, and he had no desire to intrude on it. The fact that Trip Holloway was willing to allow a stranger to see it—even in a fit of anger against her—diminished Jake's already lowering opinion of the man considerably.

Trip turned from the window, nodding toward the book in Jake's hand. "Nora kept that journal after the accident," he said, offering an unnecessary explanation. "She asked me to burn it a few years ago when we were cleaning out her old room, but I didn't. I thought one day she'd put her life back together, and then she'd want to reread it and know how far she'd come."

Jake shook his head and held out the book. "I don't think I need to see this."

"No. You keep it for a while."

Jake frowned. "Why?"

"Nora doesn't need a baby complicating her life right now. There are things in that journal that would make any judge wonder if she could handle the responsibility of raising a child."

"You'd allow me to use this against your sister?"

"I want what's best for her."

"Do you?" Jake asked with a narrowed glance.

"Or do you just want to take out your anger on Nora?"

Trip had the grace to look uncomfortable. "Yes, I want the money we could get from selling this place. I think I have the right to pursue my own goals in life. But I'm thinking of Nora, too. This place is too much for one person to handle. If she stays, she'll only work herself into an early grave like my mother did. And if she adds the burden of raising a child, she'll work herself into that grave that much sooner."

"Don't you think those kinds of decisions should be hers?"

Raking a hand through his dark, disheveled hair, Trip walked to the registration desk, disregarding Jake's outstretched hand holding the book. "Use it, or don't," he said. "I've been over our finances. Sooner or later, she'll have to come around to my way of thinking. The bank will see to that."

IN THE END, Jake didn't take the journal back to the cabin with him.

He knew he could never use the book against Nora, no matter how nasty a court battle he might find himself embroiled in. For what Thea had done, he'd been willing to nail her buffed and polished little hide to the courthouse wall, but Nora Holloway was different. She was a decent human being, and she didn't deserve to have her most anguished inner thoughts paraded in front of a courtroom full of strangers.

Neither did she deserve to have such a selfish,

money-hungry brother who could hold that journal as his ace-in-the-hole, to be played like a trump card in the event Nora didn't cooperate with his plans. Which was why Jake didn't return the volume to its hiding place behind the books on the shelf. Instead, he crammed it under a stack of fishing magazines he found in one corner of the lobby.

He told himself that when the time was right, he would personally hand it over to her. If she still wanted the book burned, he'd help her himself. But he'd never place the damn thing in Trip Holloway's hands again.

There had to be other ways to win custody of Bobby's child.

So the next day, while Charlie was inside the grocery store choosing items—surprisingly without an argument—Jake used the pay phone outside to call Gregg Sanstrom to discuss what those ways might be.

"So how's everything in Hicksville?" the attorney asked.

"Not as bad as you'd think. It has its appeal."

"And Charlie?"

Jake couldn't help smiling into the receiver. "Believe it or not, I think we're making headway. He actually made a pot of coffee for me this morning."

"Uh-oh. Did you drink it?"

"No cyanide," Jake said with a laugh. "I checked for the smell of almonds."

"Well! That is progress. And the adoption issue?"

Jake ran his fingers through his hair, feeling the frustration that had been building within him suddenly take hold. "It seemed so simple when I first called you with the idea," he admitted. "But I've spoken to Nora Holloway, and she seems determined to fight for the baby."

"Then a fight is what she's going to get," the lawyer replied.

"I don't know, Gregg. I'm not sure I want it to come to that."

"Why? Because you don't think we can win?"

"No, it's not that—"

"Then, what? You can't have it both ways. Either you make a stand for the kid, or you let this go." There was a long silence while they both gave his words consideration. Then, Gregg said in a softer tone, "You're under no moral obligation to do this, you know."

"I want to."

"It won't bring Bobby back."

Jake frowned. "I know that."

"And what happened wasn't your fault."

Jake shifted uneasily. "Put away your couch, Sigmund. This isn't about guilt. I have good reasons for wanting Bobby's child."

"Then we'll have to come up with a way to make Nora Holloway change her mind. I've spoken to her attorney. He's young, not a lot of courtroom experience. I'll apply some pressure, but I doubt it will do much good. He'll take the case to trial if need be." Gregg sighed heavily. "I do hate to go up against his kind."

"Inept?"

"No! An idealist. They never want to give up, even after you bloody their noses thoroughly."

"Maybe it won't come to that," Jake said almost to himself. "If I keep trying to convince Nora that it's in the baby's best interest for me to have custody—"

The attorney made a rude sound. "Listen. Rely on smooth talk if you think it will help. But just in case you're not as good as you think you are, we need ammunition, my friend. Surely she has a few skeletons in the closet we can rattle?"

"I don't know..."

"Hell, Jake! What are you waiting for? Ask around. In a town that small, she's bound to have pissed off someone. Friends, business associates, family. Can you find a cousin who'd testify against her, say she abused Grandma or sold the family jewels and pocketed the money?"

Jake swore softly, hating the suggestion that they resort to dirty tricks. This wasn't the way he wanted to see things play out. But what if Gregg was right? What if Nora wouldn't give in even when she saw that the deck was stacked against her?

Thinking aloud, he said, "Her brother's the only family she has left that I know of. He'd probably do it, the bastard. He tried to give me a private journal she kept a few years ago."

"A journal?" Gregg said, sounding excited for the first time. "That's perfect! Take it. Send it to me, and I'll see if we can make anything out of it."

"No."

"What do you mean, no?" The man went from elated to incredulous in a matter of seconds.

"I mean, that's not an option," Jake said, staring down at his feet while he let the words sink in to Gregg. "It's her personal diary, Gregg," he tried to explain further. "Full of a lot of pain that she must have been going through at the time."

"You read it?"

Jake's head jerked up as he gripped the receiver tighter. "Hell, no, I didn't read it! What kind of low-life son of a bitch do you take me for?"

"The kind who's going to lose this case if he doesn't give me something to impress a judge."

"I'll get you something," Jake promised. "Just not that. All right?"

"All right. But let me ask you one question."

"What?"

"Are you sure you know which side of this thing you're supposed to be on?"

DURING THE NEXT FEW DAYS, Jake did his best to come through for Gregg Sanstrom. He and Charlie began working on their boat for the race, and with every trip he made to town for supplies, or groceries or fishing gear, he took extra time to make idle conversation with the locals.

He'd learned quickly that Blue Devil Springs was filled with the kind of salt-of-the-earth citizens who kept close watch on their neighbors and knew each other's business. Some of them, Jake figured, would surely have a story to tell about Nora Holloway.

At the bank, as he cashed a check, he talked to

the president. When he purchased nails at the hardware store, he listened as the manager went into a long-winded story about the time Hurricane Betty tore the roof off his place. At the Cut 'n Curl he let an aged beautician give him a trim—taking an inch of hair more than he liked—just so he could ask her about the history of the Hideaway and the family that built it.

They opened up all right, but there wasn't a single bit of information Jake could use against Nora Holloway in court. If the good townspeople of Blue Devil Springs were to be believed, she was a shoe-in as the next candidate for sainthood.

She paid her taxes on time. She made the best blackberry cobbler in the county. She gave blood three times a year and chaired the semiannual Save Our Rivers cleanup days.

No one had a cross word to say about the woman. No axes to grind. No unneighborly disputes over property lines or barking dogs. Nora Holloway probably didn't even get parking tickets.

After the fourth day of coming up empty-handed, Jake was disgruntled, demoralized, but not defeated as he stopped for a glass of iced tea at the Whispering River Café. The place was nearly empty, and he slipped into a table in a far corner. Ben, the owner, came over to take his order immediately.

"Iced tea," Jake said, then held up a forestalling hand. "No. Make it a beer. Whatever you've got that's cold and strong."

"That kind of day, huh?" Ben asked with a grin.

"I've had better."

The man strode away. Jake rested his chin on his hand and turned his head to stare at the wall. He tried to make his mind go blank, but one of Saint Nora's odd little paintings was all he could see. Herons on a riverbank. At least he thought that was what he was looking at.

That lack of talent with a paintbrush seemed to be Nora Holloway's only failing. He shook his head. It wasn't enough. *Judge, she can't adopt this baby because she's a lousy artist.* Yeah, that would work.

The restaurant emptied, and Ben came back carrying a few beer bottles laced between the fingers of one hand. He angled them out toward Jake. "I've got domestic or imported. Pick your poison."

Jake chose a dark one and took a huge sip. Letting out a sigh, he smiled up at Ben. "Perfect," he pronounced. "Care to join me?"

Seeing that there were no customers, Ben nodded and took the second chair, tilting it outward so that he could keep an eye on the room. Jake watched the man's Adam's apple work as he polished off half a beer in just a few swallows.

Ben emitted a satisfied sound and looked at Jake. "So how are you finding life in Blue Devil Springs? Not exactly the fast lane, is it?"

"It's pretty quiet," he admitted.

"Wait a week. River rats own this town in the summer."

"I don't see how one good season can keep a business afloat for an entire year."

Ben shrugged. "Most of us do all right. We're

the closest town to the national forest, and tourists come here for supplies and a change of scenery." Lifting his eyebrows, he made a face. "They think we're quaint."

Jake took another swig of beer, letting the cold bite of the brew wash away some of his frustration. It occurred to him that in this relaxed, casual atmosphere he might be able to learn a few things about Nora and her life here. Ben was easy to talk to, and he had dated her for a while. Jake floated an innocent, lead-in comment. "Quaint certainly describes the Hideaway."

"Yep. The small, independent family resort. Last of a dying breed."

"Do you think it will come to that? Extinction?"

"Not if Nora has anything to say about it. She's determined to make a go of it." Ben glanced over at him. "Heard you were staying there, so you probably know what I mean. She's not a quitter."

"No, I suspect she's not. But I imagine it's hard to keep fighting, especially when her own brother seems to want her to sell the place."

"Trip? He's wanted that for years. Doesn't mean he'll ever talk her into it."

"He seems to think he knows what's best for her."

"Trip knows what's best for Trip," Ben said with an arched smile. "He's always been a selfish SOB."

That pretty much matched Jake's assessment of the man, but it made him feel better to know he wasn't alone in that opinion. "Still, I'm surprised she's willing to stick it out, running the place almost by herself. Considering all the upkeep, a husband would probably come in handy.''

''I imagine she could use the help.''

With a frown, Jake finished the last of his beer. He wasn't certain why he'd let his quest for information about Nora Holloway take this particular tack. Her romantic life was nothing that could help him in court, but he found himself eager to know all the same. In fact, he even pushed a little by saying, ''I understand she had one at one time. A husband, I mean.''

''Yeah. About five years ago.''

''Someone local?''

''No. She met a fellow in the national forest tracking black bears for the Park Service.'' He tossed a look at Jake. ''You probably know by now how fond she is of the wildlife around here. I guess they had a lot in common. Next thing we hear, they'd gotten married.'' He frowned, then nodded minutely. ''Peter, that was his name. Nice guy. You want another beer?''

Jake took a sip from the bottle Ben pushed across the table. ''So what happened?''

''They'd been married about six months. Had a kid on the way. A boy, I think. Anyway, Peter brought Nora into town one day for a doctor's appointment. I ran into her outside the office trying to keep out of the rain while he got the car. She was so excited about the baby, and laughing because her stomach was too big to get her raincoat buttoned.'' Ben grimaced and shook his head. ''I remember thinking I'd never seen her that happy before. And I haven't since then, either."

Jake went cold at his words. "Trip Holloway mentioned an accident."

"On the way home, Peter took one of the curves too fast in the rain. He ran off the road and hit a tree. Killed him instantly. The baby, too, although they didn't know that until they got Nora to the hospital."

"Was she injured?"

"Hardly a mark on her." Ben slid a knowing glance Jake's way. "None that you could see, at least."

Jake listened in thoughtful silence, remembering the quick glance he'd gotten of those desperate, slashing entries in Nora's journal. No woman ought to suffer that kind of loss, and yet here he was, trying to find ways to keep her from making some kind of peace with the past.

He felt torn. Obviously Nora viewed adoption as the chance to rebuild her life, and he couldn't honestly say she was wrong to think that. Even if she never remarried, she'd still probably make a good mother. A baby would be lucky to have her for a mom.

Just not *this* baby. Not Bobby's child, damn it.

He didn't like himself very much in that moment. The beer tasted bitter on his tongue, and he frowned down at the bottle in his hand.

Ben noticed and inclined his head toward the beer. "You don't like that brand?"

"Stronger than I'm used to." Jake offered the

excuse absently. Then, "It must be very difficult to recover from a loss like that."

"Even for someone as normally upbeat as Nora," Ben agreed.

Remembering Trip's claim about her stability, Jake couldn't resist asking, "Did she ever seem...I don't know...unable to cope?"

"No," the other man said with a frown, as though wondering where such a question had come from. "Not Nora. She came around eventually. Took back her maiden name and started getting out more."

"But she hasn't remarried."

Ben smiled. "Nora's had plenty of offers, but so far as I know she's rejected all of them."

"You think she's still grieving over her husband?"

His companion shrugged. "Could be, I suppose. She's never mentioned his name since the day of the accident."

Jake sat still, letting his thoughts sort through his feelings and this unexpected peek into Nora's past. He supposed Gregg Sanstrom could turn it into something ugly enough to sway a judge, but Jake didn't think he could live with himself if he allowed that approach to be taken.

Expelling a heavy, frustrated sigh, he turned his head. He was tired of trying to figure it all out. Maybe a change of subject was in order. Nora's poorly executed riverbank scene snared his attention. "These paintings are really bad," he said to Ben.

Ben cocked his head. "I know. But that doesn't matter."

"Have you considered the possibility that these paintings might actually drive business away?"

A slow grin spread across the man's face. "I'll take my chances. I owe Nora a debt I can't ever repay."

"How so?"

"Last year during the busy season I fell over a box in the stockroom." He parted his hair with his fingers to show Jake a thin, white line against his scalp. "Twenty-six stitches, and I was unconscious for almost a week. By the time I got out of the hospital I figured this place was going to be in the red, big time. Instead, I discovered that Nora had kept it open —cooking, waiting tables—whatever it took, she did. I didn't lose a single hour's worth of business. And this was while the Hideaway was overflowing, too. She saved my butt." With a tight smile, Ben looked back at Nora's painting. "So if it pleases her to think that people see her work and appreciate it, she can hang them upside down for all I care."

Jake didn't doubt the sincerity of Ben's feelings. Nora was turning out to be a more formidable opponent than he'd ever have imagined. And yet, in that particular moment, he wasn't really thinking of her as the person he might have to face in court some day. He was thinking of her as a woman...

Ben gave him a sudden sidelong glance. "Why all the questions? You interested in her?"

Jake pulled himself erect, sliding the empty beer

bottles toward the center of the table. He shook his head decisively. "Just curious."

"Uh-huh," Ben said, and his smile broadened into a grin. He turned to lean across the table. "Let me tell you something. There isn't a man in Blue Devil Springs who hasn't been 'just curious' about Nora Holloway at one time or another. You want to see what the competition looks like, drop by the Moose Hall next Thursday night. The town's having a fund-raiser for the Volunteer Fire Department." He winked. "You can compare notes, and maybe get to dance with Nora, too."

Jake looked Ben in the eyes for a moment, prepared to deny his interest, then gave the whole thing up and asked, "How do you know she'll be there?"

"Oh, she'll be there," he assured him. A young couple had walked into the café and Ben took a last swallow of beer, then rose from the table. "She's head of the fund-raising committee."

It figured.

THAT NIGHT THERE was an unexpected development in Jake's relationship with Charlie. Nothing earth-shattering, but enough for Jake to feel he was making headway with the kid.

With the boat race coming up, they'd spent the afternoon on the river, practicing strokes in one of the Hideaway canoes. They capsized twice. By the time the sun set, they were both tired and hungry, and Jake's effort to fix dinner—overcooked spaghetti and meatballs—was met with a look of open rebellion by Charlie. Finally, they settled in opposite corners of the cabin, Jake trying to drum up enthusiasm for the book on shipbuilding he'd found in the Hideaway library, and Charlie retreating once again into battle with his video space villains.

They were both ready to call it a night when they heard the sound of a dog howling—like a Baskerville hound coming over the moors. It was enough to make the hair on the back of Jake's head stand on end, and Charlie looked up from Space Scow.

"Sounds like Larry," the boy said worriedly and slipped off the couch to go to the screen door.

Jake joined him, his eyes scanning the property. The Hideaway looked tucked in for the night. The main lodge was dark. The only light came from the rehab shed at the edge of the woods. That didn't seem odd. Charlie had told Jake that Nora often worked with her animals all hours of the day and night.

More agitated barking floated across the darkness, definitely coming from the direction of the rehab shed.

"Nora's up late," Jake commented.

"She's only got the eagle left," Charlie said. "We turned loose the raccoon and the birds yesterday. She could be painting, I guess. She keeps her supplies in the shed."

"I'm going for a walk," Jake said, edging past his son and out the door.

"I'm coming, too." The boy was behind him in seconds.

The moonlit path to the rehab shed was a bright ribbon ahead of them. As they neared the small building, they could hear Larry whining, and Nora's voice raised in displeasure. The door was open, and when Jake and Charlie looked inside, the sight before them stopped them in their tracks.

The place was a mess, covered with paint that had been squeezed out of a dozen tubes. Red. Green. Blue. Splotches. Splatters. Paw prints stamped in rainbow colors and canvases littered across the floor. In one corner, the injured eagle sat in its cage and glared malevolently at them.

In the center of the room was Nora, crouched in front of her mongrel with a ragged, paint-splattered towel in one hand, the other curled tightly around Larry's collar. The dog's eyes were downcast. His tail dragged the floor, and his coat was flecked with paint.

"...ought to put you up for adoption at the next pet fair," Nora was scolding. "As if there aren't enough annoyances around here lately without having you up to your old tricks."

She rubbed powder-blue paint off his muzzle, then tilted his head up so that their eyes met. Larry offered a conciliatory swipe of his tail. Moss-green paint smeared across the pine flooring.

"Don't give me tht pitiful look," she told him. "You are a bad dog. A very bad dog. And you are one lousy artist, you know that?"

Larry tried to look contrite and invisible.

Jake cleared his throat to let Nora know she had company. She looked surprised to see the two of them standing there.

"Artistic differences?" Jake suggested.

Nora held out a forestalling hand. "Don't come

any closer if you don't want paint all over you. I don't know why, but Larry has a thing about my art supplies. He loves to chew up my brushes and claw the canvases. This time he got to my paint box. Thank goodness none of this is toxic to animals.'' She shook her head at the dog as he tried to pull away. ''Hold still, you miserable mutt, until I get this paint off you.''

''We'll help you, won't we, Dad?'' Charlie offered, and immediately he began picking up paint brushes that were scattered everywhere.

''Sure,'' Jake agreed. He bent to retrieve a nearby canvas that had globs of wet, yellow paint across one side of the picture.

''Thanks,'' Nora said, and seeing the ruined canvas in Jake's hands, she added, ''Oh, no! I just finished that one last week. I was going to take it down to Ben's tomorrow. Now look at it. It's ruined.''

Both Jake and Charlie gave the picture a closer look. Beneath the paw prints and rivulets of fresh paint, he recognized Nora's traditional beach landscape. Yep, there were her trademark flying worm/seagulls. Frankly, he thought the addition of Larry's handiwork improved the darned thing. One exchanged glance with Charlie told him that his son thought so, too.

''It's not so bad,'' Charlie said.

''Actually, the paw prints give it an interesting abstract look,'' Jake added, tilting his head to one side as he held the canvas at arm's length. ''Maybe you ought to consider taking your work in a new direction.''

"You've got it upside-down," Nora said. "And you two can stop trying to pretend you like my work. I saw your faces that day in the glade." She ran the towel over the dog's front paw. "I don't care what you think. I like it, and I'm not using Larry for a paintbrush."

"No, really…" Charlie began, and Jake placed a hand on the boy's shoulder.

"Forget it, son. We're busted."

Together, they made quick work of the clean-up. When the last canvas had been restacked in a corner, salvageable paint tubes recapped and Larry looking more his old self again, Jake surveyed the room.

"Did we miss anything?"

"Looks good," Nora said. She shook her finger at Larry, who had skulked into a corner behind Charlie's legs. "Tomorrow I'm getting a lock for the door, and you'd better keep a low profile for the next few days, mister, because I'm still mad at you."

"I'll keep him out of your hair," Charlie offered with sudden enthusiasm. "He could stay with me in my room." Then he looked worriedly at his father and quickly added, "No, that's probably not a good idea."

"Why not?" Jake asked. "If Nora doesn't mind, I don't."

He knew how Thea had always felt about indoor pets, and Charlie had never mentioned wanting or having one. But he seemed to like animals, and Larry in particular, so what harm could it do? He turned toward Nora, who had a tiny smudge of red paint on her cheekbone. He lifted the towel out of her hand and brought the tip of it to her face. "Hold still, you've got paint here. So you don't mind if Larry keeps Charlie company for a while, do you?"

Nora's mouth parted slightly, and her body seemed tense. He realized that his unexpected touch had surprised her.

"No," she said softly. "No, that's fine."

"Good," Jake said. He dropped the towel on the workbench and headed toward the door. "It's late. Come on, Charlie. Grab Picasso there and let's go to bed." At the door, he turned back toward Nora, who stood watching them silently. "Call me if you need help with the lock."

She nodded.

On the way back to the cabin, Larry trotted just ahead of Charlie, his tail wagging furiously now that he sensed he was out of trouble. Jake watched the dog absently, his mind still on the fact that Nora had seemed pleasantly unsettled by his touch.

Charlie looked back over his shoulder at his father. "He won't be any trouble, Dad. I promise."

"I know."

"I'll keep a close eye on him."

"Good."

"Dad?"

"Yeah?"

"Thanks. For letting him stay, I mean."

Gratitude from Charlie? That was even more un-expected than Nora's reaction. "No problem, son."

Charlie sprinted down the path, chasing Larry. Jake smiled as he watched his son's shadowy figure bobbing in the moonlight. He inhaled sharply, pull-ing in night scents that were intoxicating.

It was a beautiful night, wasn't it?

CHAPTER NINE

NORA SMILED as she stepped up to the microphone.

"Welcome, everyone!" she began enthusiastically, and then launched into the short, prepared speech she used every year to begin the festivities at the annual fund-raiser for the Blue Springs Fire Department. The crowd, bless them, gave her their full attention, as though they'd never heard it before.

She was halfway through the speech, just about ready to introduce Chief Quinn, when she spotted Jake Burdette at the hall's entrance door, and the rest of her words stuck in her throat. She had to swallow to get them out, so that when she did she rushed through the introduction. Chief Quinn gave her an odd look, and there was a titter from the crowd.

What was he doing here? She watched him take a ticket for a door prize from the attendant, then hand another to his son. The fact that Jake was here, and had managed to convince Charlie to come as well, stunned her into complete silence.

Not good. Chief Quinn—always a man of few

words—finished his welcome and now waited for her to jump in with closing comments.

It took her a moment to find her place. She told herself to be calm. The fund-raiser was open to anyone. But the adrenaline kept pumping through her system anyway.

This man is dangerous, the little voice in her head sent the warning. *Stay away from him.*

Behind her, the band, perhaps sensing something wrong, went into their first number. She and Chief Quinn scurried off the stage and down the steps to the dance floor. She headed for the refreshment table where Isabel was overseeing the sale of baked goods.

For days she'd tried to forget about that afternoon in the forest when she had nearly made a complete fool of herself. Bad enough that Jake had caught her in a weak moment—tearful and idiotically sentimental. Exactly the kind of vulnerability her enemy might be looking for.

But she had almost kissed him, wanted him to kiss her. And that night, when he'd made a casual attempt to wipe the paint off her cheek, her stomach had flipped at his nearness. Her windpipe had narrowed until she could hardly breathe, and his touch had blinded her to everything but the look in his eyes.

In a panic of pride and humiliation, she had decided to keep her distance. For the past few days, things had seemed to return to normal. She'd made uneasy peace with Trip. She managed to spend some time with Charlie and she'd never allowed herself to be alone with Jake, although she made every effort to play the amiable innkeeper when their paths crossed.

She reached the refreshment table. Isabel stood behind it, looking pale and ill at ease. In spite of the doctor's recommendation to rest often, the girl had insisted on coming tonight to help out, but now Nora wished she'd convinced Izzie not to attend. She wished Trip had come. He could have driven Isabel home. But he was sick himself, nursing a summer cold in his old bedroom with all the drama of a third-rate actor in a deathbed scene.

"Are you all right, Izzie?" Nora asked.

"Oh, Nora, I don't think I can stay here."

Nora had lost sight of Jake for the moment, but she caught Isabel's frown as the girl gazed off toward the front door. Evidently Isabel had seen his entrance, too.

Damn him! No matter how much she wanted to avoid him, she didn't want Isabel to be uncomfortable. Clenching her jaw, Nora rubbed Isabel's arm consolingly. "That horrible man. Hold tight, honey. I'll ask him to leave."

Isabel's head turned to pin her with a confused look. "Who?"

"Jake Burdette."

"Why?"

"Because he's upsetting you."

"No, he's not." Isabel placed a hand over her mouth. "It's the smell of cheesecake. It's making me sick. Damn it, I hate being nauseated all the time."

For a blank second Nora stood and looked at her friend in annoyance. It would have helped enormously to think that Isabel shared Nora's resentment of Jake's presence. "Do you want to go home?" she asked at last.

"No. I just want this to be over."

"Me, too," Nora replied.

"Did you say Jake was here?" Isabel glanced quickly around the room. "Where?"

"Somewhere. Who cares?" Nora took Isabel's elbow and began steering her around the table. "Come on. I'll have you switch with Mr. Tuttle at the front door."

"Why do you suppose he's here?"

No use pretending she didn't know who Isabel meant. "I don't know. Bored, perhaps. Or maybe he just wants to confirm what he probably already thinks—that the Springs is too backward a place to raise a child."

"He's never said that, has he?"

"No," Nora reluctantly agreed. "At least, not within my hearing."

"You know, maybe he's not going to be a problem after all. Maybe he's changed his mind about fighting for the baby."

"I'm sure John would have contacted us if that was the case." Nora was irritated to find Isabel so willing to give Jake Burdette that kind of credit.

"Well, he's been awfully pleasant to me the few times I've seen him lately. And he's certainly left you alone."

Yes, he has, she thought sourly. She got Isabel

settled in a folding chair by the door. Leaning down to catch the girl's ear over the music, she said, "Don't trust him for a moment, Izzie. All this good behavior probably means he's taken his investigation underground."

"DAD—"

Charlie touched Jake's sleeve, and he turned his attention from the dance floor, where a dozen couples were gyrating wildly to the band's rendition of "Rock Around the Clock."

"I know," Jake said. "You hate this place, you don't know why I dragged you here, and you want to go back to the cabin."

"No," Charlie said with a look that indicated he didn't know where that accusation had come from. "I think this old music's kind of cool. I just wanted to know if you'd give me some money for a piece of pie and a soft drink."

Jake dug into the pocket of his jeans for change, hiding a smile of satisfaction. Getting Charlie to come along with him to the local Order of Moose Hall had taken a Herculean amount of persuasion. The fact that the boy actually didn't seem to mind being here was something short of a miracle.

They'd been at this fund raiser nearly an hour now, and though the room was crowded, with clusters of friends and neighbors spilling out into the parking lot and around a small banquet area where a potluck dinner was being served, not once had Jake managed to run into Nora Holloway.

He wasn't avoiding her, but she seemed to have

that in mind for him. He'd caught sight of her dancing occasionally, making announcements about the
bake sale and upcoming Memorial Day festivities,
ferrying a tray of refreshments to the band members. Not once did their gazes meet, and he would
have bet money that was the way she intended to
keep it.

He wasn't particularly bothered by her efforts to
avoid him. His purpose for coming tonight had not
been to make her life miserable—although he felt
certain she probably thought otherwise.

No, he had taken Ben's advice, come to the place
where most of Nora's former boyfriends would be
gathered. Surely one or two of these guys would
reveal any…problem…she had that he should
know about for the baby's sake. Any moral inade-
quacies, sexual misconduct.

But as the evening wore on, he began to wonder
what had possessed him to think that approach
would work. Not one guy in the room had anything
bad to say about Nora. Jake drank a half-dozen
glasses of punch and more beers than he wanted,
laughed at the worst jokes and talked sports until
his tongue went numb.

And to what purpose?

Walt Clevenger. Steven Westmeyer. Bud Langi-
zano. Every one of them thought Nora Holloway
was the answer to a man's dreams. Pretty enough
to get them hot, sweet enough to make them feel
strong and manly, bright enough to make them feel
clever for managing to snag her interest. Relationships that had lasted three weeks, a month, six. And

when they were over, not a one of them felt cheated, manipulated or resentful. The closest thing to a complaint came from Alan Harcourt, a ranger at the park, who told Jake that Nora had too soft a heart and had loaned him money when she was short of funds herself.

Try making a judge see the downside to that! Jake groused inwardly as he walked through the room to check on Charlie. He could picture Gregg Sanstrom running with it. *Your Honor, Miss Holloway's too generous. She'll spoil this baby.*

Yeah, that had a snowball's chance in hell of working.

He found Charlie at one end of an empty banquet table, showing a pretty young girl with long, blond hair how to kill invaders on the video game he always carried in his back pocket. The kid looked guilty and flustered when he caught sight of his father and stood up immediately.

"Did you need me?" the boy asked.

"No," Jake said. "I thought you might be ready to leave."

"I'm doing okay," Charlie said nonchalantly. He jerked his head in the direction of the girl, who turned a sweet, innocent smile on Jake. "This is Darlene. I'm just showing her how to get through the first level of Space Scow."

"And then I'm going to show him how to dance," Darlene spoke up.

Charlie went red and mumbled, "I know how to dance."

Darlene rebuked that claim with a laugh and a toss of blond curls.

Jake gave his son an encouraging smile. "Come get me if you need anything, Charles. I'll be in the other room."

He turned to leave, but Charlie caught up with him before he got to the door, catching Jake's sleeve.

"Just one thing," he said softly, flicking a quick look at Darlene. "If you see me out on the dance floor, don't make a big deal out of it. Okay?"

"Okay," Jake promised. He looked into his son's grave eyes, saw the small, straight shoulders and stubborn chin that he had inherited from Jake's side of the family.

"And call me Charlie," the boy instructed firmly. "It's more macho, don't you think?"

Before Jake could answer, Charlie was heading back to Darlene.

Jake stood there stupefied for a moment. Maybe God had decided he couldn't handle a battle with both Nora Holloway and his son, and was giving him a little break from the hostilities. Whatever the reason, Jake decided to just shut up and let things happen.

He wandered back into the main hall. The band was evidently on a break. The dance floor had cleared, and Nora stood on the stage, turning a large jar of tickets in her hands, over and over again. The spotlight made the healthy shine of her hair seem like a halo. The red dress she wore swirled around her knees like living fire, and Jake wondered why, with legs like that, she didn't wear dresses all the time.

He found a spot in the back of the crowd, next to a bespeckled teenage boy who held his admission ticket in one hand and smiled at Jake. "Last of the door prizes," the kid said and wiggled his eyebrows hopefully.

Jake didn't bother pulling out his ticket. He never won those things, and anyway, he'd seen the door prize—the big one. What would he do with a cypress knee clock the size of a wagon wheel?

He settled back on his heels, feeling the effects of the beer, prepared to wait. Wondering what he'd have to do to get Nora to dance with him. Hell, just to get her to look at him...

"...and this clock has a retail value of forty-five dollars," Nora was telling the audience. "Thank you, Ed Hansen of Ed's Hardware for donating it." A hush descended on the crowd. Nora fished around in the jar with her free hand. "And the winning number is..." The band provided a drumroll. She plucked out a ticket and cocked her head to read the digits printed on one end. "Six-two-eight-one," she called out, then shaded her eyes against the spotlight's glare. "Do we have a winner? Six-two-eight-one?"

The crowd stirred, waiting for the winner's shout. The kid next to him was fumbling with his glasses, trying to check his ticket in the poor light. Jake read the numbers over the boy's shoulder. Six-two-eight-one. *Congratulations, son,* was on the tip of his tongue.

He actually nudged the boy's shoulder. And then he had an idea. He clamped his fingers around the kid's forearm, pulling him a few steps away from the mob of people pressing around the stage.

"You're the winner, kid," Jake told him in a low voice. "You really want a forty-five dollar clock? Or the hundred-dollar bill I've got in my wallet in exchange for your ticket?"

The teenager's eyes went wide. "You serious, man?"

The crowd was growing restless. On the stage Nora was shaking the jar once more. "We may have to draw again…"

Quickly, Jake slipped his wallet out, peeled off the last of the money he'd withdrawn from the ATM this morning and showed it to the boy. "Make a smart decision," he told him. "But make it quick."

Almost in one movement, the boy snatched the money and thrust the ticket in Jake's hand. He shook his head. "You must really like cypress wood."

"Crazy about it," Jake said, already maneuvering through the crowd.

"If we don't have a winner…" Nora leaned to speak into the microphone.

"We do!" Jake shouted. He raised his hand over the throng of people, jabbing the ticket in the air. "Here! Right here!"

The audience peeled back. He moved forward, his eyes on Nora, who was scanning the crowd. When he stood directly in front of her, he smiled.

With the spotlight no longer directly in her eyes, she recognized him for the first time.

And frowned.

"Six-two-eight-one." He offered up the ticket cheerfully. "The winner."

She took the ticket out of his hand as though it were radioactive. "I'll have to check the numbers," she said sharply, and gave him a look that wasn't at all what the good townspeople of Blue Devil Springs would have expected from one of their favorite citizens.

"Of course."

She matched the ticket with its mate. Reluctantly. Recovering some of her poise, she spoke into the mike, "It's official, folks."

Over the groans of disappointment—considerable when you took into account that it was just a clock, after all—Jake put his hand around his mouth and stage-whispered up to her, "Go again."

She had to lean down to catch his words. "What?"

"I'm giving the clock back. Pull another number and make someone else happy."

"Why?"

"Just do it."

She eyed the crowd, which had begun to break off into little groups, waiting for the next set from the band. He could see her weighing possible reasons for his request, coming up empty.

With one hand angling the microphone away from her, she leaned down farther, until she was almost balanced on her knees. "And in return, what do you get?"

He grinned up at her. "In return, you give me one dance. A slow one."

She shook her head, didn't even blink. "That's not the way this works."

"You're the lady with the power here, aren't you? You can do what you want. Tell them I'm just a visitor, and I can't take the clock with me on the plane. That's not quite true. But you say it, and they'll believe it. These people think you hung the moon."

"This is silly. If it's just a dance you want, I'll—"

"Uh-uh," he cut her off. "You've spent this entire evening trying to avoid me, so don't pretend you'll dance with me if I ask you to. You're afraid to be near me. Admit it."

She shot upward in outrage. The microphone stand clanked loudly back into place, screeching and drawing everyone's attention as it picked up the words she rasped out, "Why, you shifty, arrogant—"

The crowd went silent, turning back toward the stage. Nora's cheeks had gone nearly as bright as her dress, but to her credit she hardly missed a beat. She smiled into the spotlight, tossing a stray curl away from her face and wetting her lips with the swipe of her tongue.

"Ladies and gentlemen," she said hurriedly. Then with more composure, "Friends and good neighbors." She tossed an affectionate look down at Jake, and he wondered if anyone else knew how patently false it was. "It seems that our winner tonight has graciously declined the prize. He's just passing through, and I'm afraid he doesn't have any room for it. However, he's suggested that we draw again for a new winner..." She stopped, again favoring him with a toothy smile. "And in addition, he's generously donated two hundred dollars of his own money in support of our efforts to buy a new pumper truck for the fire department. Let's hear it for him, folks!"

Donating a cypress knee clock was one thing, but two hundred dollars was enough to pull several gasps of delight from the crowd. The band went into a few, sudden bars of "For He's a Jolly Good Fellow." The people closest to him clapped him on the shoulder and shook his hand.

And all the while he managed to keep the grin on his face.

Above him, Nora looked immensely pleased with herself, and he had to give it to her—she'd one-upped him.

She pulled another ticket. The clock went to an older woman in the back of the hall who whooped as though she'd just won the state lottery. His two hundred dollars went to Chief Quinn, who looked at him suspiciously when he confessed that he'd have to give him a check.

The band dribbled a few notes and then slid into "Smoke Gets in Your Eyes," making the song sound soulful and dreamy. Nora had come down from the stage.

She held out her hand with a teasing arch of her eyebrows, her eyes sparkling. "Your two-hundred-dollar song, I believe. I hope you'll find my dancing ability worth it."

He took her into his arms, catching her close with a breath of triumphant laughter. "Let's find out," he whispered against her ear.

His arm was around her waist. He brought their entwined fingers next to his chest. His eyes were on her face; hers were on some safe spot over his shoulder, but she was as close to him as she'd been in the glade, and he could feel his heart reacting just the same way.

Keep it light, Burdette, he lectured himself sternly. *You've got her. Don't chase her away.*

They moved without words for a few moments. He pulled her nearer, making her aware of his balance and command. He hadn't danced in years, but it came back to him fast. Besides, she was so pliant in his arms. She made it easy. She made it wonderful. He wanted to close his eyes and float with the music.

Eventually she pulled her head back, far enough to catch his eye. "You're not angry about the two hundred dollars?"

"No. It's for a worthy cause."

A second or two passed while she digested that. "So?" she quizzed lightly. "How am I doing?"

"Worth every penny, I think. But I may need another dance to be sure."

"Well, you only paid for one."

Jake laughed.

Her glance narrowed. "How did you get the winning ticket? I know you didn't come by it honestly."

"God likes me," he explained simply and gave her a broad, silly grin.

She frowned. "If that's true, I'm giving up all faith in a higher power. The truth, please. If you're capable of telling it."

"I bribed the kid who had it. A hundred bucks."

"A hundred—" She gasped and missed a step. "Are you nuts? I'm not even that good a dancer."

"You underestimate yourself."

To prove that statement, he led her into a sudden, exultant turn, which she followed beautifully. But when he pulled her against him again, she stiffened a little. The suspicion in her eyes had darkened.

"Are you drunk?" she asked.

"No."

"Then what's this all about, Jake?"

"Exactly what it seems." He gave her a speculative look. "Do you always overanalyze things?"

"I don't usually. But with you I'm suspicious." She shook her head at him quickly. "If you think you can charm me out of adopting—"

He stopped her by tightening his arm against her back, letting his eyes travel over her. "So...you find me charming?"

"Not nearly as charming as you find yourself."

"Ouch! Where's the angel everyone else in this town sees?"

"What?"

"Nothing."

"I'm not going to give up Isabel's child, Jake—"

Again he stopped her with a jerk of his arm, giving her a serious look this time. "Just for tonight, let's not fight," he said softly. "Let's talk. Like two adults who've discovered an interest in one another."

"Oh," she said lightly. "Fiction."

"You don't think we have things in common?" he countered with a small frown. "By the way, how's my dancing?"

"Fine."

"I like it, too. See? We do have things in common."

She laughed a little at that. Then she gave him a level look, and he could almost see her mind searching for a safe topic. "I think we should talk about something else."

"Name it."

She was silent for a moment or two. Finally she asked, "Can you really speak six languages?"

"Oui, mademoiselle." He smiled at her. *"Tu eres muy preciosa. Voglio fare l'amore con ti.* That's three of them. Want a translation?"

"I don't think so," she said softly, and he watched a warm blush of color slip down her cheeks and throat, all the way to her shoulders. Even if she didn't understand French, Spanish or Italian, she obviously recognized his tone. And maybe the longing he didn't bother to keep out of his eyes.

"I can talk sexy in eight," he pursued. "Want to hear?"

"No."

"I'm very good, *Fräulein*. How about a lesson? It's all in the way you roll your tongue."

He leaned close to her, letting his tongue slide along the soft shell of her ear. He heard the breath stall in her throat, felt the shivery reaction of her body. Then she jerked her head back in a rush, glaring at him with a look that bore all the signs of panic. He thought: She's afraid. Not of me. Of feeling too much alive.

"Stop that!" she hissed at him. "People are watching."

"Of course they are," he said in mild agreement. "I'm the mysterious benefactor of the fire department."

"You know, you really are the most—"

He never heard her opinion of what he really was the most of, because he nuzzled his lips against her ear this time. She made a little sound of protest, but she didn't pull her head away, and her fingers around the back of his neck tightened.

"Beautiful," he murmured. "So beautiful... Shall I stop?"

Her head moved, a small rejection of that idea.

Suddenly he didn't care if the whole damn room was watching. If the dance had ended and they were the only two people left on the dance floor. He brushed a gentle kiss along her jawline, and she moaned softly in pleasure.

He wanted to make love to her.

Impossible here, of course. But someplace, some haven…

His gaze flickered idly over the crowd around them. He spotted Ben talking to a pretty young woman at the edge of the dance floor, a couple devouring two plates of cheesecake with almost identical speed, the shimmer of a metallic red contribution bucket being passed around the crowd by the fire chief.

And then his eyes drifted toward the front door…and his heart stopped.

"Oh…my…God."

Nora angled her head back to look at him. Her pupils were vast and dark, as if she had been falling into a drugged state.

"What in all that's holy is she doing here?" he said in a low growl.

"Who?"

With a jerk of his head, he indicated the front entrance, where the late arrival of a beautiful woman was creating a stir of interest. "Don't you recognize her?"

"No," Nora said, trying to focus, trying to get a closer look. "You know her?"

"Unfortunately, yes," Jake said and dropped his arms from Nora as the song ended. He knew her, all right. "It's Thea. My ex-wife."

CHAPTER TEN

JAKE WAS STUNNED to see Thea standing at the front entrance. Still holding on to Nora's wrist, he pushed his way through the crowd. Behind him he heard a whispered remark or two as a few people recognized La Paloma's beautiful spokesmodel.

He didn't waste time with pleasantries. Thea wouldn't expect them from him anyway. He stopped directly in front of her as she started to move into the room, so quickly that Nora nearly overran his back. She pulled her arm from his grasp.

"What in hell are you doing here?" he demanded in a low voice.

Thea smiled thinly up at him, all silk and perfume in a room full of denim and fake fire. "Really, Jake, what kind of welcome is that?"

"The only kind you're likely to ever get from me," he snapped back.

She pouted prettily, probably for the benefit of the people around her who had fallen silent. Jake could feel their curious stares. "Why don't you ask Charles why I'm here?" she said. "He's the one who telephoned me."

Jake couldn't bear to believe that. He didn't want to think that he'd been wrong about the past few days. He opened his mouth to refute that claim, and in that moment he became aware of movement behind him as someone broke through the crowd.

"Mother!" Charlie exclaimed. "You're here!" He stopped just short of launching himself into Thea's arms. Maybe he didn't want to embarrass himself in front of Darlene, who was close on his heels, staring at Thea with wide-eyed excitement.

Thea laid delicate hands on the boy's shoulders. "Of course, darling. Would I let you down?" A cautious, sideways glance up at Jake. "Your call sounded so desperate."

"That was days ago." Charlie flicked an uncomfortable glance toward his father.

"I can't just drop everything, Charles. But I'm here now. You remember my personal assistant Anthony, don't you?"

She linked arms with the man who had just come through the door, and Anthony gave them an all-encompassing nod. Two hundred pounds of steroid-enhanced muscle filling his clothes as though they had grown on him. Silent and attentive. The perfect lover.

Charlie had no interest in Anthony. He frowned up at his mother. "How did you know we were here?"

Thea straightened. "Well, I have to admit, this is the last place I would have expected to find you—" Another glance in Jake's direction. "Even you. But a drippy-nosed young man at that quaint little place where you're staying said you were here, and of course, I couldn't wait another minute to see you." She turned an accusing eye on her ex-husband. "This is quite an interesting place you've brought our son to, Jake."

"It's not so bad, Mother. I'm—"

"I suppose you've got your reasons," Thea went on, her attention fully focused on Jake. Then she spotted Nora standing at his shoulder. Extending a slim hand, she gave her the smile a dozen photographers loved. "Hello, I'm Thea. And you are...?"

"Nora Holloway," Nora returned with a sweet smile of her own. "That drippy-nosed young man you met at the Hideaway is my brother, Trip, and we own that quaint little place."

"Oh. So sorry," Thea apologized. "It's just a little more rustic around here than I'm used to." She scanned the room for the first time, taking in the scene with a show of wide-eyed interest. "Have I barged in at an inopportune time?"

"Not at all," Nora returned graciously. "It's a fund-raiser for our fire department. In fact, we'd be delighted to have a donation. It was very nice to meet you, but I hope you'll excuse me now. There are so many things to tend to before the night's over." She turned to look at Jake. "Thank you for the dance, Jake."

"Nora..." He didn't want her to go. But she was already moving through the crush.

"Lovely girl, Jake," Thea said with approval.

Charlie remembered his manners and pulled Darlene forward. "Mother, this is my friend, Darlene. She—"

"Charles!" Thea said sharply, ignoring the girl completely. "What are you doing in jeans?"

"I—"

"You're the lady in the fashion magazines," Darlene said in an awed voice.

Suddenly Thea noticed Darlene. She tilted a smile at her. "Very wise, dear. Always befriend a boy's mother. But, you still can't steal my son's heart without my permission, you know," she said with a laugh.

Charlie went a mortified red. "Mother—"

Enough! Jake thought, and stepped closer to grab Thea's arm. "Could I speak to you? Alone?"

Before she gave an answer, he ushered her away from the door, into a little alcove where a fiery red curtain of metallic flames cut them off from the rest of the crowd.

"I don't know what you're doing here—"

"I told you, our son called me. It sounded to me like a cry for help. So I came."

"Then that would be the first damn time in years that you've paid any real attention to him. Understand me, Thea. I don't know what you expect to accomplish with this little visit. But you violate one word of our custody agreement, and I'll haul your scrawny butt into court." He shook her arm for emphasis. "Got it?"

She jerked out of his grasp and stepped back. "Charming as ever, I see," she said with a lift of her chin. "But I know this nasty attitude isn't really about us. It's about Charles. Because no matter how much you try, you can't stop my son from missing me. Can you?''

"No," he admitted. "I wish to God I could. But I can make sure he doesn't go down the same stupid, self-indulgent path you're on.''

"Don't play the loving-father role for me, Jake Burdette. You weren't around often enough to make a difference in his life.''

"You're right. I've made some mistakes. Big ones. But I'm doing the best I can to correct them now. I won't let you undo what little progress I've managed to make.''

"I didn't come here to fight with you," she said, pushing a blond curl back into place. "I came for Charles's sake. The truth is, I have to be in Japan in three days. La Paloma's taking the ad campaign worldwide. Commericals, personal appearances. I'm booked solid for the next three months.''

"So you thought you'd just pop in to say goodbye before you go?''

"I *wanted* to see him before I go," she protested. "Three months is such a long time to be away from him.''

Jake shook his head. "I'm not buying this act.''

She sighed heavily, as though giving up this particular tack. "Okay, here's the situation. Charlie thinks I've come to rescue him from you, but for once, I'm on your side. He still doesn't seem to understand our...new arrangement. And I don't have the time to explain it to him. Again.''

He stared down at her. How could he ever have

thought he loved this woman? "God, Thea," he said softly. "You used to spend hours telling Charlie stories when he was little. When did you lose interest in your own son?"

Her cold, blue eyes sparked fire. "Don't talk to me like that. You know I love that boy."

"But never as much as you love yourself."

She blinked, obviously offended, but unwilling to show it. "I put my career on hold once before. Which is more than you ever did, by the way. I'm not going to let a second chance slip through my fingers. Not even for Charles. Now, are you through berating me?" she asked, her mouth tight with displeasure. "I'd like to get back to my son."

She made a move to leave, and he caught her arm. "One more thing. No time alone with him unless I know about it. Is that clear?"

"For God's sake, Jake! I'm not a monster. I took care of Charles for years while you were off traipsing around the world."

"Yes, I know how well you took care of him. I saw the pictures in the tabloids, remember?"

She exhaled slowly. "It was one time. A silly party that got out of hand. I thought he was still upstairs in his room. If I'd known he'd come down, I'd have blistered his behind."

"And yet you're still with that son-of-a..." Jake jerked his head toward the outer room. "You're still with Anthony."

"Anthony's my personal assistant, and a damn good one. And I'm not going to apologize for being in love with him." She wet her lips, glancing up at

Jake with a resentful look. "You're wrong about him. He's got it under control now. He's not using—"

"I don't care if he fries the last brain cell he has in his head," Jake snapped. "I don't want him around Charlie. I mean it, Thea. You think I won't take what I know to the corporate suits that make all the decisions at La Paloma? I imagine they have a roomful of lawyers who spend all their time figuring out ways to break contracts with spoiled spokesmodels who misbehave."

"Fine." She acquiesced at last by throwing up her hands. "I won't let him within fifty feet of Charles. But not because of any threats you've made." Her eyes narrowed. "Don't think you can dictate to me forever, Jake."

Throwing him one last, murderous look, she parted the shimmering red curtain and stalked away.

THE DANCE WAS OVER for another year.

Wearily Nora surveyed the hall, glad that she'd asked Alan Harcourt to take Isabel home. She wasn't sure she was up to answering any more of the girl's questions about this evening.

All around her the cleanup crew of volunteers had gone into action. Wordlessly, she joined them, hoping that by keeping busy, she'd have no time to think.

For now, she was determined not to revisit the evening's events. Especially after what she'd found out.

Then, a voice from behind stopped her in the middle of tearing down the last red streamer.

"Need any help?"

She looked back over her shoulder. Jake stood in the middle of the dance floor, smiling up at her.

She shook her head at him and focused on dragging the podium to the back of the stage.

"Stubborn as ever," she heard him mutter, and from the corner of her eye she watched him approach the stairs.

She let the podium thump into place, then turned a look his way. "Don't," she said firmly. "Go home."

He halted with his foot on the first step, a small frown creasing his forehead. "Nora?".

She was so tired. Her mind was fighting to hold on to control, to her temper, and losing, losing…

"I'm almost finished here," she told him.

"Then let me buy you a cup of coffee to celebrate your success."

It *had* been a successful event, but celebration seemed impossible right now. "I just want to go home," she said.

"Are you all right?" he asked, a worried tone suddenly in his voice. "I can take you home if you like."

"No!" She turned a harsh look on him. "Don't you understand? I don't want anything from you." She shook her head, advancing a few steps. "Why did you come back here? Did you think it would be an opportunity to gloat?"

"What are you talking about? I came back because I didn't like the way we left it tonight. Our dance was over so abruptly, and I know you must be wondering—''

"I'm not wondering anything. You got want you wanted, didn't you?"

She tried to go around him, but he caught her hand, pulling her back. "Nora, what is it?"

"Let go of me."

"Not until you tell me what's wrong."

She gave him a venomous look. "While you were getting reacquainted with your ex-wife, Alan Harcourt asked me to dance. He didn't pay three hundred dollars for the privilege, but I said yes anyway, because he's been such a good friend all these years." She cocked her head at him. "But then, you'd know that, wouldn't you, since you've made it your business to find out everything you can about my personal relationships with men."

He didn't look stunned by this revelation, but his fingers relaxed, so that she slipped from his grasp. With the accusation out, the fight had left her body. Her legs folded up under her, so that all she could do was sink to the top step of the stage, miserable. Elbows balanced on her knees, she cradled her hot cheeks in her hands.

The long silence between them helped her get her emotions under some control. When she spoke at last, her voice was strong. "Tell me something, Jake, was there any man in the room tonight that you didn't pump for information about me?"

He came to join her on the step, lowering himself

beside her in one fluid motion. She stayed where she was. She wouldn't give him the satisfaction of thinking he could send her fleeing.

"Nora," he said at last. "I just wanted—"

"I know what you wanted," she cut across the explanation, meeting his eyes squarely. "You wanted dirt. Some sleazy, disgusting life-style you could parade in front of a judge. Does that just about sum it up?"

"Yes." His answer was hardly a whisper.

"That's probably the first honest answer you've given me all night."

"Listen to me—"

The world began to throb to the rhythm of her pounding pulse. "No! You listen to me. I know I've been the worst kind of fool for letting a few turns around a dance floor lull me into believing you were something you're not. Whatever entertainment you're getting out of all this, I'm not going to be a willing participant while you plot your next move against me." She looked away from him, running both hands through her hair as she steadied her voice. Almost to herself, she said, "I'm not going to be a fool any longer. I'll get as tough as I need to be to keep you from taking Isabel's baby." She turned to look at him again. "So I'm putting you on notice. Don't expect to be able to sweet-talk or seduce me into giving up, because I won't. And you can dig around in my past as much as you want, but it's not going to do you any good. Do we understand one another?"

"I think you've made yourself pretty clear," he answered somberly.

"Good."

She was down the stairs and halfway across the empty dance floor before she realized the tears were rolling down her cheeks.

TRIP MET NORA at the front door of the lodge— excited. He'd checked Thea and her assistant, Anthony, into Cabin One. For all the woman's snide complaints about the lack of sophistication in this part of Florida, she'd evidently realized that if she wanted a bed for the night, she had darned few choices.

The irony did not escape Nora—a fitting ending to the evening, she thought.

Isabel had given Trip a few sketchy details before turning in, but he wanted more. A celebrity staying at the Hideaway. A gorgeous one at that. What was it, Nora wondered, that made men so blind to everything but physical beauty?

She wasn't up to dealing with her brother's questions so she shut her bedroom door firmly. Time enough to make amends over breakfast the next morning, when her head wasn't thumping so badly, and her heart didn't feel like stone.

CHAPTER ELEVEN

WITH A RESIGNED SIGH, Jake rose from bended knees beside Cabin Two and stared down at the pitiful excuse for a boat that he and Charlie planned to enter in the Spring Bash and Dash race tomorrow. From the looks of it, no one would ever guess he knew anything about construction.

Initially he'd conceived of something bold and sleek and fast—a cross between a canoe and a Polynesian outrigger. But somewhere the vessel had taken a turn for the worse, a very bad turn, and ended up looking like a snub-nosed wooden dinghy instead. Even the waterproof sealant he'd just liberally coated the blasted thing with probably wouldn't help. Once on the river, this disaster was bound to sink like the *Titanic*.

Of course, it probably didn't matter to Charlie one way or the other now. With his mother having checked in right next door last night, he'd probably have no interest in boats or races. Or fathers.

He'd been quiet over his breakfast cereal, especially after Jake had refused his request to pay an early-morning call to Cabin One. The sullen boy Jake had hoped he'd seen the last of had come back full force after that, and had spent the morning sulking in his bedroom.

Jake glanced down at his watch. Nearly ten-thirty and still no sign of him. Maybe lunch would bring him out.

He capped the can of water sealant and scanned the area. He seemed to be the only one stirring today. Cabin One stood a good fifty yards away, but there were no signs of life. Of course, Thea had never been a morning person.

The Hideaway was dead quiet, too. Jake had been working on the boat all morning and only caught one quick glimpse of Nora as she hurried down the stairs and into the company truck. She didn't so much as glance in his direction.

There was a water spigot on the side of the cabin, and Jake turned it on to clean the brush he'd used on the boat. As he finished the task, Nora's dog sidled up to him for a scratch. "Hey there, Larry. Want to take a ride on the river? See if this thing will float?"

"No way that's going to work."

Jake looked up; Charlie was standing in front of him, his gaze focused on the boat.

The boy looked neat as a pin, his hair combed precisely, the jeans he'd conceded to wearing the last few days replaced by his former attire.

Jake kept his features calm, noncommittal. "You're too late to help with the boat," he said lightly. "At least until the sealant dries. We'll have to give it a test drive. Maybe this afternoon. The race is tomorrow, you know."

His son turned toward him. "You might have to do it alone," he said. "I might not be here to help you win."

Jake felt his smile vanish. "Why not?"

"Because Mother's come to get me. She's going to take me with her."

Just like that. No doubts. "Did she tell you that last night?"

"No."

"Then how do you know that?"

The boy shrugged. "I just do."

They stood together in silence for a few minutes, while a woodpecker drilled away at a nearby tree, and the breeze set the pines to whistling. Jake didn't know what to say, how to begin to tell his son the truth. The kid looked so confident, so reassured by what he believed his mother's arrival meant for him. How could Jake take that kind of faith away?

It was Charlie who broke the silence.

"I'm sorry," he said, and sounded truly contrite. "I know it probably makes you mad that I called her. But I want to be with her. And she wants to be with me."

Jake gave his son a regretful smile. "I thought we were doing pretty well lately. Just the two of us."

"You're not so bad, I guess," Charlie acknowledged. His cheeks worked as he chewed the inside of his mouth. "It's been different than I thought."

"So why not give us a little longer to make it work?"

"Because Mother needs me. You don't."

He couldn't let that one pass. "Charlie—"

The boy scowled. His eyebrows dipped so low Jake could hardly see the boy's eyes. "I want to see her," he said. "And you can try to stop me, but I'll find a way."

Jake watched him swallow quickly, as if too many words had gotten out. In spite of the little tremor of anxiety that had been in his voice, there was determination there as well. His jaw was clamped shut, like an old turtle.

Jake took a deep breath and calmed himself. Much as he wanted to shake some sense into Charlie, he knew that his son was in for a huge disappointment. Soon Thea would have to break the news about her trip to Japan. Charlie would finally realize how expendable he was to her life. And Jake planned to be there to pick up the pieces. There was nothing to be gained by a show of force now.

"All right," he agreed, then jerked his head toward Cabin One. "But not there. Go back inside. I'll ask her to come over."

Charlie looked momentarily surprised by his father's words. Then he said, "You don't like Anthony, do you?"

"No."

"Why? Because he's her boyfriend?"

"No."

Charlie looked at him with heart-melting directness. "Mother doesn't really love him, you know," he said in a rush. "He's just someone who makes her feel good. She needs people around her to do that." When Jake said nothing to that, he added in a quieter voice, "I'm sorry you don't love her any-more. But I do."

"It's all right, Charlie," Jake said with an encouraging smile. "A boy should love his mother. Now go inside and wait."

He watched Charlie take one last look at the boat, then the boy walked away. When Jake heard the screen door squeal shut, he exhaled his anger and frustration in a long, slow breath and headed down the path to Cabin One.

The place was still quiet. The drapes were drawn tightly to keep out the day. Time to face the music, Jake thought, and two strides carried him up the stairs to the screen door. He knocked loudly, and kept knocking until the inside door opened. A disheveled, silk-robed Thea stood behind the screen.

"Somebody had better be dead," she said thickly.

He could see now why La Paloma had chosen her. Even in the morning, with no makeup, her skin was flawlessly beautiful—pale, but without the puffy remnants of sleep.

"Sorry," Jake said, determined to be firm but pleasant. "Your son wants to see you."

"Couldn't we do this later?"

"The problem isn't going away, Thea. And the longer you wait, the harder it will be on everyone. Tell him the truth, and then you can be on that plane to Japan."

There was a little whisper of silk as she folded her arms tightly across her stomach. "You just want me out of here as quickly as possible."

"I'm not going to deny that. But Charlie's got it in his head that you're here to take him with you—"

"I never said that," she protested.

"I believe you. But that should give you an idea of what we're dealing with. He needs to hear it from you. He's waiting for you in our cabin."

"All right," she said, raking her hand through her long hair. "All right. I'll get dressed. Might as well get it over with."

He nodded as the door shut in his face.

For once, she was true to her word. She met him on the porch of Cabin Two less than thirty minutes later. She wore too much jewelry and a silky royal blue skirt that flared around her legs. Something completely inappropriate for the Hideaway, but he wouldn't have cared if she'd donned a potato sack, as long as they got this over with once and for all.

She swept past him. He caught her arm. "No matter what you say, it's going to hurt him," Jake said in a low voice. "But don't make it any worse by playing the poor abused victim in this."

Her nostrils flared at that, but she didn't say a word. After the cabin door opened and shut with a faint click, Jake settled on the top step of the porch and waited.

In less than half an hour she was out on the porch again. There was no sound from within the cabin, and when Jake lifted his eyebrows at her questioningly, she stuck out her chin, looking tense and nervous.

Jake took her arm. "Let's walk a little bit."

He led her down the railroad-tie steps to the overlook of the spring, the same place he'd spoken to Nora only a few days ago.

"Well?" he asked, turning her to face him. "Did you tell him?"

"No."

"What?" he asked, stunned.

Her lips compressed in a tight line. "I couldn't. I tried, Jake. Really, I did. But he's so…so determined to believe we're going to be together."

"The longer you let him think that, the tougher it's going to be for him to accept the truth. You have to tell him, Thea."

She gave him a desperate, impatient look. "No. It's too hard, Jake. I know I should be able to do this, but I can't. You know how I dislike emotional scenes and bad news."

He stared at her, this immature, sophisticated beauty who had never been forced to face up to the unpleasant things in life. It made him think suddenly of Nora Holloway, who had struggled so hard for everything she had, and who had probably never run away from anything.

"God, Thea," he murmured. "When are you ever going to grow up?"

She heard him and swung around, frost in her eyes. "Just because I'm not like Nora Holloway—"

He frowned. "What does Nora have to do with this discussion?"

"I saw the way you looked at her last night."

He wasn't going to explore his relationship with

Nora with his ex-wife. He shook his head at her. "Don't try to change the subject. When are you going to tell Charlie he's not going with you?"

She tossed her hair back over her shoulder. "And that's another thing," she said, her timbre darkening. "When did he become Charlie? He corrected me twice when I called him Charles."

"He did?" Jake replied, unable to stop a small smile for flitting across his lips. "Well…that's interesting."

She stalked back toward him, hands on her slim hips. "It's your doing, isn't it? I saw his clothes last night. His hair. He's even starting to sound like you. You won't be happy until he's completely unrecognizable to me, will you?"

He sighed, exasperated. "Let's not argue about this. Just tell me, when do you leave for Japan?"

"Tomorrow night."

"Then sometime between now and then you'll have to get up the courage to tell him the truth." He let his voice drop to a near growl. "I mean it, Thea. By tomorrow night, you tell him the truth. Understood?"

Eyes flashing daggers, she nodded.

NORA STARED DOWN at the boat Charlie and Jake Burdette had hammered together, critically eyeing the craft's center of gravity and its sleek, compact lines. The Bash and Dash was only a few minutes away. The judges had approved the vessel's construction, but that high middle section… Nora didn't like the looks of it. A long shot to win, she figured, and they'd be lucky to keep the craft from capsizing.

"What do you think, Nora?" Charlie asked. "Are we gonna win?"

He was looking up at her with excitement and hope in his clear, blue eyes. Jake, whom she had not spoken to since the night before last at the Moose Hall, stood a few feet away, trying to tighten the leather straps he had secured around one of the homemade paddles he'd rigged out of broom handles and plywood. He didn't look up at her.

"It's got winner written all over it," she said, crossing her fingers behind her back for telling what God would surely consider only a little white lie. "I don't see a single entry that's got a better chance."

That was certainly true. All around her were vessels that could easily have come from some sea captain's nightmare. Inner tubes stretched over canvas. Logs strapped together. Washtubs and huge plastic skimmers and floating bicycle-like structures that could be peddled to churn the river water. Not a seaworthy specimen among them.

She waved at Trip across the spring, who was busy trying to stop his own homemade craft from listing to one side. This year he'd thrown together some sort of sailboard, with one of the Hideaway's flowered bedsheets now flapping in the breeze as a sail.

Doomed. Every one of them.

At least the morning couldn't have been more perfect. A cloudless sky. The sun warm as a balm on her bare arms and legs. She settled on the riverbank, feeling the tickle of grass against the backs of her thighs where her shorts had ridden up to her hips.

The weekend's festivities were barely under way, but Nora felt proud of what she'd managed to accomplish. Since the spring pool was the bubbling headwaters of the river, the Bash and Dash had always been conducted on Hideaway property, and with a glance around her, Nora decided that the place had never looked more festive.

Breeze-whipped pennants had been strung from tree to tree. Trip had trimmed the grassy areas along the river so that picnickers and spectators could enjoy the race. The overlook had been turned into the judge's platform by the judicious use of helium balloons, streamers and a huge banner tied to the railing.

Everywhere around her people were laughing and talking excitedly. No one could take the boat race seriously, but it had always been a favorite event for the town.

She smiled, thinking how wonderful it would be to someday share a day like this with Isabel's son— *her* son—when he was old enough to understand the value of having friends and neighbors whose company you could count on and enjoy.

She wished Trip could understand that, but they seemed destined to disagree. Nora had a feeling that as soon as all the excitement of the holiday was over, round two of their battle would commence.

Every day he seemed more and more eager to be away.

Behind her, Nora heard the crunch of thick grass as someone approached. She turned, shading her eyes against the mild sunlight. It was Thea, looking crisp in all-white. Her eyes were hidden behind an enormous pair of sunglasses, and even with that protection, her body language oozed one message: boredom.

"Mother!" Charlie exclaimed excitedly, and when he stood up, the boat tipped precariously. "You came! Is your headache better? You'll stay and watch us, won't you?"

"Sit down, Charlie," Jake said from his spot behind the boat. Wearing only a swimsuit, he stood in water up to his knees.

Thea glanced around the area worriedly. "Jake, do you really think this is a good idea? Charles could get hurt."

"Mother!" Charlie protested.

"I'll be with him, Thea," Jake replied. "It's just a little harmless fun. The water's so shallow on this stretch that no-one over ten is required to wear a life jacket. Besides, Charlie can swim like a fish."

Thea looked unconvinced. "I don't like this," she said, brushing a blade of grass from her skirt. "It's all so...so..."

"Provincial?" Nora couldn't resist suggesting. Over a span of twenty-four hours, her curiosity about this woman had turned into active dislike.

Thea frowned down at her. "I was going to say crowded."

The announcer for the race began calling entry numbers. The racers had been broken up into four groups of eight. Charlie and Jake's number had been drawn for the first heat. Charlie whooped excitedly and hunkered down in his place at the bow of the boat, calling for his mother to sit and watch.

Jake tossed one of the paddles to his son, slipped the other one back in the boat and tried to swing one leg over the side. The moment he took his weight off the bottom of the spring, the boat tipped dangerously, sending Charlie grabbing for the edge. With the third try, Jake got aboard, but the vessel continued to rock.

"Move forward a little," Jake told his son.

Charlie scooted forward, then back when that didn't work, but no matter how he positioned himself, the boat refused to cooperate. Jake hopped out, inspecting the sides of the boat. The vessel began listing to the point of taking on water as Charlie leaned far in the other direction to keep from being pitched out into the spring.

"Dad, they're calling our group number," Charlie said anxiously.

"Didn't you try it out before now?" Nora asked Jake. After the fire department fundraiser, she'd decided to ignore him as much as possible. But it would be unthinkable to let Charlie take a dunking because she was too mad at his father to offer advice.

"It floated," Jake replied. "Charlie was too busy elsewhere to test it with our weight."

She didn't have to guess what Charlie had been

too busy doing. Since his mother's arrival, he probably hadn't budged from her side for more than fifteen minutes.

"You need center weight to stabilize it," Nora said as she rose to her feet. Then she grinned, unable to resist an opportunity to tease. "I thought you were such a hotshot in construction."

He scowled up at her. "Bridges, not boats."

She picked up a large rock from the riverbank. "Try this," she said, and passed it to Jake, who placed it in the boat, dead center.

The rocking motion settled a bit, but it was still bound to overturn once Charlie and Jake started paddling toward the finish line. Definitely not heavy enough.

"Get in, Mother! Hurry!" Charlie coaxed with a beckoning arm. "We need you."

"Sorry, darling, I don't think so," Thea said incredulously. "This is a Takardi original I've got on."

With the announcer making the last call for their group, Charlie became almost frantic. He didn't waste time trying to convince Thea to participate. He swung his head in Nora's direction, his eyes desperate and pleading. "Nora, help us! We need you for dead weight."

"Oh, thank you very much," Nora complained, but she was already slipping off her sandals. "I believe it's called ballast."

As she tried to slip gingerly over the side, Jake shocked her by placing his hands around her waist and lifting her bodily into the vessel.

"Sit still, and don't do anything," he told her. "Charlie and I will do all the work."

Nora nodded and sat uncomfortably where Jake had placed her. It hadn't really occurred to her that she'd be this close to him once she was in the boat. His knees touched the small of her back, and she could practically feel his soft exhalation of breath on her neck. Not unpleasant, but it didn't do much for her comfort level, either.

They pushed off from the water's edge, heading toward the starting lineup. The boat was surprisingly swift in spite of a few shaky strokes from Charlie in front of her.

A starting rope had been strung across the river, and the racers could take any position along the line they wished. With one hand, Nora motioned toward the left.

"Keep to that side," she directed. "The current's swifter as we go around the bend."

"Oh no, Charlie," Jake called over her head. "We've got a back-seat driver in our boat."

The boy looked over his shoulder and grinned at her.

"Fine," Nora said. "Just don't come crying to me when the trophy goes to some guy in water wings."

She noticed that he took her suggestion. Every racer had more than one passenger, and in an effort to get them all starting evenly, the boatman in the back of each boat had to jump out and keep the vessel from moving into the current. Jake slid over the side again, holding on to the boat with one hand and keeping his paddle ready in the other.

In another minute one of the judges fired off a starting shot. Icy drops of water showered Nora and Charlie as Jake leaped back into the craft and immediately dug his paddle into the clear spring. "Like we practiced on the porch, Charlie," Jake yelled. "Stroke! Stroke!"

And they were off.

Considering how little experience Charlie had, he did a good job keeping up his end of the task. Jake encouraged him with every stroke, and Nora, getting excited as they passed a trio of men on a Huckleberry Finn raft, took up the call as well. All she could hear was the sound of the crowd screaming encouragement for their favorites, laughing hysterically as the worst of the racers floundered and splashed water everywhere.

Ahead of them, a couple of teenagers on a log wagon flipped over. The river spat them up again and they scrambled to get out of the way.

"Dig right!" Nora shouted. "No! Too much. You're overcompensating!"

Somehow they made it around the sinking debris. Nora looked back over her shoulder. Of the eight racers, two had already fallen victim to the river, five were behind them and closing fast, only one was ahead. Pushing hair out of her eyes, she grinned at Jake, who was working hard to keep the boat from zigzagging from one side of the river to the other.

"We need more power, Captain!" she called to him. "They're gaining on us."

Jake growled something at her she couldn't understand over the noise of the crowd, but the twinkle of sunlight she glimpsed in his eyes told her he was enjoying this as much as she was.

The finish line was in sight, though still far away. The announcer was screaming into the electric bullhorn now, and people were elbow to elbow along the riverbank. The boat slid by the crowd, turning the onlookers into almost a blur. Nora's excitement took a dramatic leap forward as it actually began to seem as if they might catch the leader and overtake him.

Charlie evidently felt it, too. His thin, childish muscles strained as he leaned into each stroke. He was panting hard, completely focused on the craft ahead of them. But it was still too far away, and as though he could make the boat more aerodynamic, Charlie bent low into the bow.

"Charlie, don't," Jake warned.

But it was too late. The boat rocked wildly, and when Charlie tried to compensate for that movement, the vessel tipped even more in the opposite direction. Then Charlie tried to stand. Sensing he was about to go head first into the river, Nora made a grab for him and snagged the back of his T-shirt. He fell onto his seat, hard.

The vessel bounced. Unfortunately, Nora couldn't maintain her balance by then, either. In a cartwheeling smear of movement and sound, she

heard Charlie's yell and saw Jake's hand come out
to snatch her back from the brink.

Luck failed her this time. She went over the side,
into the icy water.

CHAPTER TWELVE

She was a sopping, freezing mess. Her shorts and blouse clung to her like a second skin, and her flesh was nothing but goose bumps. Water dripped and soaked into the grass around her feet.

"Should have gone for the trophy, man," someone around her laughingly suggested.

Nora looked up and was surprised to see that Jake and Charlie had dropped out of the race. Jake was in the water, guiding the boat to shore with one hand.

He shook his head at the bystander who'd offered such a ruthless suggestion. "You know how women are. We'd never have heard the end of it," he explained.

She made a face at him and continued to squeeze excess water out of the hem of her blouse. "I was prepared to be sacrificed for the good of the team," she sniffed indignantly.

Jake pulled the boat on land and helped Charlie get out. "Doesn't matter," he said. "Once we lost you for ballast, it was only a matter of time before we were going to end up taking a bath, too."

"Oh. And here I thought you were being gallant by coming back for me."

"Are you really all right, Nora?" Charlie asked worriedly. "Your lips are blue."

"I'm fine. But next time, you sit in the middle. I'll paddle."

There was a flurry of movement at the edge of the crowd as Thea pushed her way through. She tilted her sunglasses up over her eyes, her concern centered completely on her son.

"Charles!" she nearly gasped out. "My God, are you hurt? I saw you bobbing and weaving out there like a drunken sailor before I lost sight of you completely. Someone said you'd capsized."

The boy looked horrified by all this attention. Jake merely looked disgusted. "As you can see, Thea, he's dry as a bone. Nora's the one who went in."

The woman ignored that. She flashed an annoyed look up at Jake. "I told you this was a mistake. He could have been thrown out of that ridiculous toy you call a boat and drowned."

"Mother, stop," Charlie said on a pained note. "I'm all right. Really. We lost, but we couldn't go on without Nora. Could we, Dad?"

By now, Nora's teeth were clanking like castanets inside her mouth. Numbness was spreading through her body. She didn't want to spend any more time listening to this infuriating woman. She wanted dry clothes or a hot bath. Or maybe both.

Jake suddenly spoke up, cutting off Thea's complaints. "I'm walking Nora back to the lodge so she can change clothes," he said unexpectedly. "Charlie, why don't you and your mother watch the rest of the race together? I'll meet you at the judge's stand afterward."

He didn't wait for their agreement. Instead, he inclined his head toward one of the spectators seated in a lounge chair by the river's edge. "Can I borrow your blanket?" he asked, motioning toward a small quilt that was folded across the back of the chair.

The man nodded, and Jake whipped the quilt off the chair. Before Nora could react or protest, he stood in front of her and brought the blanket around her body. It was warm, and smelled sweetly of oranges. The icy water was freezing her thoughts, slowing her reflexes, but his touch against her throat, along her arms, still came through loud and clear.

"Come on," he said when he'd pulled the edges of the quilt as tightly around her as he could. "I'll walk you home."

"You don't have to," Nora protested past lips that felt as cold and lifeless as marble.

"I'm going to, all the same," he replied, giving her one of his level, unwavering looks. He placed his hand along her back to guide her toward the beaten-down path that led back to the spring steps.

"Are you doing this just because you want to get away from your ex-wife?"

"No," he said with a little smile. "I'm doing this because you've been a good sport and didn't deserve a dunking in the river."

She felt silly cocooned in the blanket, but it was definitely warmer, and no one seemed to think anything of it. They wove past several of her friends and neighbors, clustered in small groups along the riverbank. Several of them offered consolation to her and wished her better luck in next year's race.

She and Jake had reached the bottom of the spring steps when the announcer officially called the winner of the first heat. The crowd applauded and yelled.

Nora looked back over her shoulder. "We could have caught that guy, you know."

"Maybe," Jake agreed. "It was my fault. We had a design flaw. But we certainly gave it our best shot, didn't we?"

She nodded and started up the stairs. The blanket began to drag a little, and she tugged it closer around her throat. She felt the weight of Jake's hand even through the material as he made sure she didn't trip or lose her balance. Neither one of them spoke as they maneuvered the steps.

When they reached the top, they began walking side by side. Nora turned her head to look at Jake. "I've never seen Charlie so excited. He's certainly come out of his shell recently."

"His mother's presence here has a lot to do with that," he said. "Although I'd never have guessed he'd want her to see him actually enjoying this kind of stuff."

"Maybe that's really what he wants to be. A normal kid having ordinary fun on a beautiful day."

"It would be nice to think that. Nice to believe I'm making progress with him."

They went up the wide front steps of the lodge. At the double doors Nora turned to face Jake. He was studying her pensively. She was unnerved, and had to clear a sudden tightness in her throat before she could speak. "Thanks for walking me back."

"You're welcome. Will we see you later?"

"Perhaps. Isabel wants to check out the community rummage sale they're holding in the park today."

"How is she doing?"

"She's still in bed. The doctor put her on new antinausea medicine. She's not used to being physically ill, so it's taking quite a toll on her spirits. That, and the fact that the baby's future is still such an uncertainty."

He frowned at that. "I'm sorry. It was never my intention to create stress for Isabel. I want you to believe that. But I know raising Bobby's child is the right thing for me to do. I feel it in my gut."

"Then that's no different from the way I feel about it."

His forehead creased again, and for a moment she thought he would argue that statement. Then he sighed and shook his head. "No matter what happens, Nora, I'd like you to believe that I don't want to deliberately hurt you, either."

She wanted to tell him that it was already too late for that, but she didn't. In spite of the lecture she'd given herself about remaining unmoved by Jake's presence, she could feel her will crossing the divide, wanting to connect with him in ways that had nothing to do with Isabel's child. She drew a deep, steadying breath, repeating the simple mantra she'd created for herself. Eventually, it slipped out between her cold lips. "I won't give up."

He seemed to expect that. "I know," he said. "In a strange way, it's one of the things I've come to admire most about you."

His gaze locked with hers again. Neither of them spoke, and before she could react, he pulled the blanket toward him, taking her with it. Her body trembled a little, but it wasn't because of the cold. Jake bent his head and touched his lips to her cheek. Then he placed light, warm kisses along her jaw, the side of her mouth. Her thoughts threatened to lose focus, and with what was left of weak determination, she turned her head away.

"You only want Isabel's baby," she accused softly. "And you think a few kisses will soften me up to the idea."

He shook his head, but didn't stop what he was doing. "I'm not thinking about the baby right now. I'm thinking about us. And how much I've wanted to kiss you for so long."

She closed her eyes. This man was her enemy, and however enjoyable his touch might be, he would always be the enemy. "You think you can seduce me into surrendering."

"Will you surrender?"

He stopped long enough to give her a wicked, mischievous smile, the one that melted her right down to her bones. She swallowed hard. "No."

"Then, why worry? I can't change your mind, so there's no harm."

"There's no reason, either."

"So, kiss me now," he coaxed. "And find your reasons for it later."

He covered her mouth with his, and this time she didn't try to hold anything back. His touch was too strong to be overcome; or else she was too weak. Suddenly it just didn't seem to matter, and she knew that decision had come from her heart and not her head.

CHARLIE WAS SO TIRED, his bones ached.

The boat race had been challenging and fun, even if they hadn't won. Charlie thought he'd handled his paddle well—at least he hadn't looked like a complete dork.

By noon, his mother had lost interest in the activities and left him with his father, claiming she had business to take care of if only she could find a telephone. Secretly, Charlie knew that she liked to nap in the afternoon when she wasn't on a photo shoot. Although disappointed, he tried not to mind. His mother's beauty required a lot of care.

He and his father had gorged themselves on hot dogs, French fries and soda from the makeshift concession stand. They planned to watch the rest of the day's events from a nice, safe distance, maybe go into town later to see what was happening in the town square. It wasn't thrilling, but it was okay.

And then Charlie spotted Darlene White in the crowd. She looked really pretty in a bright green shorts set, with her long hair caught in a braid at the back of her head. Surprisingly, his father left them alone...well, as alone as you could get with a million people around you eating cotton candy and playing Frisbee. They sat on the riverbank and talked, and he thought Darlene was the funniest, smartest girl he'd ever met.

Unfortunately, she seemed to take it for granted that he would enter some of the afternoon's contests. Personally, he thought a one-legged sack race and a turtle race were stupid, and agreed with his mother—the prizes they offered were not worth the effort it took to win them. But Darlene claimed he was strong enough to make a real difference in the tug-of-war, and before he knew it, he had signed up for just about everything and had almost forgotten his mother's warning that he should try not to get overheated.

With his father and Darlene cheering, Charlie's side won the tug-of-war. Each member of the winning team got free hamburger coupons—oh, boy!—from the local hangout, but the blue ribbons that they passed around as well were kind of cool. At least, Darlene seemed to think so.

"Congratulations," his father said as they all stood around Charlie to admire his prize.

"You see, I told you," Darlene pointed out in that superior way girls had. "You were wonderful."

He felt a little light-headed all of a sudden, and yet his cheeks burned as much as his muscles. It must have been all the pulling and pushing he'd done.

When Darlene slipped a few feet away to locate her family in the crowd, Charlie pulled his father aside. Indicating the ribbon in his hand, he asked, "Can I go show Mother?"

"Looking that way?" Jake's glance took in the shirt hanging in shreds on his body. "Do you want to give her a coronary?"

"They've started to pick teams for the relay race," Darlene interrupted, with a glance over her shoulder. "My dad's planning to enter, and I promised to root for him."

His father inclined his head toward the line of Hideaway cabins at the top of the slope. "Why don't you go up and change your shirt, Charlie? I'll walk Darlene over to the race and we'll wait for you there."

Charlie nodded and headed up the steps, taking them two at a time.

By the time he reached the top, he was breathing hard again, and he had to bend over to catch his breath. He looked in surprise at his right knee. It was bleeding slightly from a small scrape. He didn't remember falling, and it didn't even hurt. Instead, he felt good. Important. Strong. The ribbon lay lightly in his palm. He wasn't just a dumb kid with no talent. The ribbon was proof of that. He could do anything.

What would Mother think to see him like this— bruised and torn and sweaty? She'd probably blame his father for not stopping him from entering the event, which really wasn't fair, but Mother sometimes got ahead of herself and didn't think things through. It would be funny to see her face, and sorta nice to show her the ribbon. It was already three o'clock. Surely she would be up from her nap by now.

He reached Cabin Two, and almost without consciously making the decision, he continued to Cabin One.

Just in case she was still asleep, he went quietly up the porch steps. He saw that the inside door was open, though he couldn't see much through the screen. He glimpsed movement, but in the moment when he would have called out, he realized that his mother and Anthony were on the living-room couch.

Kissing.

Mashed up against each other as though they were lovers in some movie.

He felt himself go beet red. He'd never seen anyone kiss like that before. Like they were trying to become one person. Like they didn't have any control. It kinda made him mad. He didn't remember much about his parents' marriage, but he knew he'd never seen them smooching like that.

He started to back away slowly, but in the next instant, they pulled apart. He could only see the sides of their faces, but he thought they looked angry, out of breath. Quickly, he pressed against the side of the doorway, knowing he could get into trouble for eavesdropping, but unable to stop himself.

"Does that tell you where my feelings lie?" his mother asked. "Don't ever accuse me of not loving you again."

"I didn't say you didn't love me," Anthony replied with a soft sigh. "I just asked how much longer you expect me to take a back seat to your son."

"Tony, darling. Are you really jealous of my little boy?"

"I'm not jealous, Thea. I'm bored. I want to get out of here."

"God, I can't wait to leave either. And we will. We'll pack and be gone by dinnertime. I promise."

"Just the two of us?"

"Just the two of us. On that long, long flight to Japan." His mother's voice became teasing, almost indiscernible. "Have you ever done it in the bathroom of a plane at twenty thousand feet? We could be members of the Mile High Club before the night is over."

Charlie didn't know what the Mile High Club was, and maybe Anthony didn't either, because he sounded unimpressed and impatient when he spoke. "Have you spoken to Charles yet?"

"You sound just like Jake," his mother complained. "No, I haven't. But I will."

"He can't come with us, Thea. You know that. I didn't sign on to be your baby-sitter."

Charlie felt his anger rise to the surface. Who was Anthony to tell his mother what she could and couldn't do? He waited expectantly, knowing that she was probably going to take his head off for telling her she couldn't be with Charlie.

"Of course he can't come with us," his mother agreed. "I never intended for him to. Let Jake find out how difficult raising a child can be. I've got my career back, and I'm not going to waste the few good years I have left."

There was silence after that, and Charlie wondered how they couldn't hear his heart hammering, even from the distance of the porch. His vision blurred with tears. For a moment everything around him went white, and it only receded when Anthony spoke again.

"It's not like your ex will let you have him, anyway," Anthony said, and he sounded meaner than someone in love ought to.

"Yes, and I have you to thank for that."

Charlie blinked as Anthony swore under his breath. "Does he still think I'm a threat to the kid's safety? I ought to sue that son of a bitch for defamation of character."

"Well, it was really stupid of you, darling. Leaving your stash lying on the coffee table where Charles could see it. Making jokes about getting him high…"

"It was just a joke, for God's sake! And anyway, he was half-asleep. He didn't have a clue what I was talking about."

"No, and neither did you. Which is why I was willing to forgive such bad behavior and give you a second chance."

There was another short silence, full of soft

moans. He suspected they were kissing again. Charlie wiped the tears off his cheek. He hated them both. And he hated himself most of all for being stupid enough to think his mother actually cared about him.

At last, Anthony asked, "When are you going to tell him?"

"All this commotion down at the spring should be over soon. I'll find Jake and convince him I can't do it alone. He doesn't want to see Charles hurt, so he'll try to make it easier for him."

"I don't want to spend the next couple of hours listening to the kid bawling because he can't have his own way."

"He won't cry," she told him. "He knows I don't like it. Charles will understand. He always understands." She sounded as though she was smiling, full of laughter. "And he loves me too much to make a real fuss once he knows I'm serious."

"Poor guy. Loving you is one heck of a full-time, high-maintenance job."

"Don't be cruel. You know you mean everything to me."

"Come here. Show me how much I mean to you."

Charlie couldn't stay to hear any more.

Somehow he peeled himself away from the doorway. Without a word or glance inside the cabin, he avoided the front steps and slipped quietly down the length of the porch. He lifted himself over the railing and jumped to the ground, landing on his hands and knees.

He headed toward his father's cabin. He needed time to think, and not even being with Darlene White would make him feel better right now.

At the cabin steps he heard the sound of cheering coming from the spring area. The relay race had probably started by now. His father would be expecting him back. Charlie looked down the sunlit slope, seeing nothing but people having fun, being families, sharing good times. He turned his back on the sight, and instead of going inside the cabin, headed toward the front drive of the Hideaway.

WHEN CHARLIE didn't make it back for the start of the relay race, Jake wasn't concerned. He could imagine the kid wanting to clean up and look his best for Darlene, who seemed to think he was pretty special.

After the race, Jake shook hands with the girl's father, who was excited that his team had come in second. He listened politely, making conversation with the White family while he waited for Charlie to come back.

But by the time the next event was called, Charlie still hadn't reappeared. He had made an agreement with Darlene White that if he entered the tug-of-war, she'd have to do her part by entering the egg toss. Now, with a last glimpse over the crowd and a look of disappointment clearly drawn across her face, the girl ran to take her place with the other entrants.

Excusing himself, Jake jogged up the slope, scanning the crowd as he went. Charlie's tardiness seemed strange. The boy probably wouldn't have hesitated to ditch his father—Jake had no illusions about that—but Darlene was another matter completely. He wouldn't have missed the opportunity to be with her.

Their cabin was silent and looked empty. Jake strode to Charlie's bedroom, hoping that he'd misjudged the situation entirely, that he'd find his son still changing clothes or asleep on the bed, exhausted from the day's events.

Instead, it was clear Charlie hadn't been here. No torn and dirty clothes were hanging neatly over the back of the chair. None of his other clothes were missing from the bureau. There was no sign in the bathroom to indicate he'd taken a shower or even washed the dirt from his face.

Jake supposed Charlie could be with his mother. If it was possible for anyone to snag the kid's attention away from Darlene, it would be Thea.

He left his cabin and walked quickly toward Cabin One, passing more than one knot of tired revelers who were headed back to vehicles that lined the front driveway of the resort. The afternoon was getting cooler, and nearly all the day's activities were over.

Reaching the porch of Thea and Anthony's cabin, Jake knocked on the screen door. His ex-wife appeared in the doorway. She'd changed clothes and touched up her makeup. On the couch behind her Jake noticed that her luggage was nearly packed. Clearly she and her lover were about ready to leave for the airport.

"Is Charlie with you?" Jake asked without pre-amble.

"No, I thought he was with you."

"Have you spoken to him this afternoon?"

Thea looked annoyed and defensive. "No. But I told you I would, Jake."

"I'm not concerned about that right now," he said. "I'm trying to find him."

"Well, you'll have to look someplace else. I'm not hiding him from you." She lifted her chin. "You're welcome to search if you like. Come out, come out, wherever you are, Charles," she called, turning her head first in one direction, then the other. "Daddy's here, and he thinks I've kidnapped you..."

"Not funny, Thea." Jake said. "For once in your life, think of someone besides yourself."

"Well, I told you, he's not here."

"Who's not here?" Anthony said as he came through the bedroom door, suitcase in hand.

"Charles," Thea said. "His father's looking for him."

Jake leaned one hand against the door frame and stared down at his feet. If Charlie hadn't come to see his mother, then where was he? A soft breeze whispered across the porch, cooling the sweat that had begun to trickle down the small of his back. Movement at the corner of his vision made him turn his head a fraction of an inch to the right. An object lay on the raw, pine flooring of the porch.

He bent to retrieve it.

Across his palm lay the blue ribbon Charlie had won in the tug-of-war.

"You said you hadn't seen him," Jake cut across Thea's explanation to Anthony. "This is the ribbon he won this afternoon. He wanted to show it to you."

"Well, he didn't," the woman replied.

"Damn it, Thea! He was here."

"He wasn't! Ask Anthony. Although I don't suppose you'll believe him any more than you believe me."

"He wasn't here," Anthony agreed. But a moment later, he seemed to rethink that answer and added, "I guess he could have been, though."

"How?" Jake demanded.

"The screen door's been open all afternoon. He could have come up without us knowing it. We were on the couch...talking..."

Unfolding her tightly crossed arms, Thea gasped, and one slim hand flew to her mouth. Her gaze went to Jake, to Anthony and back again. "If he saw us while we were...if he heard us—"

She broke off. She looked stricken, and Jake felt the first icy fingers of fear touch his spine.

CHAPTER THIRTEEN

"I NEED YOUR HELP," Jake said.

He'd found Nora down at the spring, helping the cleanup crew store away what was left of the day's concession food. She turned to look at him, packets of Ketchup clutched in one hand. Either the grim tone of his voice or the look on his face was enough to convince her that he was deadly serious, because she tossed the handful of condiments onto the table in front of her.

"What is it?" she asked.

"Charlie's missing."

She didn't ask for details. She pulled the apron she wore over her head and tossed it on the table with the rest of the concession supplies. "Where have you looked?"

"Everywhere I can think of. I don't think he's on the property."

Jake turned again to scan the area he'd already searched.

"Did you look in the rehab shed?" Nora asked.

"That was one of the first places I thought of."

"There are a couple of others around here he

may have found during the past few days. Let's check them out.''

They walked together in silence, past the common areas where diehard participants of the day still played, along the edge of Hideaway property where the woods began.

The maintenance shed yielded nothing, nor did the ramshackle barn that had once housed a couple of horses for the Hideaway guests to ride. At the boathouse, they stumbled across a passionate young couple, but no Charlie.

Sending the teenagers away, Nora turned to Jake, biting her bottom lip thoughtfully. "Do you think he's run away?''

Jake drew a long, slow breath. It was the same question he'd been asking himself for the last thirty minutes. He'd pressured Thea into confessing what Charlie could possibly have heard at her cabin. With that abbreviated and chaste version of the conversation clear in his head—and knowing it had probably been a lot worse than that—he still didn't believe Charlie had run away.

No matter how hurt Charlie had been, the kid was smarter than that. He wouldn't take off in a part of the country he didn't know. None of his clothes were gone. The backpack still sat in a corner of the cabin's living room. He had no money, and no resources to get any. Frankly, there was no one to run to. Darlene White was the closest thing to a friend he had, and Jake had seen her leave with her family twenty minutes ago.

He shook his head. "I suspect he's been hurt by

what he might have overheard at his mother's cabin, and he's gone someplace to cool off and think things through.''

''Then maybe you should leave him alone for a while.''

He thought of Thea's anxious, halting admission to him, the sly enjoyment Anthony seemed to take as he watched her try to explain. If the boy had been there…if he had seen one-tenth of Thea's true self…

''I've got to find him, Nora.'' Jake stared off into the late-afternoon light, with its dreamy, lengthening shadows. ''There's only about another hour of daylight left.''

She started off down the path. ''We can contact the county sheriff's office. Have them form a search party.''

''He can't have gone far.''

She stopped suddenly. Her hand tugged on his sleeve to bring him around to face her. ''No, he can't,'' she agreed, and he saw the gleam of a new idea catch fire in her eyes. ''It's a long shot, but there's one more place we can look—the glade where we set Marjorie free.''

With Nora at the wheel, the Hideaway truck bounced off the rutted front driveway that led from the resort and onto the asphalt. To keep from sliding across the front seat, Jake made a grab for the dashboard and tilted Nora a sideways glance when he saw her punch the speedometer up immediately.

''I want to get there before dark,'' she explained.

He watched the woods and wilderness stream

past the window. The last remnants of a dying sun
flickered between the trees, so that the scenery became nothing more than a magic show of strobing
light—green, gold, green, gold.

Are you out there, Charlie? Jake called silently.
Please. Just give me a chance to make it better.

He turned his head to look at Nora. Her profile
was unmarred, except for the tiniest twinge of anxiety over her eyebrow. Clearly sensing his scrutiny,
she slid her glance away from the road and gave
him a small smile. "He'll be there," she said in a
determined voice. "I'll bet you a week's free stay
at the Hideaway."

"And what if you're wrong?"

"I won't be."

Jake tried to take comfort, but his senses felt entirely apart from him. He was hardly aware of the
moment they left the main road and entered the
gates of the national forest.

Nora slowed to comply with the park speed limit.
"How is your ex-wife taking all this?" she asked.

"I wouldn't know. She and Anthony left for the
airport almost an hour ago."

She glanced at him sharply, disbelief in her eyes.
"With her son missing?"

Jake found it in him to smile. "Thea's maternal
instincts have been dulled by all this newfound celebrity. She's like a child with a new toy. It makes
her careless with people."

"Is that why you won't let her have custody of
Charlie?"

He had to think a moment just how much to tell

her. Nora was someone he felt he could trust with the truth, but it was ugly, and not one he was particularly proud to have been a part of.

"I was halfway around the world," he began, "when I picked up a paper and saw a picture taken at one of her parties. Charlie was asleep in the background, curled up on one of the couches. I was so mad I called my attorney on the spot, asked him to find out what the hell my kid was doing there."

"What did he find out?"

"He couldn't reach me for quite a while." Jake looked down. "That was the day Bobby and the bush crew were attacked, and I spent the next couple of days at the hospital. When that was...over, I made arrangements to come home. The first thing I did was see Gregg about challenging our custody agreement. That's when he told me he'd found witnesses who swore they'd been at the party and seen Anthony offer drugs to Charlie."

"Oh my God," Nora gasped. "What could that man have been thinking?"

"I doubt if he was." He drew a deep breath. "Anyway, the threat of exposure was enough to get Thea to back off a public fight."

"What did Charlie think about all this?"

"He doesn't even remember it. It was three o'clock in the morning. Thea planted the idea in his head that I was taking her back to court just for spite, and he's believed that ever since."

They'd come to the end of the lane. Ahead lay the glade where they'd picnicked and fished and watched Marjorie regain her freedom. Nora cut the engine, and the sound of the stillness all around them took over.

Jake felt his heart drop. The boy wasn't here. No one was.

Oh, God, he thought. *Help me. Tell me where I go from here.*

And then, just at the bend in the river, there was movement. Charlie. The radiance of the sunset had caught the gleam of gold in his hair. He sat on the sloping edge of the riverbank, lost in thought, his back to them. If he'd heard the truck's arrival, he chose to ignore it.

With a sudden flush of relief, Jake exhaled a broken laugh. He looked at Nora quickly when she touched his sleeve. The glance they exchanged felt as warm and reviving as a kiss on a cold night.

"I told you he'd be here," Nora said with a wide grin of satisfaction. "Now go tell him it's time to come home."

ALL IN ALL, it hadn't gone too badly, Jake thought an hour later. He heard the shower cut off, and a few minutes later, Charlie emerged and went into his bedroom. Jake finished making a couple of sandwiches, slipped them onto paper plates and joined him there.

He watched Charlie pull on the expensive pajamas he insisted on wearing. The boy's body was lean and nearly hairless. There was a darkening bruise along his rib cage, and red scrapes across one knee. The injuries, though slight, made him seem so vulnerable.

"I made you ham and cheese," Jake said, and placed the paper plate on the bedside table.

"I'm not really hungry," Charlie replied. His mouth lifted in a small, valiant attempt at humor. "Probably too many hot dogs this afternoon."

"How about a glass of milk, then?"

"Dad, I'm all right. Really."

"I know."

The boy slid between the sheets on his bed, then drew air between his teeth as his wounded knee touched the covers. He pulled it up, tilting his head at the reddened patch of skin.

"Do you want something for that?" Jake asked. "There's a first-aid kit in one of the drawers in the kitchen."

"Nah."

"Tell me something. How did you get to the glade on your own?"

"I saw a couple of guys packing up their truck for the day. There was a campground parking sticker for the forest in their window, so I figured they were probably headed back there. I just wanted to be by myself for a while, so when they weren't looking, I slipped in the back. Once they pulled into the campground, it was easy to hop out." Excitement glittered in his eyes. "Pretty cool, huh?"

"Pretty cool," Jake acknowledged. "And if I ever catch you doing something like that again, there'll be no Space Scow for a year."

"I figured you'd say something like that," the boy groaned. But one corner of his mouth twitched in amusement.

Jake dug his hand into the back pocket of his jeans, suddenly remembering the blue ribbon. He held it out to Charlie. "I picked this up at your mother's cabin. I hope you'll still want to keep it."

"Sure," he said. "Why wouldn't I?"

Jake sat down on the edge of the bed. He handed the ribbon to his son. With a shrug he said, "Today was rough on you. Maybe you don't need or want any reminders."

Charlie looked at the ribbon, then ran one finger down its satin smoothness. "Some of today wasn't so bad. I liked being with Darlene, and the boat race. We did all right, huh?"

"Better than all right," Jake agreed.

Charlie placed the ribbon on the bedside table, next to his sandwich, then drew his arms up behind his head and was silent for a long time. The boy's eyes captured Jake's, froze him in place and made his heart beat harder.

"I thought she needed me more than anyone else," he said softly. "But she doesn't need anyone. Except maybe Anthony."

"Your mother loves you, Charlie. It's just that she's the kind of person who needs attention from a lot of people. She's always been treated very special. By her parents. Even by me at first. But for years it's just been you, looking after her. And you've done a really good job of it."

"That didn't keep her from leaving."

"No," he had to agree. "But she had commitments to honor. And until she comes back, I plan to honor mine to you." He leaned forward to tuck the covers around his son, drawing his gaze again. "I need you in my life, Charlie," he said in a low voice. "I screwed up by staying away so long, and I don't blame you for giving up on me. But I'm trying hard to earn a second chance. Do you think that's possible for the two of us?"

The boy was silent for a long time. And then something in his eyes changed, and with a smile full of fatigue and childish hope, he said, "I guess we could give it a try."

FORTY-FIVE MINUTES LATER he left Charlie sound asleep. He took a shower, letting the hottest water he could stand steam away the day's punishment and fear. Slipping into a fresh pair of jeans, he picked up Charlie's damaged clothes and stuffed them into the garbage along with the sandwich.

Tomorrow he and Charlie ought to go shopping in town. New T-shirts and shorts for both of them. Maybe they'd check out the rest of the weekend activities in the town square. Tomorrow he'd find Nora and thank her for helping him.

Restlessly he walked out onto the front porch. The night breeze was a cooling whisper against his bare chest. There were lights still on at the main lodge, and along the line of cabins that sat on the opposite side were one or two cars belonging to guests. The season had evidently started for the Hideaway.

To his left he heard muted movement. Lights were on in the cabin Thea and Anthony had vacated, and behind the sheer curtains Jake caught a glimpse of Nora. What was she doing over there at this time of night, when everyone else was settling in for the evening?

EXHALING AN ANNOYED SIGH, Nora squirted liquid cleaner on her sponge and attacked the soapy film that formed a ring around the bathroom sink.

She would never, ever, buy a single La Paloma product again as long as she lived. Not mascara. Not lipstick. Not even the tiniest vial of perfume. Any company that could hire someone like Thea didn't deserve a cent of Nora's hard-earned money.

In spite of their short stay, Thea and her lover had managed to turn Cabin One upside down. After a brief inspection, Nora had discovered a chocolate stain on one of the living-room couch cushions, broken dishes in the trash, a cigarette burn in the brand-new sheets, and finally, residue from a spewed soda can all over the kitchen walls, cabinets and countertop. She only hoped that was the worst of it. Short-term visitors seldom had time to really make an impression on a place. She should have known Thea would be different.

No use grumbling, Nora supposed. She had most of what she needed in the housekeeping tray she always carried with her to clean, and the rest of the night to work if that proved necessary. It wasn't as if she'd have any luck sleeping.

Not after today.

What a crazy, mixed-up day it had been. Charlie's disappearance had been frightening, of course, giving her a few bad moments when there seemed to be nowhere else to look for him. The boat race had been good, silly fun, a chance to forget about cash-flow problems and the possibility of court-room battles. But it was the memory of Jake's kisses that still floated around in her head, banging up against every sensible thought she'd ever had.

She caught a glimpse of herself in the bathroom mirror. Color heightening her cheeks. The gleam of some indefinable something twinkling in her eyes. *Oh, Lord, suppose I'm head over heels in love with the guy?*

She made a helpless sound and shook her head. *I just won't be, that's all. Get a grip, Holloway. He can't make you fall in love with him.* Squirting more cleaner into the bathtub, she scrubbed with renewed vigor.

A few minutes later, with the bathroom finally spotless, she sighed and straightened from bending over the tub. She capped the cleaner, and when she looked up, Jake was there, leaning against the bath-room door.

To have the object of her private thoughts ma-terialize in front of her, especially dressed in noth-ing but sneakers and jeans and that gloriously naked male chest, made her heart jump. "How long have you been standing there?"

He grinned at her. "Long enough to wish my own tub needed scrubbing."

"Your place better not look like this, or I'm keeping your deposit."

Jake's eyebrows bunched over his nose. "With

as little time as we spend indoors and a neat freak for a son? Not hardly.''

"How is he?''

"Sound asleep.''

"And his attitude?''

"I think there's hope.''

She stripped off her work gloves and rinsed her hands in the sink. Drying them on the towel she kept tucked in the back pocket of her shorts, she smiled up at him. "I'm glad.''

"Me, too.'' He paused, drawing a relaxed breath before continuing in a low voice, "And I'm especially glad that I had you to help me get through today. I think I was on the verge of losing it when you suggested the glade.''

Under his scrutiny, Nora suddenly realized that the small bathroom seemed even smaller, warmer. She slapped the gloves into a compartment of her work tray and came toward him. He backed out of her way, into the living room.

He watched her a few moments while she arranged the bouquet of flowers she'd brought from the lodge into a glass vase. Pleased with the simple arrangement, she set the vase on the table in back of the couch. The scent of roses drifted lightly across the room.

"So what are you doing down here this late?'' Jake asked.

"Check-ins tomorrow.'' From the front pocket of her shorts she pulled out the preregistration card she kept on all guests. "The newly wedded Mr. and

Mrs. Derrick Beiderbaum,'' she read. ''From Tallahassee.''

He motioned toward the champagne bottle she'd brought along with the flowers. ''So the champagne isn't your way of celebrating another housekeeping triumph?''

''Not unless I find anything else that's been dismantled or destroyed in here.''

Jake glanced around the room and shook his head. ''Typical of Thea. She's fastidious in her appearance, but she lacks organization in her personal life. Can I help?''

She cocked her head at him. ''Are you serious?''

''I build bridges where they've never seen a cake of soap,'' he replied. ''I'm not afraid of a little dirt and grease.''

She passed him a handful of cleaning supplies and then placed the bottle of champagne on top of the stack cradled in his hands. ''The champagne goes in the fridge, after it's been wiped down inside.'' As he moved to do her bidding, she added, ''Make sure the welcome card faces out.''

''Got it.'' He entered the kitchen, and a few moments later she heard him exclaim, ''Damn! What happened in here?''

''You want to resign?'' she called out with a laugh, realizing he'd discovered the soda-can accident.

She heard him grumbling under his breath, but he didn't come back into the living room. In another instant she recognized the sound of the refrigerator door opening. She smiled. It was going to be a sticky mess to clean up, but at least, with Jake's help, she'd have a head start.

She went into the master bedroom. Stripping off the bedcovers, she placed the dirty sheets on the porch where she could grab them on her way back to the lodge, then stretched fresh ones over the mattress.

Honeymooners always got the deluxe treatment. A small box of chocolates went on the bedside table. She filled a dish in the bathroom with little bottles of bubble bath, lotion and oils. Behind the door she hung two terry-cloth robes—his and hers—on lightly scented, padded hangers.

In the living room, she dusted and polished, plumped pillows and swept debris off the hearth in front of the fireplace. The chocolate stain on the couch cushion was more problematic. Nothing in her bag of cleaning tricks seemed to work. Still, the cabin looked warm and cozy, the perfect place for the Beiderbaums to spend the first few days of married life.

Jake appeared in the doorway. He tossed the cleaning towel over one well-formed bare shoulder. ''Ready for the white-glove inspection,'' he said.

She followed him back into the kitchen, and her mouth gaped open. The place was spotless, not just the fridge, but the walls, cabinets, even the toaster gleamed. There wasn't a sign of its previous occupants anywhere.

''It's terrific,'' she told him, touched. ''You wouldn't be looking for full-time work, would you?''

"Sorry. You're out of luck. Are we done yet?"

"Almost," she said, and began turning off the lights in the cabin. "I want to give the stain on the couch pillow one last chance to surrender."

Moving to the couch, she placed the pillow across her thighs and sprayed the spot with her strongest cleaner. Jake joined her, settling back against the cushions with a sigh. His gaze traveled around the room.

"What do you think?" she asked. "Will it pass muster?"

"The place looks great, Nora. Stop worrying."

"I can't help it," she explained, still scrubbing at the stain. "I just like the Hideaway to be some-place special for newlyweds. A place they'll re-member for the rest of their lives together."

"Ah," he said with a knowing nod of under-standing. "No Beiderbaum wedding rings thrown down the drain."

She lifted the pillow and slapped him across the chest with it. "I told you, that was a freak incident. I'm not even sure those two people were really in love. They probably shouldn't have gotten married in the first place."

"Like half the population," he said sourly, then plucked the pillow and damp cloth out of her hands. "Let me try." He rubbed at the stain. His forehead creased as though he were trying to will the damage away, then he lifted it to his nose to take a sniff. "Good grief, it's chocolate! Thea will be out of a job if she keeps indulging her sweet tooth."

Her eyes narrowed at him, taking in firm, aggressive lips that could kiss with such exquisite tenderness. "Don't you believe in love anymore?"

"After Thea? I don't know." His eyebrow lifted as the spot on the pillow disappeared. He held up the cushion so she could see, then tossed it back in her lap. "Do you?"

"I want to." Nora said the words slowly, carefully. "I try to picture myself sometimes, living here alone, taking care of the place until it falls down around me." She shook her head. "That isn't the way I always dreamed it would be."

"The mistress of a honeymoon haven without a husband," Jake said in a low voice, and when she turned her head toward him she saw that the hard, cynical look in his eyes had softened. "Not much of a personal recommendation."

She grimaced, feeling suddenly uncomfortable seated this close to him, as though her body was warming and tensing all at the same time. "I suppose if it turns out that way, I'll just have to try that much harder to make the Hideaway successful."

"You're already making it successful, Nora," he said. His smile started slowly, then curved teasingly. "Your newlyweds are going to love their stay here."

"Don't make fun. This place is very special to me."

"I think I know how you feel about it," he said. "The Beiderbaums will sense it, too."

"Do you read tea leaves, as well?"

"I don't need to. I just know. The Beiderbaums

will still be keyed up from the ceremony, exhausted by the drive here, but too excited to wait any longer.'' His hand found hers curled upon the pillow. He lifted it, touching his lips lightly to the back of her fingers. His eyes never left hers, not for a glance, not for a second. ''Derrick Beiderbaum is going to carry his lovely new wife…'' He halted, arching an inquiring look her way.

''Lucinda,'' she supplied on a breathy little note of pleasure. Jake's lips were soft against her knuckles.

''Lucinda…across the threshold of this cabin. She's going to admire the flowers in the vase. He's going to eye that champagne in the fridge and wonder how many glasses it will take to calm her nerves.''

''How many will it take?''

''That depends on how long he's known her. He doesn't want to frighten her.''

''I'll bet she's not easily frightened.''

''No. Definitely not the shrinking-violet type,'' he said, and she watched his mouth quirk upward. ''So even though it's too warm, she'll ask him to light a fire in the grate.''

''Mmm, yes. I like that. A romantic fire.''

''They'll drink half the champagne, sitting in front of it.''

He had turned her hand over, and his mouth was doing something delicious, something lovely to her palm. She swallowed hard, wanting to continue to play this game, and knowing the danger of it.

"Only half the bottle?" she asked. "Maybe I should start buying half magnums."

His lashes lifted. With his head still down, he frowned at her, a playful warning not to ruin his scenario. "They'll finish it later. They'll be too busy looking deeply into each other's eyes."

Suddenly he tossed the pillow aside and leaned across the distance that separated them, stopping just short of actually touching his lips to hers. She felt his breath against her cheek, smelled the scent of the soap he'd used. Something took off in her system, like bottle rockets on the Fourth of July. Unnerved, she inhaled violently.

"He'll start to sweet-talk her," she murmured slowly. "Maybe even suggest they change into something more comfortable."

"She'll giggle and get embarrassed," he added with a grin. "But she'll want to hear more."

"He seems very sure of himself."

"Can't help it. She's on fire for him."

"She is?"

"Uh-huh." He teased her lips with his tongue. "He's irresistible to her."

"But it's been such an awfully long day," she managed to get out.

"Doesn't matter. It's the moment they've both been waiting for." The thought of his coming nearer still sent a shiver through her, and when his tongue touched her lips again, she could no more resist than she could stop breathing. "Such a long…long…time," he whispered against the side of her mouth.

And finally, his lips took hers, and she fell deep into the kiss that was waiting for her. He was gentle at first; he seemed to sense her need. Then he began to use his mouth and tongue like a relentless weapon, roughly stroking, plunging, claiming possession of her. It was easy, oh it was so easy to respond to that demand.

Suddenly he wrenched his lips from hers. "Stop me now if that's what you want," he said. His chest rose and fell rapidly, as if he labored against some emotion that savaged his senses. "Much further and I can't promise that I'll be able to. I want you so much, Nora."

She remained trapped between his hands, her mouth parted and the blood galloping through her veins. Was she crazy to allow this to happen? She didn't know. But right now, she knew that only a fool would look beyond tomorrow, and wise and lonely was no way to live out a life.

She pressed her hand against his chest, feeling his heartbeat sprint against her fingers. Lifting her chin, she found his eyes. "I don't want to stop," she told him softly. "I want you to kiss me again."

Desire flitted through his eyes. With a sound somewhere between a growl and a purr, he swept her high in his arms suddenly, and she gave a little cry of surprise that was stilled on the next heartbeat when he buried his face at her throat, nuzzling kisses along her neck.

"Your honeymooners. Derrick and Lucinda," he

murmured against her flesh. ''Will they like that bed in there?''

''We should make sure,'' she said, her breath punctuated with little gasps.

''My thoughts exactly.''

CHAPTER FOURTEEN

THE SOFT, STEADY DRUMMING of rain on the cabin roof woke him.

The bedroom was drowning in pools of night shadows, but of the objects Jake could see—curtains, bureau, rocking chair—none looked familiar. He scowled, trying to get his bearings. After a moment, his twisted swamp of a brain clearly began to remember. And when he did, his confused frown turned into a smile.

He rolled his head to one side, encountering a mass of soft, sweet-smelling hair. Nora was snuggled against him, one arm draped across his chest. Her breath moved in and out in her sleep, gentle puffs of air that warmed his shoulder and teased his senses.

He inched sideways until he could see her face in the poor light filtering in from the outside porch lamp. She looked tired—there were smudges of exhaustion beneath her long lashes—but a small, peaceful smile curved her lips.

He wanted to place his mouth against those slightly swollen lips, pull her into his arms and feel her fevered response to him again, but he didn't.

She deserved her rest. They'd made love twice during the night—so wildly, so wantonly, that even he was convinced that a third time was impossible for now.

Later, he thought with a slow grin. Later. But not too much later.

She moved suddenly, frowning and sighing heavily. "Izzie…drink your milk," she mumbled. "Good for the baby…"

"Yes, ma'am," he said softly. He hugged her closer, and evidently satisfied, she burrowed deeper against him.

Wonderful Nora. She tried so hard to be everything to everybody. Isabel, her brother. The animals in her rehab shed. The Hideaway. Even the people of Blue Devil Springs demanded so much of her energy and attention. It wasn't right or fair that someone so good and decent should have had such pain.

He wanted to change all that.

And he knew he could. He could help her realize the dream of having a child of her own to love. All he had to do was drop his custody suit.

He knew in his heart that she'd make the good parent for the baby. Bobby's son would be fine and flourish in her care. There could be no argument to a judge about her worthiness as a mother. There simply wasn't one to make, and Jake knew that soon he'd have to call Gregg Sanstrom and tell him that.

But his greater challenge was to find a way to convince Nora that he loved her. It seemed as though it should be so easy. His feelings for her were clear. Irrefutable. She was the first woman in his life that he was afraid to lose, the first he knew his life would be empty without.

They could raise Bobby's child together, as husband and wife. But he could imagine saying those words to her, then seeing the suspicion in her eyes. She wouldn't believe him for a minute. She'd wonder whether he was asking her to marry him because that was the only way he could get his hands on the baby.

He stared up at the ceiling for a long time, watching while lightning fingered the edges of the curtains. He wouldn't say anything right away. He didn't want to blow it. He needed time to marshal the arguments to convince her.

A roll of distant thunder rattled the windows and sent rain in a mad tattoo across the roof. It was enough to stir Nora from sleep.

"What is it?" she mumbled against his shoulder, her eyes still closed.

"The rain."

"Oh, hell…another leak?"

"No," he said with a smile for her confusion. He placed a kiss against her temple. "Go back to sleep."

"What time is it?"

He lifted his free arm to read the luminous dial of his wristwatch. "Nearly five o'clock."

"I should get up," she said with a sleepy yawn. "There are things that need to be done. If Isabel isn't up to watching the desk today—"

She made a move to rise, and he pulled her gently back down beside him. "Relax, Nora. No one's doing anything this time of day."

She was more awake now. One hand came up to play across his chest, and her lips placed a trio of kisses against the wall of his rib cage. "Not even us?" she asked, her voice full of drowsy regret.

Just like that, he wanted her again. He groaned and lifted her hand from its exploration of the hair that grew low across his chest, replacing it on her sheet-covered breast. "I'm trying to let you sleep. Don't push your luck and my control past its limits."

Her fingers came right back, descending beneath the sheets to find his arousal. Her touch drew a harsh gasp from him, and she tilted her head back so that she could find his face. "Oops! Too late."

He turned suddenly, so that they were face-to-face. In a gruff, passionate voice, he said, "Damn it, Nora! You're asking for it."

"Yes," she agreed with a husky laugh. "Yes, I believe I am."

She planted a lush, juicy kiss against his mouth. He groaned an exaggerated complaint, but he was already pushing her back against the pillows, ready to ease into her again as the last of his objections dissolved.

"JAKE, wake up. Jake."

Pinned beneath him, Nora grasped Jake's shoulder and began shaking him in earnest. He groaned and settled more heavily against her. The sun had pushed its way into the bedroom, and the light was so flat it had drained away any vestige of last night's magic. Panic knocked in her chest. She'd slept too late.

She twisted around until she could see the face of his watch. Oh, God. Nearly nine-thirty. What had she been thinking?

"Jake."

"Hmm?"

"Get up," she commanded him urgently, trying to wiggle out from under his warm, wonderful weight. "We have to go."

"Why?" he muttered.

"Lucinda and Derrick."

"Who?"

"The Beiderbaums. My newlyweds."

He shot upright, the look of alarm in his eyes almost comical. "They're here?"

She scooted out of bed, pushing hair out of her eyes as she tried to find her clothes strewn all over the room. "No, but they will be soon. I've got to get this cabin back in order before they arrive."

Jake flopped back against the mattress, dragging one arm over his eyes to block the invading sunlight streaming past the curtains. "Call housekeeping," he mumbled.

"I *am* housekeeping," she pointed out with a laugh as she slipped into her shorts and zoomed the zipper up. Sitting on the side of the bed, she pushed into her sneakers and began quickly lacing them up. "Now, rise and shine."

"We need to talk."

She turned and leaned back across the bed on one elbow. Giving Jake a quick kiss, she smiled at him. "I know, and I want to. But now is not a good time. I'm going to be running behind all day, and Charlie must surely be up and wondering where you are by now. This is what we get for being too…energetic last night."

He took hold of both her forearms. Pulling her close, he gave her a lingering, tempting kiss. "Charlie's like his mother. He'd sleep until noon if I let him. And I've still got some…energy left," he whispered encouragingly.

"Don't even think it, Burdette," she said, and pulled away and off the bed before he could urge her back.

"How about lunch?"

"I can't. I promised I'd staff one of the booths in town between noon and two."

"Dinner?" he asked with a resigned sigh. "I'll take you anywhere you want to go. We can have a nice, romantic meal and a long talk over a bottle of expensive wine. There's so much I want to say to you."

He sounded so serious that Nora stopped tucking the hem of her blouse into her shorts and swung her head to look at him.

His thick, dark hair was as tousled as hers, but on him it looked sexy, inviting a woman's touch. The smallest shadow of a stubbled beard lay along his jawline, and she remembered how he had rasped it against her flesh during the night—hard enough to make her blood tingle, light enough to make her shiver. A tightness corkscrewed into the pit of her stomach, and there was nothing more she wanted in that moment than to cross the room and let Jake work his magic.

That, she realized with a burst of self-awareness, was where she had wanted to be for so long. In Jake Burdette's arms. She knew herself well enough to know why she had allowed last night to happen. Casual flings and one-night stands had never been her style, and if she'd given in to lusty teasing and erotic touches the night before, that response had its foundation in only one thing: love.

She didn't know when it had happened. Perhaps when Jake had held and comforted her in the glade. He had not been her enemy that afternoon.

It didn't matter, really. She loved him.

"All right, Jake, it's a date," she said softly. Trying for a more normal tone, she added, "Now, get up and get moving, before I make the bed with you in it, and you have to explain to the Beiderbaums how you got there."

NORA LEANED her elbows on the counter of the quilting booth, then settled her chin in her hands as she people-watched the crowd that had come to enjoy the activities in the town square. Well, at least her shift was nearly over. In another few minutes someone would be coming to relieve her so she could return to the Hideaway.

Where still more work awaited.

The day had been difficult. Straightening up the cabin where she and Jake had spent the night. Making sure the part-time help she'd hired for the summer understood how to do towel service for stay-overs and clean up after guests checked out. Feeding the menagerie in the rehab shed. When she got home, she'd have to take up where she'd left off. By now, Isabel was probably desperate for a break from the registration desk.

Of course, there was tonight to look forward to. A candlelit dinner. Wine. Maybe a few kisses in the moonlight. Who knew where that would lead?

Nora smiled, just thinking about the possibilities, and wished she could conjure Jake up just by concentrating. But he'd told her that he planned to spend the day with Charlie, fishing in the glade and getting to know each other better. As glad as she was that their relationship seemed to be making progress, she missed him already.

Coming back to earth from daydreams, Nora straightened as she realized that John Forrester was making a beeline for the quilting booth. He was holding hands with Michelle Mitchell, the woman he'd been dating for the past six months.

"What are you two up to?" Nora asked.

"I'm your relief," Michelle replied, and with a quick kiss for John, she moved behind the counter to join Nora.

"Business is slow, I'm afraid."

Nora turned over the keys to the cash box and picked up her purse. Quickly she went through a few simple rules for Michelle's benefit, then left the booth. John was still standing at the counter, and he approached her as she dug into her purse for the keys to the truck.

"Do you have a few minutes, Nora?" he asked. "I'd like to talk to you."

"Sure. Walk with me, why don't you?"

They strode side by side through the throng of people strolling around the square—a knot of kids enthralled by a magician, a smattering of well-heeled collectors picking through antiques spread across the grass, a family watching Mom's and Dad's caricatures being done by Chief Quinn. By all signs, the weekend was a success.

"I was going to give you a call first thing in the morning," John said beside her. "But since I've run into you here, I figured we might as well touch base."

"Do you want to go to your office?"

"No, that's not necessary. I know you're probably eager to get home. How's Isabel?"

"About the same. She's really looking forward to all this being over."

"As I'm sure you are."

They had reached the truck. Instead of unlocking the vehicle, Nora turned and leaned against the driver's door. Something in John's demeanor made her nervous. She steeled herself for the worst and gave her attorney a long, scrutinizing look. "John, what is it? Is something wrong?"

"I'm not sure. I got a call from Mr. Burdette's lawyer late yesterday. A lot of what he had to say was just showmanship, I believe. He's very good at trying to intimidate those of us who are less ex-

perienced.'' He tried a smile, but it failed in the
face of her frowning concentration. "One thing he
said did disturb me, though, and I think you should
be aware of any potential damage it might cause
our case.''

Her heart was galloping now, her nerve endings
treacherous. "What is it?'' she asked, attempting to
tame the tremor in her voice. "Just tell me.''

"Nora, after you lost Peter and the baby, did you
keep a diary of some sort?''

The question was completely unexpected. She
felt a little relieved, because her mind had feared
so much worse, but obviously John was worried
about something. She tried to think back to that
horrible time in her life, and through the numb, rac-
ing pattern of her thoughts, she did remember the
journal. "Yes, I kept one for a while. It helped me
get through the rough patches.''

"Do you still have it?''

"No, it served its purpose and was destroyed a
long time ago.''

"Are you sure?''

"I gave it to Trip. He burned it.''

"Think very carefully about this. Are you positive he burned it?''

The odd, gone-in-the-middle sensation was back
in her stomach. "Why are you asking me about
this?''

He stared at her a moment, looking uncomfortable, as though trying to find the right way to begin.
She was ready to scream by the time he drew a
deep breath and took her hand. "Gregg Sanstrom—

Burdette's attorney—insinuated to me that a very damaging personal journal, written by you, was going to be made available to him. So damaging that it would raise serious questions about your ability to be a fit mother to Isabel's child. He suggested we drop the case now, before it's made public.''

He looked at her again, and waited, unspeaking, until she grasped the sense of what he was saying.

"That can't be," she cried. "No way." Then hardly able to form the question, she asked in a small voice. "Do you think he's telling the truth?"

"It could be a bluff, I suppose." John's gaze turned wary. "But how would he know of its existence?"

Everything in her screamed denial. That journal was long gone, no more than ashes. She searched her memory, trying to recall if she'd actually seen Trip burn it. What John implied was almost more than she could bear. No! What he was suggesting was a mistake. It had to be.

Looking at John's sweet, troubled features, she shook her head. "It's impossible. Trip and I have had our differences lately, but he would never betray me like that."

He flinched. And what she saw in his face drained away all the hope she had in her. "Sanstrom didn't say this information was coming from Trip," John told her in a quiet voice. "He said it had been supplied to him by Jake Burdette."

WHEN NORA PULLED into the front driveway of the Hideaway, she had no real comprehension of how she'd gotten home. She killed the engine and then continued to sit there, her body too physically exhausted to move at the moment, her mind too hazy to sort through what her next step should be.

Gripping the steering wheel, she closed her eyes and leaned forward until her forehead touched the smooth plastic. She couldn't go inside yet, couldn't face Isabel and maybe some of the Hideaway guests and try to pretend that everything was all right. Instead, she tried to draw several calming, deep breaths into her lungs, tried to clear her mind as she turned over the events that had brought her to this sorry state.

What had she done to deserve this? Dared to dream that adopting Isabel's baby could bring a little happiness to herself? Fallen too deeply in love to recognize betrayal?

Her control faltered in that moment. She thought her heart would crack with loss. Her throat thickened, and the tears came, pouring down. Disbelief. Hurt.

Eventually, there were no more tears to shed. Nora sniffed hard and wiped her eyes with tissue she found in the glove compartment. The rearview mirror revealed a mess—swollen eyelids, blotchy cheeks, but somehow her limbs found fresh strength. She got out of the truck, knowing what she had to do.

Instead of heading up the front steps to the lodge, she turned in the direction of Cabin Two. Jake's rental car was gone, but that didn't matter. She'd wait for him to return.

Movement and noise down by the spring caught her attention. Several of the Hideaway's guests had discovered the pool and were enjoying the afternoon on the sunny bank. She caught sight of Trip at the overlook deck, pulling down the last of the streamers that had been used yesterday for the boat race, and she almost detoured in that direction. It had to be Trip who had given Jake the journal. She suspected he had struck back at her, angry at her unwillingness to change their financial arrangement regarding the Hideaway. But now was not the time to confront him. Not with so many guests within earshot. Later would be soon enough.

She sat in one of the rocking chairs on the cabin's front porch. Waiting. Knowing that after she talked with Jake, none of the things she'd thought possible this morning would come to pass.

She had no idea how long she sat there. It could have been an hour, two. Time had no meaning. Eventually she picked out the sound of an engine coming down the driveway, and a moment later, Jake's sports car pulled into the space reserved for Cabin Two.

Together Jake and Charlie approached the front steps, fishing gear in hand, laughing over some joke they'd shared. They'd been successful from the looks of it; a stringer of fish dangled from Charlie's hand. The boy appeared suntanned and happy. There were flecks of dirt on both their jeans and T-shirts, and on their face and arms a gloss of drying sweat.

When he saw her seated in the rocking chair,

Jake welcomed her with a smile, but the moment they got close enough for him to see her face, it disappeared. She stood up, looking down at him from the porch.

"You have something that belongs to me," she said simply. "I'd like to have it back."

He gave her a wary, questioning glance, then turned his attention to his son. "Charlie, throw our catch in the kitchen sink. Then take a shower and get cleaned up. I'll be in shortly."

When the boy was safely inside and out of earshot, Jake came slowly up the steps. He gave Nora his full attention, his eyes searching for every nuance in her features. "What is it, Nora? What's the matter?"

"I saw John Forrester in town today. My attorney. He said he'd heard from yours. In fact, the man tried to coerce him into dropping the case. He suggested that a journal I kept a long time ago might be made public if I didn't."

She watched the puzzled look on his face change to one of disbelief. His mouth opened as he started to say something—perhaps in his own defense. But one look at Nora and he was instantly silenced. He moved toward the porch railing and stood in silence, gazing out at the springs.

Eventually, he spoke softly. "Gregg overstepped."

She supposed a small part of her still hoped he would disavow any knowledge of the journal, but clearly that wasn't the case. Through clenched teeth, she said, "Then you're not going to deny that you have it."

He turned around, crossing his arms over his chest. "No, I don't have it, but I know where it is. Gregg should never have said what he did."

"Of course not," she agreed with a shaky laugh. "Not when you were so close to seducing me into giving up the baby." Her chin lifted. "Isn't that right?"

His eyes narrowed. "Is that what you think last night was about?" he asked in a low voice.

She returned his hard gaze without fear, but as she did so images from last night began to form. Jake's arms curving protectively around her, his fingers fanning against her hips, the touch of his tongue teasing one nipple until she shivered. Deliberately, she turned her mind's eye away from those memories.

"Trip told you about the diary so you could use it against me," she stated, determined to keep control of the conversation and herself.

"Yes, but I didn't want any part of it. I knew that from the start."

"Oh, please…"

There were several seconds of silence. Then Jake said quietly, "I intended to tell you about it tonight."

"That's a rather convenient excuse, don't you think? Considering I've just caught you redhanded."

Jake's jaw tightened. "It's not an excuse," he said, his eyes traveling over her. "It's the truth."

She shook her head. "I don't believe you."

"I may be a lot of things, but a liar isn't one of them. I thought you'd know that by now. I thought we'd reached a certain level of trust between us."

"Well, so did I," she replied coolly. "I guess I was wrong."

"All right. I can't see the sense in trying to convince you if your mind is made up." He straightened, coming toward her until he was so close she could see the flecks of light in his eyes. "Where do we go from here?"

She jerked away, eager to put distance between them. "I'll fight you in court for the baby if I have to, no matter what you think that book does for your case." She tossed her head defiantly at him. In a voice dry as desert wind, she said, "Use it if you like. Writing down my thoughts in that diary helped me get through one of the worst times of my life, and there's nothing in it that I'm ashamed of. I won't let you blackmail me into quitting. All I want now is to have you leave. I don't want you on Hideaway property."

"Nora…"

He had touched her arm, and she pulled away from his grasp as though his fingers carried fire. "No, Jake. I want you out of my life. I can't bear to see you here day after day—reminding me how completely stupid I was to love you. I'm going to get your bill ready." She swallowed, trying to get past the lump that suddenly seemed to be blocking her throat. "Because of Charlie, I won't ask you to find someplace else tonight. But first thing in the morning, I'd like you to go.''

Before he could say anything, Nora ran down the steps, heading for the main lodge. She got no farther than fifty feet before he caught up with her.

He tugged on her arm, dragging her back to face him again. ''Nora, wait. We can't let it end this way.''

''Why? Because this isn't the way you planned it? Don't you ever get tired of trying to manipulate people?''

His eyes turned dark, and when he spoke, his voice was like winter silk. ''Did I manipulate you into loving me?''

She shook her head in slow misery. ''I don't love you.''

''That isn't what you said back there on the porch. And it isn't what you showed me last night.''

''Last night, I…'' It was so useless to deny it. She wasn't nearly a good enough actress to pull off such a pretense. She sighed and looked him directly in the eyes. ''All right. You want some kind of trophy to take with you out of this mess, I'll give it to you. I allowed last night to happen because I thought I was in love with you. I thought there was a way for us to overcome anything, including what to do about the baby. But I was deluding myself. It was just sex for you.'' She corrected that statement with a quick, negative swipe of her head. ''No, it was more than that. It was a way you thought you could win, which is what you've wanted all along.''

There was no accusation in this, just a statement of fact.

"You're wrong, Nora. I've known for a long time that it's more than the baby who's kept me here. It's you. Tell me how I can prove that to you."

Tears were thick in her voice when she answered, but she wouldn't let them spill over. "You can't. It's too late. Don't worry, I've learned a valuable lesson, and I know I'll be stronger for it." She gave him a grim smile that was no more than a grimace.

She turned and left. He didn't try to stop her again. There was nothing more to be said.

NORA ROSE EARLY the next morning.

The night had brought nothing but sleepless misery. After her confrontation with Jake, she hadn't had the strength to deal with her brother's traitorous behavior. Both he and Isabel knew something was wrong, but she refused to discuss it. The tension at the dinner table had been thick, dangerous, and everyone had gone to bed early.

Now, Nora steeled herself to see Jake one last time if necessary. There would be no ugly scenes, no tears, no denials or regrets for what might have been. It would be a clean, quick break. They'd meet again in court, if that was what he wanted.

She couldn't manage breakfast, but she swallowed a cup of strong coffee, hardly noticing that it was too hot to drink. She went out to the registration desk. If Jake hadn't come by the desk by the eleven o'clock check-out time, she'd slip the bill she'd prepared late last night under his door.

But when she reached the desk, she realized that he'd already been to the lodge. On the counter sat a thin book she recognized immediately as her diary, and on top of it lay an envelope with her name neatly printed beneath the Hideaway logo. She slit the envelope open with her fingernail, feeling herself turn to stone all over again.

A piece of paper fluttered out to land on the desk, and the accompanying message on Hideaway letterhead was short and to the point:

Nora—
The enclosed check should cover my stay. If there's anything left, please spend it on the baby. You were right all along—you will make the better parent. I'll take steps today to make sure nothing stands in the way of that happening.
    I wish you all the joys of motherhood.

                                          J.

Nora stared down at the note in her hand. There was no sudden surge of elation. What was Jake up to now? She knew how fatal it was to trust him.

So it surprised her how much she wanted to. Why couldn't she just hate him and be done with it?

The answer to that question, however, came quickly. Despite all the hurtful words she had hurled at him yesterday, despite the suspicions she still harbored, she loved him.

That was one reason she hadn't slept last night. Yes, there had been fear that the baby was lost to her, but more than that, she hadn't been able to sleep because every time she closed her eyes, Jake was there. Every moment they'd shared together, every taste, every scent. Branded on her mind indelibly.

But he was gone now, and there was no point in giving in to foolish speculations about what might have been. Time to accept, once and for all, that not every dream comes true. If she was lucky, Jake would keep his promise not to interfere in the adoption, and the baby would be hers. If not...then she would fight. She might have to accept the loss of them both and go on. She had done it before, and she could again.

Heartsick, but resolved, Nora unlocked the cash drawer and placed Jake's check inside. The note she folded in half and slipped inside the diary. Later she would destroy both.

She flipped through the small bin of folios that made up guest registrations, pulling out the one for Cabin Two. Jake's name and address in Virginia stared back at her from the top of the card. With deliberate care she placed the Paid In Full stamp over the face of it. Then she began preparing the rest of the bills for today's checkouts, double-checking state tax, tallying rent totals.

It was easier, safer, to concentrate on business.

Routine tasks would keep her from dwelling on Jake's betrayal. But the entire time she worked, a little voice inside her kept asking one question: When will this hollow feeling leave?

CHAPTER FIFTEEN

September 1999

THE AIRLINE RESERVATIONS CLERK handed Isabel her ticket, and the girl turned toward Nora, offering a scared, hopeful smile. "Well, I guess this is it," she said.

"I suppose so," Nora agreed. Shifting the baby onto her hip, she captured Isabel in a quick hug. "Knock 'em dead, Izzie."

"I can't believe this. I'm really nervous about facing the internship committee. Giving birth was easier."

Not for me, Nora thought, remembering how she'd stayed by Isabel's side through every moment of the young woman's labor. Nora had been a nervous wreck, though she'd never let on to her friend how frightened she'd been for her that day three weeks ago. Dr. Brewster spewing agitated orders. The nurses rushing about in organized chaos. Isabel weak and panting with pain. But in the end, the delivery had been quick and uncomplicated, and little Robert William had come into the world screaming at the top of his lungs. A perfect, beautiful little boy.

Now, content and sound asleep, he lay cradled in his adoptive mother's arms.

"Blakely-Forbes is lucky to get you," Nora told Isabel. "The committee will see right away that they made the right choice. You're going to be a great surgeon."

"I hope I'm half as good at being a doctor as you are at being a mom."

"Do you think so? Three weeks, and I'm still trying to tell the difference between a hungry cry and a wet one."

"Something tells me you'll get plenty of practice in both," Isabel said with a smile. She leaned forward, pushing the blanket away from the baby's face so that she could get a better look. "I still don't see much of me in him. Or Bobby either, for that matter. Actually, he looks a little like…"

The comment fell away unfinished, and Isabel ducked her head.

"You don't have to avoid saying his name," Nora told her. "The baby looks a lot like Jake. Even I have to admit that." When Isabel still looked uncomfortable, she added, "It's all right. I don't think about him much anymore."

That was so far from the truth it was laughable, but Isabel didn't need to know that.

There was silence then, just short of being awkward. To fill it, Isabel said, "I'm sorry, Nora. I wish things had turned out differently. There was such a…a spark between the two of you. I saw it right away.''

"You did see something,'' Nora replied, trying for a light tone. "But it was nothing good.'' She smiled down at the baby, running a finger gently across the soft, silky cap of Robert's hair. "At least Jake kept his promise. John called this morning while you were packing. The petition to adopt remains uncontested. In a matter of days, Robert will legally be mine.''

"Did you ever let Jake know the baby's been born?''

"Yes, I sent him a birth announcement.''

"Then maybe he'll want to see Robert someday.''

Nora shook her head. "I don't know, Iz. I suspect he'd like to put everything behind him. I know I would.''

"You wouldn't like to see him again? Maybe try to make it work this time?''

During a weak moment, Nora had confessed to Isabel her feelings for Jake. She hadn't told the girl everything—that in a moment of foolish hope she'd added a personal note to the announcement she'd sent Jake. A suggestion that they arrange a visit. It would be a chance for Jake to meet his nephew, she thought, and to know that she was prepared to offer an olive branch.

She'd wanted that. Needed it, really, because now she knew in her heart that she'd been so wrong about everything. He'd known about her journal—

Trip had confessed that he'd shown it to Jake—but he obviously hadn't given it to his attorney.

She'd wracked her brain trying to come up with a logical reason for that, but nothing made sense. The kind of ruthlessness she'd accused him of didn't fit the man she'd spent time with, the one who had agonized over his son's feelings, the one who had been so gentle as he'd carried Marjorie. The man who'd been so gentle with *her*.

From the beginning he hadn't tried to hide his intentions. He'd said openly that he would fight for his brother's child.

It mortified her now to think of the angry words she had thrown at him. She'd overreacted, and even as she'd tucked Robert's picture into the announcement and sealed the envelope, she'd known that it was probably an exercise in futility. It was too late. Their parting had been too terrible. But hope was stubborn, and some dreams just refused to die.

A week later, when Jake's package arrived, the last of that dream withered.

In response to her note, he'd sent a photograph album. Old and worn and visited many times, from the looks of the cover. When Nora had opened it, she saw that page after page was filled with pictures of Bobby Burdette. Baby pictures. Childhood antics by a lake. Teen years full of school accomplishments.

It was the letter at the bottom of the box that Nora could see in her mind even now. She'd read it with shaking fingers, and Jake's short message had remained engraved in her heart ever since.

Nora—

I'm relieved that the baby arrived safely, and pleased by the thought of your happiness. I think a meeting would be unwise. However, I'm sending you my mother's album. I hope someday you'll share these pictures of Bobby with his son.

J.

The olive branch had been rejected. Politely, but firmly. There was nothing she could do to change the outcome. She should never have tried.

"Do you hate him?" Isabel's question brought her out of those painful memories.

"No. I wish I could."

That much was true, at least. How much easier that would have been than knowing that she'd had a shot at real love and blown it so completely.

"Then it's not hopeless," Isabel said.

"I accused him of terrible things," Nora told Isabel. "He'll never forgive me."

"Why is that so impossible to imagine? You forgave Trip."

She had. But Trip had been almost in tears, begging her forgiveness. And now, after swearing that his betrayal had come only in the heat of anger, and after a few months of flawless behavior around the Hideaway—where he did everything from patching roofs to cleaning out the chimneys—he was gone again, earning money somewhere in South America by taking tourists down whitewater rivers.

He was selfish. Shallow. Completely irresponsible. Sooner or later he'd lose patience or run out of money and the issue of what to do about the Hide-away would come up again. More arguments over the dinner table. But he was still her brother.

"I couldn't stay angry with Trip," Nora answered. "He's the only family I have left other than Robert."

The airport speaker called the latest arriving flights, and both women looked up, knowing the time was drawing near to say goodbye. Isabel picked up her tote bag and gave Nora a kiss on the cheek. Her eyes glistened with unshed tears, but her smile was optimistic.

"Goodbye, Nora. I'll never be able to repay you for what you've done for me. I couldn't have gotten through any of it without you."

Nora's own eyes began to fill. "You'd better go. Before we both end up bawling like a couple of kids."

Isabel nodded, quickly wiping away wetness from her eyes with the back of her hand. "Before I go, I just want to give you one thing to think about." She looked at Robert again, then touched her finger to his pudgy little hand. "Robert's so lucky to have you for a mother. But he could use a daddy, too. I can think of only one man who ever applied for that job, and if Jake was willing to do it, don't you owe it to the baby and yourself to see if there's anything left to the relationship?"

Nora gave Isabel a non-committal smile. She already knew the answer to that question. There was no relationship. Jake had made that perfectly clear.

A meeting would be unwise...unwise...unwise.

CHAPTER SIXTEEN

New Year's Eve, 1999

NORA DIDN'T GO to bed early on New Year's Eve. Robert William Holloway had other ideas.

She'd let him nap too long during the day, and now, two hours before midnight, he was wide awake. She fed him and changed him and sang him a silly lullaby. She even reread him Isabel's Christmas letter—full of excitement and stories of her success at Blakely-Farber, but he just kept blinking up at her from his crib, like a curious baby bird expecting to be entertained.

Nora frowned as a loud trio of pops crackled from the direction of Blue Devil Springs—early revelers getting a head start on the celebration. But instead of being frightened by the noise, Robert seemed to find it intriguing, and he gave her one of the smiles she could never resist.

"All right, my little angel," she said, drawing him gently into her arms. "You want to welcome in the millennium? Let's see what kind of show Blue Devil Springs puts on for us."

Although there was probably no need for it tonight, she bundled him warmly in blankets, then sat him in his portable car seat. By the time she finished, only his bright, inquisitive eyes were visible. Satisfied, she headed out the front door of the lodge. Larry appeared to ingratiate himself against her leg, and the trio trooped down the steps to the spring's observation deck.

The night was beautiful. Unexpectedly warm, but flavored with the pungent scent of pine. A nearly full moon. The light on the surface of the spring pool moved in mesmerizing eddies. She found a good spot on the bench to see the fireworks from town over the trees, positioned Robert close beside her and settled down to wait.

Not a bad way to greet the new year. And certainly different than the way she'd ushered in last year. So much could change in a mere twelve months.

She checked on Robert, making sure his head was still covered. She had discovered obstinacy in him already; he never failed to try to slip out of his cap. She had a feeling as the months went by he would become more and more of a handful.

But all the work, all the worry was wonderful. Motherhood was every terrific thing she had expected it to be, and so much more. She loved Robert more than she'd ever imagined possible.

She could go days now without thinking of Jake. Throwing herself into work and caring for the baby made the days pass quickly.

Nights were the more difficult. Robert was sleeping straight through now, and those lonely hours in bed did nothing but remind her of how wonderful it had felt to lie beside Jake, secure and warm in his arms.

She was eager to be beyond that longing for him. Perhaps in time...

Larry made a warning sound in his throat and rose from the deck, tail wagging. Nora turned her head, saw someone coming down the steps and tried to hide a grimace of disappointment. Only two of the cabins were occupied tonight, and she'd hoped not to have company.

And then her heart jumped as the newcomer moved out from the shadows of the trees and into the moonlight. He came toward her with his hands buried in his jacket pockets, his collar turned up to frame the face she saw every night in her dreams.

In dreams, and out of them...

"Jake—"

The rest of her words failed her. All she could do was sit on the bench and wait for him to reach her.

He stopped directly in front of her. "Happy New Year, Nora."

She looked up at him, stunned. "What are you doing here?"

"I suppose I could say that curiosity got the best of me, that I came to see the baby. But that wouldn't be entirely true." He glanced at Robert, then raised an eyebrow at her, asking for permission. "Do you mind?"

"No. No, go right ahead. He's still awake."

He bent closer and carefully unwrapped the blanket from around Robert's face. "Hello, little guy," he said softly. Robert responded by taking hold of Jake's finger and pulling it into his mouth. Jake looked delighted, spent a few more moments smiling down at his nephew and then tucked the child back into his warm cocoon.

He straightened. "He looks like a great kid, Nora."

"He is."

"Thank you for naming him after Bobby."

"It's a good, solid name."

"Yes, it is." He cocked his head at her. "What's the matter? You look pale."

"It's the moonlight."

"Do you think I've come back to try to take him away from you?"

"No."

"Good, because I haven't. Even if I could."

"So why are you here?" she asked again, thinking it was time to do more than exchange banal pleasantries. "From your note, I got the impression that you didn't want to have anything to do with me."

He made a self-deprecating sound. "I left here thinking that the best thing I could do for you would be to get out of your life. For months I wouldn't allow myself to reconsider. Then when I got your note, your tone was so distant, I was afraid you were just doing what you thought was best for the baby.''

"What changed your mind?"

"Finally I couldn't stay away. I began thinking that it was a damn shame we never got to go out to dinner that night, and I never got to say all the things I wanted to. It might have made all the difference in the world."

She looked up, a tightness in her chest that made it difficult to draw breath. "Why? What did you want to say?"

He moved to sit beside her on the bench. The moonlight gave her no clue to his mood, but she sensed a sudden tension in him. "I wanted to say that I'd been acting like a jerk about the baby," he began quietly, his tone absolutely serious. "Making your life miserable because of a lot of stupid guilt I was carrying around over Bobby's death. I was the one who sent him out that day to check up on the crew." He sighed heavily. "And I was going to tell you that I wouldn't stand in your way any longer, that I had absolute faith in your ability to raise my brother's child."

"You were?"

"Yes."

"I'm sorry. I should have given you a better chance to explain. I never wanted us to end up enemies."

"That's good. Because it's awfully hard to be enemies with the person you want to marry."

Nora had to swallow twice before she could find her voice. "What?"

"After we got the business of the baby's future settled, I intended to ask you to marry me."

"Jake, I—" Nora's voice broke.

He held up a forestalling hand. "Wait, I'm not finished. I think you owe it to me to hear the rest, the best argument I've got for the two of us getting married."

"Which is…"

"I love you, Nora," he said, taking her hand between his. "I've been miserable without you. I know there's no reason for you to think I'm telling the truth here, but I'm asking you to take it on faith."

His eyes looked straight into hers. Beneath his warm regard, her heart hit the roof of her mouth. The tension that had haunted her own body flowed from her like a fleeing ghost. She smiled at him, knowing she was going to say the words she'd been longing to utter.

"I love you, Jake. Much as I love Robert—and I'm crazy about him—I've missed you so much."

She touched her palm to the side of his face. "I need you, Jake. I don't want to face the new year without you."

"You don't have to, sweetheart," he replied, taking her hand to lay a kiss against her palm. "The Hideaway is the first place that's ever felt like home to me. I'm strong and I'm not afraid to get my hands dirty. Let me be the one to help you here."

He paused a moment and continued. "I assume Trip's still in the picture, pushing you to sell?"

She nodded slowly as his words started to sink in. "South America for now. But he'll be back, eager to talk me into giving him his way."

"So let's do it. I can buy out Trip's share of the place. He gets what he wants, and you can turn the Hideaway into anything you've got a mind to. Just so long as I get to help you do it. You don't ever need to manage on your own again, Nora."

"You're serious, aren't you?"

"I've never been more certain of anything in my life. What do you say? A new baby. A new husband. New hope for your dream here at the Hideaway. Can you think of a better way to start the millennium?"

She couldn't, and to make sure he understood that, she brushed her lips against his tenderly, with just a touch of impatience.

"The fireworks should be starting soon," she murmured.

"Feels like they already have," he breathed against her lips. And then suddenly, he broke away and stood up. "Oh, hell—Charlie. I forgot all about him."

Nora rose as well. "Where is he?"

"Still asleep in the car, I hope. He sulked all the way from the airport when I told him he couldn't help convince you to marry me. Seems he thinks it's a great idea, too."

She curled against his side. "Go get him. We

can watch the fireworks together, like a family. Then you'll check in. Into the lodge, of course.''

He pulled her into his arms. His teeth flashed as he grinned down at her. "I know I was only there one night, but I'm kind of partial to Cabin Two— lots of fond memories.''

"Not available," she said, shaking her head. And then, in a delighted afterthought, she added, "But guess who's staying there?"

"Not Derrick and Lucinda?"

"No. Better. Becky and Harold Fuller."

"Who?"

She brought her hand up, wiggling her fingers in front of him. "My wedding-ring-down-the-drain couple."

He laughed in surprise, and the sound of it was just the way she remembered in her dreams. Rich and sexy. "How did that happen?" he asked.

"I sent Becky the ring. She talked to Harold. Next thing you know they got remarried. Now they're back for a second honeymoon."

"Good for them!" Jake exclaimed. He lifted her chin with one finger and looked at her with eyes that were suddenly serious, full of moonlight. "If it's true love, it's worth fighting for."

"We should make that the Hideaway's new logo," Nora suggested softly.

There was a skittering crunch of falling pebbles from the darkened springs pathway, and Jake tilted his head in that direction. With a sound that was part sigh, part laugh, he called out, "All right,

Charlie, I know you're there. Come on down and help us bring in the new year.''

The boy materialized out of the shadows cautiously, his thumbs hooked into the belt loops of his jeans. ''Everything okay, Dad?''

Jake nodded, pulling Nora even closer against him. ''She said yes.'' He glanced down at her, his eyebrows arched. ''Didn't you?''

''Yes,'' she said and wrapped her arms around him. ''Oh, yes.''

Even in the pale moonlight, she could see Charlie's broad grin. ''Cool,'' he replied. Catching sight of Robert, he bent to let the baby clutch the tip of one finger. ''Hey, this must be Robbie. I'm going to be your big brother. Okay?''

She watched Charlie entice a silly smile from the baby.

He's going to be so good with Robert, she thought, and then she couldn't think at all because Jake bent his head and placed a nibbling line of kisses against the nerve-rich flesh at the base of her throat. Heat flooded her veins, making her feel drowsy, as though she was living the dream she'd imagined for so long. She closed her eyes, only to open them again when a thundering boom from town announced the first fireworks.

''Look, Robbie,'' Charlie said in an excited voice. ''Those are fireworks. Aren't they pretty?''

Nora turned her head to glimpse a constellation of livid red, white and blue sparks thrown up against the night sky. She curled against Jake's chest. "Can you believe it?" she asked softly. "It's the year 2000."

Jake didn't even notice. He was too busy kissing her again.